PENGUIN BOOKS

The Wrong Girl

Zoë Foster Blake enjoys writing her biography because she can write things like, 'The literary world was shocked when Foster Blake was controversially awarded the Man Booker prize for the third time', despite the fact that this is patently untrue.

Things that *are* true include a decade of journalism writing for titles such as *Cosmopolitan*, *Harper's BAZAAR* and *Sunday Style*, as well as being the founder of all-natural Australian skin care line, Go-To.

Zoë has written four novels, *Air Kisses*, *Playing the Field*, *The Younger Man* and *The Wrong Girl*; a dating and relationship book, *Textbook Romance*, written in conjunction with Hamish Blake; and *Amazinger Face*, a collection of her best beauty tips and tricks.

She lives in Springfield with her husband, Homer, and her three children, Maggie, Lisa and Bart.

T0363517

BOOKS BY ZOË FOSTER BLAKE

Air Kisses

Playing the Field

The Younger Man

Textbook Romance
(with Hamish Blake)

Amazinger Face

The Wrong Girl

Zoë
FOSTER
BLAKE

The WrONG Girl

PENGUIN BOOKS

PENGUIN BOOKS

UK | USA | Canada | Ireland | Australia
India | New Zealand | South Africa | China

Penguin Books is part of the Penguin Random House group of companies
whose addresses can be found at global.penguinrandomhouse.com.

| Penguin
Random House
Australia

First published by Penguin Random House Australia Pty Ltd, 2014
This edition published by Penguin Random House Australia Pty Ltd, 2017

Cover design by Allison Colpoys © Penguin Random House Australia Pty Ltd
Text design by Laura Thomas © Penguin Random House Australia Pty Ltd
Author photograph by Michelle Tran
Typeset in Fairfield by Laura Thomas © Penguin Random House Australia Pty Ltd
Colour separation by Splitting Image Colour Studio, Clayton, Victoria
Printed and bound in Australia by Griffin Press, an accredited ISO AS/NZS 14001
Environmental Management Systems printer.

National Library of Australia
Cataloguing-in-Publication data:

Foster Blake, Zoë, author.
The wrong girl / Zoë Foster Blake.
9780143784883 (paperback)
Subjects: Romance fiction.

penguin.com.au

*Dedicated to whoever it was
who invented peanut butter.*

I – we all – thank you.

I

Lily pulled her phone out of her pocket and checked the time: 7.25. Pete was meant to be here at seven p.m. He was bringing the new season of *Boardwalk Empire* over on his laptop, they were ordering pizza and she had a posh bottle of shiraz she'd swiped from work; things might not get much better than that.

Lily checked her appearance briefly in the mirrored splashback above the sink as she poured some corn chips into a bowl. She was wearing her trusty denim shorts and a dark-blue singlet. A small gold chain with a tiny bird circled her neck; since her long hair was freshly washed and boofy, she'd tied it up into a high bun.

She took the corn chips into the lounge and carefully manoeuvred her housemate Simone's fancy aromatherapy-humidifier-thingy off the table. Even though Simone was earning terrific coin as a *very* successful model, she was ultimately determined to open a wellness and nutrition centre, catering to the precise kind of cool, slim, beautiful people who didn't need help. Simone's fanaticism for wellbeing pervaded the entire house; there was always something sprouting or fermenting on the kitchen bench, and wheatgrass growing on the windowsills. Rooibos and oolong tea, buckwheat

1

flour and LSA had long since taken over the pantry, leaving very little room for Lily's barbecue shapes and shake-a-pancake mix.

After living together for three years, Lily was still resistant to Simone's food choices. It wasn't as though Sim had been subtle about trying . . . freshly made date and orange gluten-free cookies here, roast tamarind tofu on brown rice there – her part-time job at a health food cafe didn't help – but Lily remained resolute in her diet of Turkish bread, Corn Flakes, pasta and white rice. In fact, the more Simone lectured and spruiked her way of life, the more Lily resisted it. She actually preferred Sim's homemade quinoa porridge over her Uncle Toby's sachets, but she was too far gone to admit it.

Lily heard a knock downstairs and bounded down to get the door.

'I forgot the fucking wine.' Pete looked ruefully at Lily as she opened the door.

'I have some,' she said, as he stepped inside and kissed her on the cheek. He looked positively homemade with his scruffy brown hair, black floppy hat, vintage Led Zeppelin T-shirt and dirty old jeans. What a grub. Simone said he dressed like he was in a band to compensate for the fact he was merely a publicist for bands. Lily just thought he looked like, well, Pete.

'*And* as if I wasn't already the best,' she said, walking inside towards the lounge room, 'I ordered our pizza to be delivered at eight. Hawaiian with mushrooms and olives, and a margherita with pepperoni. *Plus* pistachio and white-chocolate gelato.' Lily beamed with pride.

'You're primo, you are.'

As she turned to see his delight at her good pizza-ordering work, her face fell. He had his phone out and was barely listening. As usual. These days he was always on Blendr or Tinder or whatever new hook-up app was cool. He had tried to get Lily to do the same, but she maintained she'd rather stay single forever than hunt on her phone for same-suburb sex with creeps.

'So!' he said as he collapsed on the sofa and kicked off his filthy brown ankle boots, crossing one ankle over the other as he lay down on his back. 'How was Byron? Have any fun? You got back yesterday, yeah? Did Simone make you do soft-sand beach runs and drink green juice all weekend while she banged on about spiritual nirvana?'

'No way. We were too busy making out with all these really cool, rich, hot guys and drinking espresso martinis.'

'You were drunk and falling off stools is what I heard. It was the best of times, it was the mess of times . . .' His eyes were flickering with mischief.

'I had fun; I'm glad I went,' Lily said indignantly as she walked to the kitchen and poured the wine. 'Here you go,' she said, handing a glass to Pete who had shuffled up and made room for her on the sofa.

'Did you get a big dirty new year's eve pash?' he asked.

Lily had, in fact, got a new year's eve pash, but it was under the duress of Simone's insistence – 'Um, you're *single,* you know' – and she couldn't recall his name or face. He'd kept calling her Eurasian, which was so tired. Her dad was *half* Japanese, which made her as Japanese as a taco, in her opinion. She had *slightly* almond-shaped eyes and *almost*-black straight hair, and that was the extent of it. Her freckles and light-hazel eyes felt pretty Aussie to her.

'I did, actually. Wouldn't know him if I fell over him, but that doesn't mean he wasn't a nice guy. A gent, from memory – walked me home and bought me a kebab because Sim was busy with her millionaire lover.'

'Walked you home. Please. Walked you to bed, more like it.'

'Actually, I remember telling him my sister was inside sick and that he couldn't come in,' Lily laughed at her deception, but Pete

3

was back on his phone.

'So who was *your* new year's eve prey?' she asked, trying to gain precedence over whatever had his fingers rapidly flicking over the screen of his phone. Lily couldn't be sure there would've been just one target. Pete was in turbo-single mode after a long relationship and making the most – the very most – of it. He'd even become flirtier with Lily, which she found slightly unsettling but not entirely annoying.

'Reply hazy, try again,' he said in Magic 8 Ball-speak, which they had done with each other for years. He finally jammed his phone back into his jeans and looked at her.

'Why are we talking about that shit, Lil? We should be talking about how great it is to hang again after weeks of you dying to see me.'

Lily rolled her eyes. Case in point.

'Oh, stop it. I'm adorable.' He put his wine glass on the coffee table and lay back, sinking into the big, plush cushions.

God, he was actually becoming a bit much, Lily thought. She didn't really know what to make of him tonight. She'd almost prefer they were back in plain old friends mode. It was better than all of this weird, loaded innuendo.

Lily got up and went to the kitchen again, returning with some lazy 'guacamole' she'd made with one avocado and some salt and pepper. Despite being a producer on the cooking segment of a TV show, she was an astonishingly average cook. She preferred being the eater, not the maker. She took a chip, scooped up some dip, and promptly dropped the whole thing on her T-shirt as she chartered it to her mouth.

Pete chuckled. 'Never change.'

'I have to, I have guacamole all over my top,' she said, without missing a beat.

'Touché.'

As she walked upstairs to switch tops, she heard the door buzzer go.

'Can you get that? It'll be the pizza!' she yelled while rifling through her drawers for something else to wear. She threw on a black tank and darted back downstairs to the lounge room, just in time to see Pete going through her bag.

He looked up. 'I'm outta cash, and the loser at the door insists on being paid for the pizza.' He grabbed two twenties from her wallet and shot down to the front door.

Something fired up in Lily's gut; he was late, and hadn't brought wine or money. This was pretty much standard Pete, but tonight it was annoying. She exhaled and tried to just Have Fun.

Two hours later, brimming with pizza and moving onto a bottle of white wine they'd found in the fridge (Lily hoped it wasn't one of Simone's expensive ones), the two friends lay watching a particularly excellent episode of *Boardwalk Empire* with only the TV screen illuminating their faces.

'What time will you drag your hangover into work tomorrow?' asked Pete as the closing credits ran. It was the first week in January, and many friends had already returned to work.

'I don't go back til next Monday,' Lily said gaily.

'Ah, yes, I forgot that TV stars need more holidays than us plebs.' One of Pete's favourite things was to tease Lily about her job, even though technically his was far wankier.

'We're not back on air until the following week; there's not much point us all being in there this early. No one would do any work anyway.'

'I probably can't drive, huh?' Pete asked, turning his head and sipping his wine, eyes locked on Lily.

'No chance. I'll call you a cab.'

'Or . . .' His eyes flashed with intent. 'I could just . . . stay . . . here?'

Lily turned and looked into Pete's eyes, and weirdly, she just knew. Knew that finally The Moment had arrived. She shouldn't have been too surprised; she *had* invited him over and shared two bottles of wine with the guy. They were both single and drunk. She knew it was a possibility; she'd assumed it might eventually happen. But still, her heart was pounding and her mouth was suddenly devoid of saliva and there was all kinds of weird twitching in her gut. She was *so* shit at this stuff.

Pete leaned in to her and kissed her gently on the lips.

'I've always wondered what that'd be like,' he said. And Lily was surprised to find it wasn't weird at all.

Lily smiled and they kissed again, this time a long, slow, gentle one that did exciting things to Lily's lower body, and confusing things to her brain. As they continued to kiss, Pete leaned back on the cushions and pulled Lily down onto him, wrapping his hands around the small of her back. He smelled intoxicating – it was the usual Pete fragrance but with the sweet, salty undertone of his skin. He gently stroked her back as he kissed her with more urgency and Lily responded, pushing herself into his body, ever so subtly. Soon he was lying entirely on his back on the sofa, with Lily directly on top of him mirroring his increasingly hungry kisses. She felt his hands move down to her arse, which he caressed and squeezed, and as she ran her fingers through his hair, gripping the occasional handful, they kissed feverishly. She knew what was happening next.

Pete suddenly pulled back his head to look at the now quite flushed Lily. 'Should we take this fun new game upstairs?'

'Mmm . . . I *guess* signs point to yes,' she said, and, deciding to just go with it – the wine happily, loudly encouraging her – she pulled herself off his body and stood up, walking upstairs, knowing he would follow.

'Well, don't be *too* excited,' he said.

'Oh, don't worry, I'm not,' she said, turning to smile at him, wondering if she was, in fact, excited or not. Either way, it had been quite a while, and who better to break a drought with than a friend. More than a friend? Maybe . . . She pushed the mind-chatter away and tried to focus on the stairs, which seemed to be whooshing away much faster than they usually did. Here goes.

2

It was *good*, Lily admitted to herself. The sex was good. She grinned and allowed a small mist of gold dust to fall over the moment: *she and Pete had done it*. After years of being genuinely, strictly platonic, almost like brother and sister, they had done it, and it had *actually been good*. Although Nick from last summer – Mr-Slap-Your-Arse-Grab-Your-Ankles-Slide-You-Down-And-Flip-You-Over – had really set the bar quite high, she mused. God, was that her last time? It was. How disgraceful. She was a few months shy of wearing a nun's habit. She shook her head and steered her mind back to Pete, who had excused himself to the bathroom after his somewhat theatrical finale.

She pulled the sheet up over her body. Actually, she wanted her bra and undies back on; she couldn't be all nude and stuff in bed with Pete! No, no, no, too weird. She scrambled around on the floor in the dark, trying to locate two small, stringy items that had been removed with very little care for their whereabouts. She found her bra and jammed it on as she heard the toilet flush, but no knickers. Fuck! Her fingers located her shorts under the bed and she pulled them on instead, just as Pete came back into the room.

'You can't do the post-shag dash. This is *your* house, remember.'

She fell back onto the bed, her shorts undone but at least in the right general area.

'What are you doing? Come on, back into bed with you. I'll feel used otherwise.'

Lily laughed, doing as she was told.

Pete kissed her shoulder softly then wrapped an arm around it. 'You smell good, like caramel.'

'It's my natural scent. My feet smell of fairy floss,' Lily said, smiling, relishing the human contact. Being cuddled by Pete felt oddly familiar. She tried not to let her mind race away with visions of them doing this frequently.

'Feel better now?'

'As in having had sex with you, or having some clothes on?'

Pete laughed. 'It was always going to happen. You knew it; I knew it.'

Lily frowned. That wasn't what you were supposed to say when you'd finally had sex with your best friend, was it? Or was it exactly what you said and she was being too sensitive? You're *supposed* to tell them how you've been thinking about it for centuries, and now unicorns are dancing and angels are singing and everything has fallen into place . . . right? She was beginning to wig out over this, she realised. Sex always made her wig out. But she'd definitely imagined the post-sex mood between them – if it were to ever happen – would be a little more . . . *something*.

Pete threw a casual arm over Lily's chest and turned to face her. 'Oi. You cool? What's happening up there?' He tapped the side of her head.

'Yeah, yeah, course, just, it's, well, I'm trying to wrap my head around the fact you're cuddling me in your undies, I s'pose.' She laughed lightly, insincerely, but he didn't seem to notice.

'All that's missing are the cigarettes.'

She suddenly felt like he was a little too confident, a little too used to this situation. It irked her. She felt a surge of territorialism and insecurity. He noticed.

His voice softened. 'You know, I wouldn't have guessed you were such a goer in bed.'

She flushed and cleared her throat.

'But you've always had a hot little bod.'

'*Jesus*. Gross. Would you stop it?'

He sighed and rolled onto his back.

Lily propped herself up on one elbow so she could look at him properly, even though the moonlight coming into the room barely illuminated enough to distinguish a nipple from an elbow. She waited, allowing him conversational space to go on.

'So, I met a good one, Lil,' he said, suddenly. 'Her name's Lou. We met at a gig just before Christmas. She's *really* cool, so self-contained and creative and funny . . . She has this short red hair and a *mountain* of tatts, which are two things I never rated on girls, but there you go . . .'

Lily tried to calm her explosive heart with a deep breath.

He went on, his voice tinged with adoration and wonder. 'With her it's just so *easy*, you know? I can be myself, and we have so much fun together, there's none of the jealousy bullshit I had to put up with with Karen . . . She manages The Wolves, too, has done since the beginning, and now that they're big in the US, she . . .'

But Lily had stopped listening. She tried to swallow, but her mouth was arid. Surely this wasn't happening. Surely Lily's close friend and extremely recent sexual partner had more tact than to ramble on like a lovesick teenager about some girl he's fallen for ten minutes after HAVING SEX WITH HER.

'Wow. She sounds super.' Her voice was equal parts sarcasm and venom.

'It's only early days and, y'know, Kaz and I only split a few months back and I'm still dealing with some shit from that, obviously, and I need to be single for a bit probably, but it could really turn into something, Lil . . .'

Pete had missed the substantial bitterness in Lily's voice and was now observably, unashamedly daydreaming about this Lou idiot. Lily felt something brewing within her that she had not felt for some time, probably since The Mechanic, who so thoroughly messed with her that she'd seriously considered ditching men altogether, and becoming a trendy lesbian with a cool deck of cards tattoo on her neck. It was fury. Pure, industrial-grade fury.

'Get out.'

'No, really, I mean it . . . She's pretty awesome, Lil.'

Lily swivelled out of bed and stood up, her arms crossed. She looked down at the black lump that was Pete.

'I mean get out of my house.'

'What, why? Lil, what's going on?'

'Are you SERIOUS, Pete? We just had sex. You and me, after being friends for, what, three years? That's a *big thing for me,* Pete. And then, as you cuddle me, in my own bed, you tell me in great detail that you think you might have fallen in love with another girl. Another girl whom for all I know you were sleeping with less than twenty-four hours ago. I know you're a pig, that you screw your way around this city like it's your profession, but to do that to *me*? *Unbelievable,*' she hissed, grabbing her favourite grey hoodie from the top of her laundry basket.

'Where'd all this come from?' He sounded genuinely baffled, which pissed Lily off even more. 'We're just fooling around. I didn't realise you were into me like *that.*'

'Oh, don't *flatter* yourself,' she mocked, mustering up every ounce of disgust she possessed. 'It's basic human decency, Pete.' And she stomped out of the bedroom and down the stairs.

Once in the kitchen, she leaned on the bench to steady herself. She was shaking and the tears were pooling dangerously in her eyes. *Pete*, of all men. She thought he might actually have been one of the Good Ones. But no, just another pig.

Footsteps descended the stairs so she quickly turned her back to him and put the kettle on. She needed a cup of tea quite desperately. And a shot of vodka.

She heard him putting his boots on and collecting his keys and (empty) wallet, and then walking towards her. Her skin prickled, knowing he was nearby.

'Can we just talk about this for a sec? I don't understand why you're flipping out.'

Quiet.

'Look, I'm sorry you're pissed off. I'm – I still don't know what I did, but I'm sorry.' He reached out and put his hand on her shoulder and she whirled around savagely, shaking it off as she turned.

'What happened just then is that you slept with me, and then told me you were in love with another person. And then expected me to workshop that with you! If you can't see what might be upsetting to me about that, then you are an even bigger piece of shit than I initially thought. I don't want you as a boyfriend, Pete. I don't need to even explain that, surely, but I'm not just some girl you fuck and then leave behind while you go back to your girlfriend.' She angrily resumed the very important task of water-boiling management.

'I thought it was just a bit of fun!' His voice was distressed, urgent. 'I had no idea you – you never told me you felt that wa—'

'*I don't feel this way!* I just don't treat sex as something as nothingy as you do! Now can you just go?'

He waited a few moments before turning and walking out the door. When Lily heard it close, she gulped back tears. Not only were all men DEFINITELY scum, but she had just lost one of her mates, too. What a terrific fucking start to the fucking year.

3

Lily woke up and stared at her ceiling. Instantly, things felt wrong. Physically, emotionally, everythingly. For starters, it was about 900 degrees in her sauna of a bedroom, which would be ideal if she were small pieces of marinated lamb, but instead she was a sad, hungover little human. Her brain was haggling desperately with other organs to get some water in order to function, but there was none to donate. Her stomach felt queasy and vulnerable, like it might need to spend a bit of time launching things up and into a toilet. Lily rolled over and smushed her face into the pillow. She smelled the faint trace of Pete's aftershave and lurched up onto her knees as if stung by a bee. The insistent pounding in her head was titanic, but she could not spend a second longer in sheets that had enabled sexual relations with Pete 'The Dog' Barnett.

She leaped off the bed, and as she did so, her left foot got tangled in the sheet. She hopped once, twice, desperate to stay upright, grabbing her wobbly, too-light wicker washing basket to steady herself, which of course leaned and fell, and they both came crashing down, Lily smacking her shoulder hard on the corner of her tallboy as she did.

'FUCKING FUCK FUCKSHITFUCK!' she screamed. She kicked the sheet once, twice, but it was now even more twisted around her foot. She gave up, and the tears flowed in streams down her cheeks. She was in huge amounts of unfair pain, she was embarrassed; she was officially the biggest loser in Sydney.

As she lay on the floor, rubbing a shoulder that would soon be adorned with a walloping bruise, sniffing and holding back tears, she wondered how she had arrived at this point. On the ground in her shorts, crying. Her mind flitted between self-wallowing and self-righteousness; she was within her rights to be pissed off: *he* kissed *her*! He started it! What a prick. She wondered if they would be able to be friends after this. She sat up and slowly untangled her foot, cursing at the sheet as she did so. She inspected the large red mark on her shoulder, shaking her head and wondering whether this was an icepack-type injury or a heatpack one. She never knew stuff like that. She needed Simone, who *always* knew stuff like that.

She turned her phone on and it immediately chimed with a text.

I'm sorry for bringing Lou up at that stupid moment. Now I see my fail. I'm sitting out the front of your place smoking like a fuckwit – please come and talk? Px

He'd sent that at one-thirty a.m., an hour after she kicked him out. Huh.

Okay. You really hate me or you're really asleep. Goin home now. Px

That one was at two-thirty. She had no idea if he was lying about staying that long. It was definitely something he'd do for points, make a dramatic and apologetic gesture, or at least pretend he did.

Maybe she should just call him. They were adults, grown-ups, they could move past this, surely. And maybe, just maybe – she allowed the admission to sneak into her brain, like a teenager creeping into her bedroom after curfew – she had to take some of the blame. After all, she was the one who'd dared to think of him as potentially more than a friend, even if she'd denied it to his face.

She flopped back on the bare mattress and closed her eyes. She needed some strong painkillers and she needed some magical person to come and sort this whole mess out and make everything happy again.

Just then, Lily heard the front door slam closed and a loud, cheerful 'Babes?' came from downstairs. Simone was back from Melbourne! *Wonderful*. She would set her straight. Together they would find some kind of There's A Reason For Everything treasure in all of this.

'Up here,' Lily hollered, pulling on an oversized singlet that could masquerade as a dress – in female company, at least – before lying back dejectedly on the mattress. She heard Simone dump some bags and her keys on the kitchen bench

'Well, *someone* had a party here last night . . .' Simone called out jovially. 'Oh, that's right, slimy Pete was here, wasn't he?' Lily heard the fridge door open, and after a few minutes of unpacking what was undoubtedly almond milk, tofu and tempeh, Simone walked up the stairs.

'Babe? Still alive?' she asked tentatively as she came down the hallway.

'Yes,' Lily said, her voice low and deflated.

Simone's gorgeous head appeared around the doorframe, all clear eyes and tanned, radiant skin, but on seeing Lily's face, her own crumpled with concern.

'Whoa. You look like *shit*. Did you have some magnesium drops before bed like I said? You *know* they help hangovers —'

'We had sex.'

'NO!' Simone said, a look of shock and delight lighting up her face.

'Mm-hmm. And then a few minutes later, he told me in he was in love with some girl. Fun night in all.' She looked at Simone with a bemused, wry smile.

'I *told* you he was a pig! I knew he'd pull something like this on you . . . God . . . And to YOU of all people, I mean, he *adores* you, Lil, so that's really saying something about what a mess he is. It's all his stuff, obviously. No reflection on you. God, he is just *so cripplingly* emotionally unaware.'

Lily sighed and shuffled her legs up so she could hug her knees. She didn't expect a whole lot of pity from Sim, who'd always disliked Pete, but she wasn't in the mood to be enlightened.

'I shouldn't have gone there . . . *Why* did I go there? Why? Am I that starved for sex that I have to resort to screwing friends?'

Simone looked at Lily as if she'd just asked to saw off her hands. 'Ohmygod, are you *insane*? Pete has had a thing for you since he was, I don't know, sperm. I *know* he has. I've seen it for years. He's just completely uncomfortable being honest about his feelings, and so he obviously self-sabotaged the situation and hurt you as a reaction to the disappointment within himse—'

Lily's brain was two self-help phrases away from shutting down completely.

'I *assure* you there is no subtext; it was a drunken accident. And you know what? I'm fine. Bit messed up, because I'm always a bit messed up the day after sex and it's been a while, but that's it. I *swear*.'

Lily was more of a boyfriend-girl than a one-night-stand-girl but the whole boyfriend thing hadn't really been happening for her lately. The last two years, lately.

She looked up at Simone, eyes big and earnest. If she were deeply honest, she *didn't* think of Pete as boyfriend material, which made all this worse – being ditched by someone you didn't even want.

'All right,' said Simone. 'Tell me he was at least good?'

'*Way* too vocal, it was grunts and sighs and "oh baby, oh baby" the whole time, but good, yes.'

'So how did it happen? The bit where he ruined everything?'

'We're lying there cuddling and it's nice and not even weird at all. And of course I'm spinning out that I've just had sex with *Pete*, and am thinking, you know, maybe would it become a regular thing, and then he starts telling me about this girl with red hair and tattoos who he's in love with.'

'Is he already with her?'

'I'm not sure. I pretty much kicked him out the moment he'd finished saying what an amazing girl she was and how much fun they have and blah blah blah, pass me the goddamn bucket.'

'What a *sociopath*,' said Simone. Then, after a few moments, 'He's actually done you a favour, babe. You could've spent, like, another six months sleeping with him, and wondering if he was the guy for you, and the way you two carry on and hang out, you could definitely be mistaken for thinking you'd be good together, but he clearly doesn't care about anyone but himself. It's The Pete Show all the way. You don't need that kind of destructive energy in your life.'

And this was why Lily loved Sim. Despite her love of psychobabble, she knew how to extract the truth, like a straw in a horrible thickshake. Which was why it was such a pity she never, ever paid attention to her own advice.

'He's ruined our friendship. That's what makes me sad.'

'Don't sleep with your friends next time then, idiot.'

'Promise not to, especially not you. Hey, so enough about me, how was last night?'

Simone flopped back onto the bed and sighed. 'You weren't the only one dealing with a complete dickhead.'

'Hang on, did Mr Ferrari fly down to Melbourne yesterday too? I thought we liked him!'

'We *did*. He was staying at the penthouse at Crown, and everything was perfect. I got off the shoot early so we had a nice dinner and went back to the room, and things were amazing, I mean, he was doing all *kinds* of wild stuff to me, like, kinky shit. He's a bit sick, actually, but anyway, we were drinking Cristal and having fun . . . and then, at like, two a.m., he buzzes in not one, but TWO hookers.'

'*No.*'

'True story,' Sim said, sitting up and shaking her head. 'I don't know what's more offensive, the fact he thought I was the kind of chick who would want a foursome with two high-class prozzies, or that I was so boring in bed he had to call in backups.'

Lily started giggling, and then the giggle built up to a chuckle, and then a full-blown, belly laugh.

Simone slapped her on the arm. 'It's not funny, babe! What if I'd laughed when you told me your story?' But she was smiling, and then, seeing Lily start to cry so hard tears fell from her eyes, she began laughing, and then she was *really* laughing. When Lily snorted, and the two girls shrieked and squirmed and rolled around on the bed in laughter.

'I bet Ferrari would love to be here right now, with us rolling around together on the bed like thïs,' Lily said, trying to get her breath.

'We could call in old Mrs O'Connor from next door to make up numbers,' Sim said between gasps, and Lily was off again, laughing and laughing, feeling the tension from the past twelve hours start to leave her body, on some level relieved that she wasn't the only one having a shitty time with men. God, if perfect, beautiful, smart, funny, wild Simone couldn't find a good man, what hope did she or any other mere mortal have?

'Oh, God, stop, no more, I can't breathe,' Simone said, clutching her tiny, taut stomach, wiping tears from her face.

'I'm sorry, Sim, what a fuckstick. What a bunch of fucksticks they all are. Are we in some sick reality show we don't know about?'

'Or *Two and a Half Escorts*?' Sim said, trying to quieten her sniffs.

'I might go lesbian,' Lily contemplated as she twirled her long, dark hair around her finger.

'Oh, because you were so good at it last time. How long did that last?'

'Couple of hours. But I mean it about meaning it this time. Men are so incredibly shit.'

Simone stood up and stretched her arms, no doubt stiff from a gruelling Yogalates class.

'I'm totally with you on swearing off men. I didn't even tell you about my run-in with Michael last week either . . . He's broken up with the Russian mail-order bride and so now he wants to' – she made bunny ears – 'have a chat.'

Michael was Simone's ex. They tortured each other constantly, regardless of geographical barriers or new partners. They made Tina and Ike Turner look functional. In Lily's opinion Simone was still deeply, irretrievably, self-destructively in love with Michael, but insisted she was over him. Lily chose not to ask about Michael any more, such was the torment he'd caused Simone in the two years they were together. He was the genital herpes of boyfriends; persistent, unattractive, painful and there for life. He didn't deserve any more airtime. He had ended it a year ago under very dubious circumstances, and it had taken at least six months for Simone to lift her head above the cloud of sleeping pills and booze, and show any semblance of confidence.

'Seriously, think about all the effort and time and money and waxing appointments we spend on those pigs, and what do we get back?'

'Confessions of love about other women, or just other women,' Lily said.

'I've really had enough, babe. Like, *really*. Maybe this is the year we reclaim, Lil. Get back to our feminine power. Clear our heads and hearts and keep our bodies pure; focus on ourselves. Realign ourselves to what and who we actually want in our lives, rather than just sailing aimlessly with no intention. Come on, Lil! Should we go on a little sabbatical? No, wait, a saBOYtical! Even just for three months?'

Lily felt a shot of adrenalin go through her. Three months of no boys was a cinch, especially as she wasn't exactly getting any action anyway.

'Make it six, and I'm in.'

Simone's eyes lit up.

'*Really?* Ohmygod, this will be incredible. This will totally make everything right. We'll keep each other strong; we'll s*mash* this. It will be like my ultimate green cleanse, but for the . . . heart.' She smiled her angelic smile.

'It'll be easy for me,' Lily said, standing up, her stomach finally feeling ready for food of a disgracefully greasy nature. 'I've got single-itis. I can't even remember what it's like to have a boyfriend. And I'm nearly thirty, don't forget, Sim; this is getting serious . . . You'll find it tough, though. You're the one who has five men a day fall in love with you and an emotionally retarded ex-boyfriend who won't quit.'

'They're bad men. They're not serving us. They've gotta go. If we want to find *real* love, genuine, mutually serving love, we need emotional clarity first,' Simone mused earnestly. 'So we're doing this?' she asked, hand outstretched for Lily to shake.

'HELL, yes, we're doing this,' Lily said, shaking her friend's hand vigorously.

4

To: Lily Woodward
From: Simone Bryant
Subject: The rules

Hi babe,

Bobby is coming to clean at four today. I forgot to leave cash, but just pay and I'll pay you back tonight.

I hope you're feeling a bit better about Pete ☺

I've had time to think about our man-cleanse and I think we need to make some rules, or we leave it open to cheating. Or as you'd say, 'technicalities'.

GUY DETOX RULES

- No physical contact with opposite sex – PURITY!!! ☺
- No dates or hanging out with guys you're attracted to (so Kevin with the ferret from apt five is fine)
- No web misdemeanours: sexy FB chat, Tinder, Skype, email flirting, etc.
- No phone sex or sexting
- No crushes

Anything you want to add?

xoxo

To: Sim Bryant
From: Lily Woodward
Subject: Call me Sister Woodward, please

I don't know what makes you think I need all this spelled out, since I am practically already a nun.

Some additions:

- No sex with rich guys and hookers
- No pretend lesbianism
- No fantasising about One Direction

I think that covers it. Pete sent sucky email . . . I just wb saying what we did was a mistake, I'm fine, but we should just leave it at that. And THAT's the last contact with men I will be having for six months.

Lx

Sent from my iPhone

To: Lily Woodward
From: Simone Bryant
Subject: Re: Call me Sister Woodward, please

Who knows, it might be the start of a big awakening for him. God knows he needs one.

See you tonight xoxo

P.S. What about fantasising about Ryan Gosling?

To: Sim Bryant
From: Lily Woodward
Subject: NO GOZZO

I mean it.
I'll be checking your web history.
Lx

Sent from my iPhone

Lily hit send and sipped her water, enjoying her last day off by spending a few hours at the beach. Fucking Pete, she thought, with overwhelming disappointment. Why'd he have to go be such a *dick*.

Lily turned her thoughts elsewhere: tomorrow was Monday, her first day back at work, which raised a mixture of excitement and anxiety. She produced the cooking segment on *The Daily*, a morning show that had been around forever and often felt like it. Her executive producer always wanted Big Name chefs, but the problem was, they usually worked until two a.m. and couldn't be bothered making the seven a.m. call time. At the end of last year Lily had suggested the show go back to the old model of one in-house chef so everyone wasn't in a complete state of panic four days a week, and amazingly her idea had been approved. A new chef had been decided on over the Christmas break, and she was nervous thinking about who it might be, since the decision would likely have been made by her series producer, Eliza, a sweet but ineffective woman with about as much chef knowhow as a pot plant. The new chef could make or break Lily's year, depending on whether they were fun and easy to work with, or stubborn, lascivious and cantankerous, which was what she had learned to expect based on her experience with a largely male chef's pool. She shook her head; she hadn't even been asked for suggestions.

Lily used to think she wanted to be the on-air talent, when she first started in TV, fantasising of her Bridget Jones moment and becoming an overnight sensation, but she soon realised she'd be terrible at it. In fact, it might be her worst nightmare. She preferred being behind the camera, with all of her mistakes and her private life protected, and absolutely no need to wear heels, or entertain the notion of hairspray. Much better. Much more Lily.

The next morning Lily pulled her long, dark straight hair up into a messy bun and looked at herself in the far-too-truthful bathroom mirror. She was wearing a pair of black jeans, ballet flats and a light-grey top she'd bought in Byron Bay that walked the line between T-shirt and dressy top. She knew today would just be workshopping; why dress up? Of course, that wouldn't stop Eliza from wearing her office-lady finest. She persisted with the idea that traditional female business attire, the stuff favoured by Melanie Griffiths in the late '80s, was 'professional' and 'polished' even though in every-one else's eyes it was just 'vividly outdated'.

There were no spots left in the car park, as far as Lily could tell. Finally, after almost ten minutes of zooming her small, had-it-since-uni VW Polo around columns and partitions, seeking that elusive car space, Lily spied one. It was a good one too, right near the lifts. She put her foot down and sped towards it, only to see a sleek black ute gracefully reverse into it three seconds before she arrived. She slammed on the brakes and her jaw plunged in shock. Who does that? It was clearly hers!

She waited to see who would exit this horrible bogan chariot, so she could fire them a greasy and then bookmark them for future greasies too. A head emerged, then broad shoulders in a simple white shirt, followed by dark denim jeans that were full-stopped with navy trainers. The man slammed the car door closed and spun around. He was *astonishing*. Tall, with dirty-blond hair with a slight curl, olive skin, three-day stubble and a body that would definitely list the gym as a close friend. He noticed Lily staring at him and frowned, as if *she* had done something wrong. Then he walked off to the lifts, leaving Lily to fume at this rude, beautiful bandit.

She reversed and did another few laps, settling for a reserved park one floor up, empty because none of the execs were in this soon after New Year's. She couldn't stop thinking about the guy who had stolen her spot; who was he and why was he parking down with the commoners? He looked like he should be presenting the evening sport segment, or selling luxury yachts. Actually, yeah, he'd definitely be in sales, she thought. Gross. If there was one thing worse than a guy in a tarted up ute who stole your car spot, it was the fact that he was a salesman too.

Lily's desk, she was disappointed to discover, was as messy as she'd left it, press releases and a pile of cookbooks balancing precariously over her keyboard. She'd secretly hoped the cleaners would tidy her pigpen over Christmas, but unless you put some-thing actually IN the bin, not next to it, not leaning against it, they didn't take it. She sighed and slung her bag over her chair. Another year of Leftovers You'll Love and Fast Feeds and stovetop burns and washing burned debris off pans. Was she up to it? She'd get there. The first week back always sucked, but she loved her job overall. Plus, she'd worked too hard and for too long at *The Daily* to simply up and find work elsewhere.

'Any ants? They're having a fucking field day on mine,' a voice from behind said. Lily spun around to see a flame of red-pink hair and a wide smile standing behind her.

'Al, you've gone all gingersnap!' She hugged her friend tightly and gave her a kiss on the cheek.

Alice worked on the home decor and renovations segment and was irresistibly dysfunctional; how she managed to hold down her job, let alone remember to shower and eat each day, baffled Lily. Despite her corrosive persona, a hangover from years of masterful work as a high school Emo, Alice dressed like a preschooler and was the office darling. Lily often wished she could be more like Alice, who was seemingly unfazed by other people's moods or attitudes or demands. She just got on with things; other people's shit was nothing to do with her, she said. It was an inspiring attitude and, as Lily had discovered, impossible to fake. Plus, Alice was twenty-five, and why wouldn't you be that carefree at twenty-five? Lily had been.

'Did it last night, saw the box at the chemist and thought, fuck it. Plus, I'm really into sunsets at the moment, and this kind of looks like one, don't you think?'

'You could wear any hair colour and it would look good.' It was true, Alice's peaches-and-cream skin and enormous, dark-brown doe eyes meant she was impervious to the usual rules about colour complementing and clashing. But mostly, she didn't care what other people thought, and *that* was why it worked.

'How was camping?'

'*Awesome.* Jules and I borrowed The Pest from her cousin, this horrible old mobile home from the '70s, and we did this huge road trip, and met these mental German B-packers and had the full summer kombi van experience. Did a lot of acid. Didn't really mean to, but on the first night Derek kissed me over dinner and slipped a tab into my mouth and it went from there, really.'

'That sounds a *little* bit like he drugged you, Al.'

'I don't know how I'm going to handle this prison after all that fun . . .' Alice spoke as though she were a bank teller who was glued to her stool all day, when in fact she was rarely at her desk, and spent her days racing around the set, or roaming the city, or filming celebrities' houses, or producing lightning-fast renovations.

'Hey, how was Byron? Did you see that gypsy I recommended?'

Lily scrunched up her face and exhaled through her nose. '*Byron* was amazing.' She looked around surreptitiously. 'But then when I got back I hooked up with Pete – don't make that face – and then he told me he was in love with some girl.'

'You're fucking with me.'

'Nope.'

'That's a *total* spin-out. I really thought if he ever got you you'd be married in, like, three minutes.' Alice, number one fan of love and sex and male-female relations in general, looked genuinely disappointed.

'Doesn't matter, I'm on a man-detox now. He gave me the perfect reason to ditch men. Won't miss them. Simone's doing it too. We're each other's support.'

Alice burst into laughter. 'SIMONE? Simone is off men? Oh, now I've heard *everything*. She won't last an *hour*.'

Alice didn't get Simone. She thought she was fake and insincere and that Lily could do better.

'She'll be fine. I'm excited. Do you even know how much energy men take up, Alice? I guess you wouldn't, since you meet a new guy effortlessly once a week.'

''Scuse me, I saw Matt for *ages*.'

'Ah, yes, the DJ who wore T-shirts of other DJs so that people knew he was a DJ.'

'He was such a lovely donut, but the DJ lifestyle is not for me. Plus he never had any cash and I could only steal enough quiche from the test kitchen to support us for so long.'

'So you'll be a Sally Single with me?' Lily asked with a smile, knowing full well Alice and single went about as well together as porridge and seaweed.

'Sure, yeah, whatever.' Alice began walking back to her desk, turning halfway across the office to say, 'Hey, have you heard about the new chef?'

'Let me guess, he's a good-looking, conceited megalomaniac with six women on the go and a long-suffering wife at home.'

'Nah, don't think so. Young. New. A good country boy straight from the pumpkin patch. But sadly, he's not handsome.'

Lily started up her computer and shook her head. 'Don't care anyway. Not interested.'

'He is *GODLY*. The bear's flares. All movie-star baby blues, big hands that could make a house from scratch, a voice like a war general and hair that's made of pure silk and you just *know* what's hiding in his pant—'

'I don't care if it's Tom Hardy himself: I'm not interested.' Lily looked at Alice with a pained look on her face.

'We'll see,' said Alice, in a singsong voice.

Dale tapped his finger on his mouse. Lily's co-worker was a small, nervous guy with a penchant for train-driver hats, possibly because he was balding, but more likely because it made him feel less visible and therefore less likely to be forced to converse. He seemed to find the world a largely terrifying place. Lily was ashamed to admit she occasionally intentionally made him squirm, with up to three or four non-work questions in a row. Dale cleared his throat.

'No TV experience, no. Just restaurant.'

'*Great*. So we're supposed to anchor the segment on this guy and he has no TV experience, no cookbook, no website, no hosting role on *My Kitchen Rules*, nothing.'

Behind Lily the office door opened, and a small woman with short black hair, impressively both flat *and* frizzy, walked in. No one who'd worked at *The Daily* for longer than a day wore anything in the same sartorial area code as Eliza's knee-length skirts, blouses, flesh-toned pantyhose and blazers.

She was thirty-five at most, but looked forty. It was her eyebrows, Lily decided. They were too arched and thin. It aged her, and made her look mean, which she wasn't. She was a big dork. As she walked towards the pair, she tip-tapped away on her chunky old BlackBerry.

'Nice break, everyone?' She was yet to look up at them.

'Yeah, really great, thanks, Eliza, how was yours? How was Port Macquarie? How are your family?' Lily asked, smiling.

'Mad and many, you know how it is!' Eliza's tinkly laugh rang through the room. 'So, I have some *very* exciting news.' Eliza's news was always at least a week old. Lily knew not to get excited.

'We have our new in-house chef! His name is Jack Winters. He was the head chef at Simmer in Mudgee, a two-hat restaurant, he trained at *all* the fancy places in Paris and London – you'd probably know them, Lily – and, between us and the doorknob, he looks like he could be a Hemsworth brother . . . but better looking! He's going to get the stay-at-home mums very worked up, let me tell you that right now . . .'

Lily winced. Dale's intel was spot on. They'd hired a no-name, no-experience beefcake to get the viewers all hot and bothered. Classy.

'Now, I won't keep you, I'm sure you've loads to do; Ben will be in touch about the planning meeting tomorrow. Oh and Lily, we should talk about some new tea towels.' Eliza was always 'urgently noticing' things that made absolutely no difference to the show. Last year she had called a meeting to discuss the importance of matching wooden spoons.

'Okay then, more soon. It's great to be back, team!' And with a smile and a swivel, she was off.

Lily waited til she was safely out of view and earshot before turning back to Dale.

'So, you'll hassle the Thermomix people again?'

'Okay,' he said at a volume better suited to a church or library. Lily couldn't help feeling like she was dealing with the work experience kid most of the time, despite Dale technically being a producer, albeit an assistant one.

Back at her desk, Lily typed 'Jack Winters Simmer' into Google and hit search. A stream of restaurant reviews, but no videos or images, which was troubling. She read with interest the first one, written by Terry Durack, which awarded Simmer 19/20. Almost unheard of.

'Stalking your kitchen Adonis, huh? That allowed on your lame detox?' Alice's finest skill was sneaking up on people and spying on what they were doing.

Lily spun around. 'Can you pipe down? It's my job to research, remember? Yours too, in case you forgot.'

Alice slurped noisily from her Diet Coke – quite possibly her third or fourth for the day – and looked at Lily mischievously. 'I'm going to make a bet with myself in my head right now that you fall for him.'

'Cool. Hope you win,' Lily said, her back to Alice.

'You've got chewy on your jeans,' Alice said as she turned and walked back to her desk.

Lily looked down at the back of her jeans and saw a wad of green mess on her left calf. She cursed under her breath. Would she ever be a grown-up? she wondered as she took a pen and started to work at the glob of gum. It was roughly as effective as casting a spell. She deleted the words 'Jack Winters Simmer' from the search box and typed in 'how to remove gum from jeans' instead.

5

'But it's RUDE, babe! And *such* bad karma.' Simone looked at her friend in disbelief.

'I actually can't believe how much you are missing the point here. Just because Chris Rich-guy texts does not mean you're excluded from the detox. That's like you, as a vegetarian, having just one meat pie.'

Lily was flicking through one of Simone's new swimsuit campaign lookbooks, shot in Cabo, Mexico, in which Simone was oiled up and depleting several layers of ozone with her smouldering gazes. It really was horrible for the self-esteem, Lily confirmed, living with a bikini model, but she loved Sim and was proud of her, and had long ago stopped trying to compare herself with Sim and her fabulous tits and perfect body and hair and skin.

'I haven't slept with him. He's just a friend, and *he* doesn't know about the man-detox, so in his eyes I'm just a *bitch*.'

'Tell me, does this "friend" of yours have a penis?' Lily looked at Simone, eyebrows raised.

Simone sighed and threw her head back so that it arched over the top of the sofa, while covering her face with one of the cushions.

Only her hair and her long silver and turquoise earrings were visible. She *loved* silver jewellery. Kaftans and crochet and soft cotton scarves also rated highly on her list.

'Do you need me to find our emails with the rules?'

Simone ripped the cushion off with a flourish, her hair messy, her enormous, green eyes wide. Despite the fact she'd been out all night she didn't look even remotely tarnished by alcohol or sleeplessness.

'Okay, no, shut up, I get it, but what about, like, business friends? I SWEARTOGOD, that's all Chris is.'

'Chris who owns houses in New York, Spain and Paris, and also a cruiser, and looks a lot like Adrien Brody? No. He doesn't seem much like your type.'

Simone smiled coyly. 'Just because the men I date are successful does not mean that's *why* I date them. And part of the reason I'm doing this sabboytical is to find a man outside my usual type, anyway ... Someone honest, and simple ... and genuine. Someone with heart.'

'You *love* painful men! You love going out with racing-car drivers and athletes and tycoons and guys who are constantly on their phone. You *love* the drama and the excitement.'

'But look what happens the moment it gets even a tiny bit serious: they freak out, or bring in hookers, or introduce their boyfriend or wife.'

'I didn't know you were looking to get serious ...'

'I don't want a bloody Tarago and a picket fence. I'd just like, I don't know, someone to be authentically, mutually happy with, I guess.' She hugged her knees and looked at Lily at the other end of the sofa.

'I mean, my birthday with the girls was *amaze* last month, but I couldn't help thinking how nice it would've been to have a boyfriend to spend a weekend in the country with, and just cook up a big meal, and slob about in trackies with. You know? Something *authentic*.'

Lily cocked her head and smiled softly at her friend. 'Do you know how many girls would kill for your life, Sim? The glamour and travel and excitement . . . and you're after a spag bol and a plumber to kiss you goodnight. Look, relax. You're going to fall over some incredible man who will adore you and be everything you dreamed of before you know it. And just in case you ever forget, that man is *not* Michael.'

Sim looked at her phone and sighed. She hated being reprimanded about Michael, but Lily didn't give a shit. She'd seen the damage he'd done.

' 'Kay. I won't text. I was having a weak moment.' She crossed her legs and resolutely tucked her hair behind both ears.

Lily stood up and chucked the lookbook on the pile of magazines that covered the coffee table. 'Maybe I will have some of that chickpea and twig stew after all.'

Simone, who was always delighted when Lily wanted some of her cooking, leaped up to assist. '*Yes!* Oh, you'll *love* it. It's really good with some Greek yoghurt and raisins, so good for you, full of all the protein white-sugar-white-carb types like you never get. I wrote all about protein on my blog last week, did you read it?' Simone stopped and looked at her friend.

In Lily's mind there was no worse sentence than, 'Did you read my blog?' except for maybe, 'I had the weirdest dream last night . . .'

'You should use some of my recipes on the show,' Simone said earnestly.

'Ha! Buckwheat and lentils and oogy-boogy smoothies on *The Daily* . . . our viewers would get diarrhoea at the very idea. It's lamb chops and sugary muffins for us, thank you very much.'

Simone could only shake her head.

*

It was only ten a.m. on the second day back at work, and Lily was already feeling the familiar grip of stress tighten around her throat.

A panicked email had come in from Eliza early that morning stating she needed the first week's segments by that afternoon, which meant Lily (and Dale) had to switch off holiday cruise control and get to work. Lily opened the largely blank planning spreadsheet with a sigh. All those empty rows and cells caused her enthusiasm for work to suddenly drop to subterranean levels. She didn't have a single decent recipe idea, let alone five strong, first-week-back-with-a-new-chef ones. She could ask around as she sometimes did, but it was usually a waste of time. If Eliza had it her way the only food they'd cook on the segment would be macarons and cupcakes. It was a running joke among the crew: she suggested a cupcake recipe pretty much every planning meeting, even when the theme of the week was India.

Lily reached for her hot tea, and instantly spilled the pale brown brew all over her keyboard, mouse and onto her jeans. Of course.

'*Shit*,' she whispered furiously, backing out from her dripping desk. She mopped up what she could with tissues, then gave up and headed to the kitchen for paper towel.

She filled the kettle and turned it on to make a fresh cup. As it gurgled, she ripped off some paper towel and started dabbing her thigh. Just once she'd like to be able to take her clothes off at the end of the day without there being an enormous patch of food, drink or olive oil on them. Was that too much to ask? No wonder she never dressed up for work.

She heard footsteps behind her and turned to see who she was about to be embarrassed by.

In walked the Ken doll who'd stolen her park yesterday. He was wearing black jeans, a dark-blue T-shirt and dorky grey New Balance trainers. His tanned arms were perfectly muscled, a fact Lily tried not to notice.

He seemed to be in a rush, and, without even a glance at Lily, walked past her to the fridge. He pulled out an enormous foil-covered tray of something, then slammed the door shut. He touched his hand on the side of the now quiet kettle and, feeling it was hot, simply lifted the whole thing and raced out with it.

Lily looked after him, gobsmacked. Did he just steal her hot water? And with it the very vessel in which to create more hot water? She stuck her head out the door in the direction he had hurried off to, but he was gone. Unless that was human blood under the foil and the boiling water was needed to save someone's life, that was the rudest thing Lily had been privy to in this kitchen. And she'd once had someone repeatedly break into her fruit salads and steal the pineapple pieces. Nothing else; just the pineapple.

With wet, stained pants and no tea, Lily returned irritably to her desk. There was a text from Sim lighting up her phone screen.

This photographer is HOT . . . I'm not allowed to take his number, am I?? What if he took mine? LOL xx

Lily shook her head as she replied.

No. Put your boner away and get back to work. x

Speaking of getting back to work, that was precisely what she needed to do.

'These are going round.'

Dale presented a tray of small friand-looking things on a plate, and then placed it on Lily's desk before scarpering away. Lily peered at them; they looked pretty good. She tried a red-tinged one, and almost spat it back out when she realised it was brimming with liqueur.

'Mmm, do I smell tasty treats?' Alice appeared from thin air, as she generally did whenever there was food circulating.

'I don't think tasty —'

'Ooh, they look fun!' She popped one into her mouth, and immediately had the same reaction as Lily, screwing up her nose and chewing in exaggerated motions.

'I'm eating a shot of tequila, aren't I? Hey, what's that brown shit on your pants, you pig?'

'Spilled my tea. Please, enjoy another one.' Lily pushed the plate back under Alice's nose.

'No.'

'Oh, come now, you love junk food.'

Alice reluctantly slid a dark-brown cake into her mouth. She screwed up her entire face.

'That good, huh?' Lily's eyes were dismayed. 'Dale brought them over. I was really hoping they'd be delicious.'

'Alcoholic six year olds will love them.'

'Hey, so we're meeting the chef this arvo,' Lily said. 'Apparently he's locked himself in the test kitchen since he arrived, which is why no one has met him yet. I like that. Makes me think he might actually want to do good stuff. Hey, want a DC? I'm going to get one.'

'Nup.'

Lily took the remaining cakes to the kitchen and set them down on the bench, relieved to see the kettle was now back, which saved her from walking to the drink machine for a Diet Coke in order to get a caffeine hit. She filled it up and flicked the switch, then opened the fridge to get some milk. When she closed it, the beefcake thief was standing at the bench, looking at the tray of friands.

'What are these?' he said.

Lily blushed; he was so *rude*.

'They're . . . liqueur friands, I guess you could say.'

'Oh,' he said. 'Any good?' He looked genuinely interested.

'Disgusting.'

Something flickered in his eyes. It looked like he wanted to laugh.

'Huh,' he said, before touching the side of the now gurgling kettle. 'Can I take this?'

He's got to be kidding, Lily thought. Again?!

'I was just boiling it for a cup of tea, actually.' She tried to keep the sarcasm from her voice.

He leaned over and plucked the kettle off its base and, stepping in close to Lily so that she got a direct hit of his woody, smoky cologne, poured hot water carefully into her cup, careful not to scorch the tea bag. Once he was finished, he walked out with the kettle, saying a quick 'Thanks' as he went.

Lily crossed her arms, her mouth agape. At least this time he'd bothered to give her some water first, she conceded.

Five hours later, Dale and Lily sat in the boardroom, waiting for Eliza, Sasha, who was *The Daily*'s executive producer, and the famous mystery chef. Lily felt like they had a firm list of recipes and even a star chef booked in, an eighteen-year old prodigy from the UK who was on a promotional tour for his new TV show, and who had already amassed nearly two million Twitter followers, most of them fourteen-year-old girls who found his floppy hair and mischievous grin utterly magnetic.

Voices came down the hallway and into the room walked Sasha, in top-to-toe black with clear cat's-eye framed spectacles, a green resin-bead necklace and fire-red lips, and Eliza looking like, well, Eliza.

'Happiest of new years to you both,' Sasha said. She was an extremely impressive woman professionally, and never forgot a person's name or role. It was testament to her terrifying attention to detail.

'I see you got some sun over the break, Dale?' Sasha grinned, and Dale smiled meekly back. Everyone laughed, because Dale was as pale as always and wasn't offended by such things, and because Sasha was lovely, and the boss. Lily had been subtly trying to make Sasha fall in love with her and promote her from the day she started at *The Daily*, but Sasha's nature was not to single anyone out, or show favourites, or even really acknowledge anyone outside of plat-itudes, so Lily had no idea what Sasha actually thought of her.

'Is Jack coming?'

'Yes, he knows to be —' Eliza started, before something caught her eye at the door and her expression became the facial equivalent of a golden sunset over fields of luminous poppies.

'Here he is now,' she said, beaming.

Lily looked up from her worksheets and her eyes grew to the size of dinner plates. It was *him*. The kettle thief. All arm muscles and dazzling blue eyes, he walked into the meeting room and pulled out a chair next to Sasha.

Instantly, the entire energy of the room changed. Eliza pepped up, and sat with what must have been extreme discomfort in a spec-tacularly straight position in her chair; Dale had flushed with nerves as he always did when someone new was in the same room/post-code; and Lily was busy swallowing back her annoyance at the new chef's various forms of theft. Yeah, good one, Alice, she thought.

He's a *real* dreamboat. Just as polite and delightful as can be.

'Sorry I'm late. I had a bit of a . . . *hiccup* in the test kitchen with the chicken.'

Eliza giggled, hurling another hundred-watt smile at Jack and waiting for his return smile. He smiled at her briefly, eyebrows raised, nodding.

The *test kitchen*! Lily had to clench her eyes closed for a second to prevent face-palming. It must have been him who'd made those awful friands, the ones she dissed when he asked about them. Oh well, she thought. Serves him right. They were horrible.

'Has everyone met . . . everyone?' Sasha asked. 'Shall we do that first?'

'As you know,' Eliza began, as though she had been asked by the teacher to tell the class about her summer holiday, 'last year I decided *The Daily* really needed a permanent, in-house chef.'

Lily's veins pulsed and the hairs on the back of her neck stood on end – *you did* not *think of that, it was* my *idea!* She shot a look to Sasha to see if the boss would give her some kind of reassuring, 'Relax, I know it was your idea' nod, but it was fruitless. Lily crossed her arms and sat back in her chair, taking a deep breath to calm herself down. Razor-sharp thoughts of quitting pierced her brain, as they did each time Eliza frustrated her, or her work went unappreciated or uncredited. There was zero chance she was sticking around if she didn't get promoted this year, she confirmed. Nada.

'We wanted someone for the audience to *really* bond with, and form a relationship with. Someone with impressive chops, as it were' – tinkly laugh – 'and the kind of obvious charm our audience goes really *wild* for. So, without further ah-*dyoo*, let me introduce you to the man who will fulfil all of these requirements and many more. Jack Winters!' She gestured towards him with a flourish.

'Wow, what an introduction,' he said, smiling shyly. 'Thanks,

Eliza. I'm looking forward to working with you guys, and trying this TV thing, and getting to know the city – all of it,' he said, with a pure country-boy grin. Oh, give me a break, Lily thought. All that's missing is the goddamn straw between his teeth.

'This is Lily, your segment producer, and this is the assistant producer, Dale. You'll be working with them closely day to day,' Eliza said, as an afterthought.

Jack threw one of his enormous, tanned arms across the table towards Dale, ready to shake. Dale actually flinched.

'Hi Dale, nice to meet you.'

Dale pulled his arm up to the table and tentatively shook the great walloping hand thrust before him, muttering a 'Nice to meet you' as he did so.

Jack pulled his arm back and slowly turned his gaze to Lily, all deep-sea blue eyes and long black lashes.

'Lily, is it? Pleased to meet you.'

Lily's eyes moved up to meet his, her chin still down in defiance. Why didn't she deserve a handshake?

'Yes, Lily. Nice to meet you too.' She knew she sounded pissed off, and half-hated herself for it, but she wanted him to know she wasn't some pushover who would forgive his rudeness just because she had ovaries.

'Thanks,' he said. 'I look forward to working with you.'

'Well! Now that we're all "besties" ' – Eliza made the bunny ears as she spoke – 'let's get cooking!' More tinkly laughter. Lily sighed quietly and opened up her notebook.

An hour later, Sasha's PA interrupted the meeting to remind her of an appointment. 'It's going to be a magnificent year, I can just feel it,' Sasha said before leaving.

'Okay then,' Eliza said, smiling widely. 'Lily will email everyone the updated schedule this afternoon, and we'll regroup tomorrow for rehearsal, okay? This segment is going be just *awesome*, you guys. I know it.' She stood up, straightening her now creased, too-tight pants, and seemed disappointed that Jack didn't immediately mirror her move so they could walk and talk their way down the hall together. But Jack was busy writing down note upon note. Lily was annoyed to realise she was impressed; most of the chefs she'd dealt with were either extremely experienced and borderline savant-like in their ability to 'get' what they would be doing on set, or so blisteringly arrogant they made it up as they went, causing hell for her and Dale, not to mention the camera and floor crew.

Sensing Jack would be a while, Eliza clutched her notebook to her chest and began scrolling down her BlackBerry fast and with importance, making her move towards the door at the rate of an injured sloth. Getting nothing after another minute, she gave up and walked out of the room. Well, *someone* had a crush, Lily thought, smiling. She didn't blame her, her boyfriend Kirk was about as charming as a mosquito, and equally as annoying.

Dale and Lily finished their notes and stood up. Dale scurried out of the room immediately, as though there were a fire alarm that only he could hear, leaving just Lily to pack up her many press releases and papers, and Jack scribbling away like a crazed fool.

Suddenly, Jack looked up, directly at Lily, straight into her eyes.

'I stole your kettle, didn't I.' It wasn't a question. He looked at her intently, as though studying her.

Lily nodded. It was probably too much to openly scowl, she thought. 'Yeah. Twice actually.'

He smiled ever so faintly.

'Sorry. The one in the test kitchen is broken and no one's replaced it yet. I'm just going to bring my one from home tomorrow.'

'You need to talk to Lionel. He's the one who gets stuff done

around here. Small guy, beer gut, Sydney Swans hat, inappropriate . . . You'll see him around.'

Jack continued to peer up at Lily, his head cocked to one side.
Another small smile – amused? thoughtful? – crossed his face. It
was disconcerting, and Lily wanted to get out of his tractor beam.
Not because he was disarmingly good-looking and his quizzical
staring made him even more handsome, but because Lily had work
to do.

'So, do you cook, Lily?'

'Not even nearly,' she said honestly.

'But you enjoy doing the cooking segment? Wouldn't you need
to cook to produce a cooking segment?'

'Not at all. I love *food*, though, and I love my segment. Sleazy,
self-important chefs aside.' As she spoke she realised how offensive
it was, but it was too late.

His face relaxed and he broke into a chuckle. It was ridiculous: the way his eyes crinkled at the edges, and that perfect smile
pushed into his cheeks, causing a couple of lines either side . . .
She wondered how old he was; maybe thirty, maybe thirty-five? She
couldn't tell; he was in that age bracket that lacked clear delinea-
tion. There was a small gap between his front teeth, she noticed.
Huh. Not so perfect after all.

'I'll try not to fall into that category,' he said, finally taking his
eyes off her.

Lily nodded as a full stop to the conversation, if you could call
it that, and walked out of the boardroom shaking her head. He was
odd, she confirmed. A real oddball.

6

Lily was feeling anxious. They went live Monday morning, and if this rehearsal were anything to go by, it would be a nuclear mess. Rob and Mel, hosts of *The Daily*, were still so utterly wedged into holiday mode that they may as well have had a margarita in one hand and a frisbee in the other; the set was incomplete, and Eliza was running on double-shot mochas and unwarranted hysteria, which annoyed the crew and made all the producers unnecessarily anxious. The general mood was akin to a crowded beach after a shark alarm. Lily decided to stop watching rehearsal and focus on her segment and set instead. She could at least make sure *that* was decent, Jack's as yet untested on-air skill notwithstanding.

Lily pulled the pre-chopped herbs and fish from the fridge and placed them next to the stove, while Tim, the lighting guy, stood on a ladder messing about with the lights, which Sasha said looked too 'train station toilets'. Jack stood at the bench, straight-armed leaning on his hands, reading his script. He was wearing a simple light-blue shirt – the memo must have reached him about no checks in front of camera – and black jeans with black trainers. Sasha had wanted him to look friendly but sexy; the Curtis Stone

46

effect, she called it. Like one of your older brother's good-looking mates. All that was missing was his white *The Daily* apron, which no one had been able to locate.

Lily took a moment to assess her set. Lighting aside, she was happy with the final product, having worked with the set designer and fitter last year to make absolutely sure there was none of the shiny, glossy chintz usually associated with TV-set kitchens. The look was a bit cool, a bit industrial, complete with second-hand wooden beams overhead, low-hanging naked globes and exposed brick behind the cooking bench. Of course, Eliza had immediately had two shelves of spices and oils and products installed onto the wall to keep advertisers happy, which annoyed Lily, but there was nothing she could do. Eliza might have the nous of a twig, but she knew how to keep the sponsors smiling. The fridge was concealed in a wooden cupboard and there was a line of unmatched antique jars acting as the holders for Jack's utensils along the bench. It would all look horribly outdated in a year or two, but for now, it was pretty cool for a network morning show. The sink wasn't actually functional – well, it could last the show, but it was the equivalent of a camping rig, and needing refilling and emptying before and after filming, and sometimes even during ad breaks. Ah, the glamour of live TV.

Jack was on set *way* too early for his segment – the talent generally rocked up five minutes before go time – but Lily was impressed that he wanted to be around and soak it all in. Not that there was much for him to do until the cameras were on him – the rehearsal recipe was a breeze. He'd chosen it himself: grilled salmon with a fennel and mandarin salad, and as with every show, Dale had chopped, prepped and laid out all the ingredients and utensils.

Jack, Lily, Dale and Eliza had at least done a brief run-through earlier, sorting out timings, and ingredient placement, where Jack would stand in relation to Rob, which camera he would be addressing, and making sure Jack remembered to 'talk to the camera, not the food', but Lily could feel Jack's nerves vibrating through the floor; he was clearly terrified. She'd written his script directly from his recipe, and made it as simple as possible so that he understood that all he had to do was cook the meal, and explain how he was doing it in a friendly way to Rob, and his new best friend, the camera.

Suddenly, Jack looked up.

'Hey, the salmon will take a little while to cook, and I reckon I might run out of things to say. What was I supposed to do if that happens?' Not even the fact that he was whispering could mask his nerves.

'That's when you switch to the salad.'

'Oh yeah, right.'

He went back to his script and made a note.

Lily smiled at him, feeling oddly fond of this new, vulnerable version of Jack. Much nicer than the abrupt kettle-stealing one. Feeling generous, she went on.

'If you ever feel like you're running out of things to say, just talk us through an ingredient. Tell us its history, what else it's great in, any surprising facts about it. Anything. Works every time.'

'Thanks.' He didn't even look up. Lily tried not to feel embarrassed.

The voice of Terry 'Grimmo' Grimstead, the floor manager, boomed through the set. 'One twenty seconds until food. Kitchen set?'

'Kitchen is set,' Lily hollered, quickly tidying the bowls and wooden spoons before leaving the set to watch offside with Dale. Normally she'd ask if Jack was okay, if he needed anything, but his vibe was one of leave-me-alone, so she did.

One of the sound guys ran over and quickly attached a mic to

Jack – way too late in the piece, in Lily's opinion – and Rob saun-
tered over to the set, ready for action. Jack and Rob seemed to get
along well, which was good, and Lily hoped some of Rob's confidence and playfulness would rub off on her nervy new chef. She
wanted Jack to do well, she realised. She needed him to.

'Ten seconds!' Grimmo began to bark the countdown.

And it was on. Rob was his usual fun self, and was genuinely
trying to make Jack feel as comfortable as possible under those
harsh lights. Jack stuttered and messed up his words when he was
introducing the dish, and constantly blocked the overhead cameras
from showing the food, but after a couple of minutes he loosened
up and the segment and chitchat started to flow more easily. Jack
was definitely behind in his timings, but that was why rehearsal
was so crucial. They would finetune it later. He also forgot to turn
the fish, Lily noticed, and watching him slice up his mandarin
while he talked down to the chopping board, it was obvious he
wasn't TV-trained. She tried not to panic about her amateur new
charge, and rather, see it in a positive light. After all . . . there was
something refreshing and adorable about that innocence, *right*? He
wasn't over-explaining everything and coaching the viewer to the
point of being patronising, which so many chefs did. You really did
feel like this nice, handsome, nervous stranger was just teaching
you how to cook some salmon.

Sensing Jack's errors would not be going unnoticed, Lily looked
over at Eliza, who was chewing her thumbnail as though she hadn't
eaten in weeks. She had forgotten how much was riding on this for
Eliza – Jack was her choice, after all. Lily threw her a faint smile
and Eliza did her best impression of one back.

Grimmo was signalling five seconds to go, and Jack, running
behind, had frantically grabbed his vinaigrette to pour on the salad,
only he knocked over the small jug in his haste, and dressing spilled

over the white bench and onto the floor. He looked up at the camera like a deer in the headlights, while Rob – rather unfairly, Lily thought – laughed uproariously.

'240 until news,' Grimmo yelled.

Rob patted Jack on the shoulder and told him not to worry, a shitty rehearsal ensured a perfect live show, then vanished out the fire exit for a cigarette. Jack, clearly rattled by his accident, and the pace and energy of live TV in general, wiped the sweat off his furrowed brow and set to work cleaning up his mess. Lily couldn't help but feel bad for him. And herself: they had a *lot* of work to do before Monday.

7

Lily took a look at Simone's outfit and physically clamped her teeth onto her tongue to stop herself from saying anything. Her flatmate was wearing denim shorts that were masquerading as underpants and while they were attempting to cover her bum, they seemed more interested in sneaking up towards her rib cage. She'd teamed them with a white cropped singlet that exposed the top of her toned belly, and heavy black boots. The shorts were forgivable at, say, a music festival or in the year 1983, the top was better suited to a gym class, and the shoes were far too heavy for the look.

But this was Simone, and Simone was not one to be told. Plus, to be fair, with her body and hair, no one was really looking at the boots.

'Where you off to?' Lily asked lazily from her position on the sofa, where she was reading a book written for thirteen year olds, but which Team Adult had greedily snatched for themselves and quickly made into a bestseller.

'The Royal for a drink with Grace and Skye. They have DJs tonight, it'll be fun, plus the weather is so yummy, the beer garden will be pumping . . . You should come!'

Lily's eyes sailed back down to her book. She'd worked so late last night, and all week, she was buggered. She didn't have the energy to go out.

'Nah, you go ahead.'

'Okay, Lil? You need to stop being such a nanna. You're young and cute and it's summer and we can help each other swat away all the boys who fall in love with us, because we're not interested in them *anyway*.'

Lily peered up at Simone, who, in the interest of understatement, was adding huge silver hoop earrings to her outfit.

'You saying you need my guard because you're a chance to falter?'

Simone turned around quickly.

'*Ha*. As if. I'm smashing this, babe. Have had, like, three guys try their best on me this week; even that Dylan guy from the races last year who I actually could genuinely like – did I tell you he imports those amazing spongy yoga mats I love? I had no problem whatsoever knocking them back.'

'Yeah, me too. They're banging down the door but I just heroically shoo them off.' Lily went back to her book, shaking her head.

'Hun, you can read your books on a Saturday night when you're seventy. But now? At this age? You should go out. Plus, it's what this thing is all about – enhanced womanhood, baby! Feeling the feminine power! A girls' night out is perfect for that. So, go get dressed. Come on.'

Lily couldn't say why she really didn't want to go, which was that Sim and her friends would be off their faces in a few hours, and not that fun at all. Plus, going out with models required a certain level of sartorial confidence that Lily simply didn't possess. She looked down at her old black shorts and singlet for proof, and then back up at her friend, standing there with her hands on her hips, all earnest and righteous, and sighed.

'Wear something of mine if you like, because you're not wearing that,' Simone said.

Lily closed her eyes and her book. 'Okay, okay, just for *one* drink.'

'Yippee!' Simone clapped, jumping up and down so that Lily was treated to the sight of her lacy bra. 'There's a *gorge* white dress on the back of my door that would look so hot on you. Go try it on while I pour us a cheeky rosé.'

The Royal was filthy with summer-loving flesh-barers. All the beautiful people seemed to have agreed to come out for a drink at once, and finding a chair, let alone a genetically imperfect specimen, was impossible. Lily was used to feeling invisible next to Simone, but add her model mates Grace and Skye, and she may as well have been one of the empty glass collectors. As she waited at the bar for a drink, she looked down at the tiny white dress she'd borrowed and felt pleasantly relieved she'd at least done that much. Her hair was needing a wash and therefore suitably scruffy and just-woken-uppy for this cool-kids crowd, and the simple smudge of eyeliner on the outer corners of her almond eyes did a decent enough job of giving the impression she'd made some effort. Couldn't go as far as heels, though, and seeing everyone else in sandals and thongs, Lily was pleased with her decision.

Simone was on a mission: after two glasses of wine at home, she was now sharing jugs of margaritas with the girls, and her volume was increasing in direct proportion to her sipping pace. Lily knew how this night would end; when Simone went out, she went *all* out. She quite often didn't return til the next evening, having enjoyed a bender with the girls, or a new beau, or whoever was in town and up for some fun and a five-star hotel room. But Lily tried not to judge; Simone was twenty-six and successful and gorgeous and enjoying her life. Good for her. Plus, she evened it all out by being a virtuous chia-seed crunching, meditating monk through the week.

Lily was not averse to going out every now and then, but was more likely to get sloppy on a good red with her mother at a restaurant, or to hit a dingy pub with Alice and drink beer and play pool all night. She was an extremely messy drunk, and it served her well to remember it, and more crucially, contain it. Simone, on the other hand, could return home after twelve hours of partying – ready for a Xanax and a cup of tea – and still look sensational.

'Lily!'

Lily closed her eyes, knowing that when she opened them, Pete would be beside her. She thought she'd feel a rush of anxiety, seeing him for the first time since their falling-out, but she felt a strange sense of calm. She opened her eyes and, sure enough, he'd pushed his way through the loud mesh of people and was standing to her right.

'*Thought* it was you! But then I thought, Lily don't wear dresses . . . Anyway, what's up?'

He'd started his sentence babbling excitedly, but by the last word he'd slipped into a serious, soft voice that was barely audible amid the boozy ruckus, and, quite frankly, it was stomach-churning to Lily. Seeing him in the flesh, eyes glazed, hair a mess, breath thick with alcohol, it was absolutely clear she'd made the right decision to cut him.

'I'm great, Pete. Really good. You?'

'Oh, lah-di-dah! I'm *well*, thank you, Mrs Over Polite,' he said in a mock-fancy voice. 'How ever do *you* do?' He laughed and took a sip of his beer, his pinky poking out in an aristocratic fashion.

Lily said nothing, and looked over his shoulder as a signal she was ready to move on.

'Saw Sim in the beer garden, thass'why I went looking for you.

Geez, she's got her pissypants on tonight, hasn' she? Good thing, I s'pose, since she forgot to wear *actual* pants.'

Ordinarily Lily would've joined in for a gentle teasing, but tonight she prickled, and felt defensive. SHE was allowed to pay out on Sim, but who was he to? He *wished* he could get a girl like Simone, or a glance or even a look of disgust from a girl like Simone.

'Yeah, well, we're celebrating.' Lily said, not entirely sure why. She didn't need to justify anything to Pete.

'Oh yeah? She marrying one of those rich fuckwits?'

He said it jokingly, conspiratorially, but everything that fell from Pete's mouth was intensely irritating to Lily. Perhaps her PMS had arrived early, but she felt unusually compelled to punch him. Or maybe she had finally come to terms with the fact he was a jerk, after having experienced the extent of his jerkiness firsthand, and now all she could see when she looked at him was the word 'jerk' floating above his head, like an unfortunate halo. She squinted at him in disgust.

'That's nine-fifty, please.' The busy and distracted bartender slapped her glass of white wine on the bar and held out his hand to snatch Lily's ten-dollar note.

'That's fine, thanks,' she said to him, picking up her drink and turning around, nudging her way carefully through the dense wall of people in line for a drink.

'Heyheyhey, what's the Geoffrey Rush?' Pete exclaimed as he scrambled to keep up with Lily.

She faced him as soon as there was some space and a bit more quiet.

'Pete, I don't really want to talk to you, okay?' The frustration Lily had successfully concealed on her face was screaming through at 100 decibels in her tone.

'You're still pissed at me? Jesus! Lil, so we slept together, big deal, I would never have gone there if I'd known you were gonna be such a sook about it.'

'Oh, go fuck yourself!' she hissed bitterly.

Pete visibly recoiled, then, only seconds later, true to Pete form, his face rearranged into an indignant mask.

'Okay, you know what, Lil? I've apologised and apologised but honestly you are *overreacting*. Chill *out* for once in your simple little life.'

'Okay, YOU know what? Don't *ever* talk to me again,' Lily said, eyes blazing.

Pete looked at Lily, shocked and wounded. No one ever spoke to him like this – he was the world's best conversational cowboy; there was nothing he couldn't charm his way out of.

With one final look at her 'friend', Lily turned and walked away.

She could feel adrenalin whooshing through her body; her hands were shaking. She wasn't quite sure where that had come from, but it felt right. Now she had closure on Pete. And, if she allowed herself some flattery, she'd given him a serve that was long overdue, and maybe, just maybe it would inspire some kind of change in him. But more likely he would fuck himself up on drugs, drink too much and wear his misery and fury proudly, like a ratty old biker jacket. Lily inhaled deeply, and whistled her breath out through her lips. She took a long sip of her wine and began patiently navigating the pushy maze to Sim and the girls.

A bottle of Moët had somehow manifested in front of the three girls when Lily arrived back at their spot, as had four flutes – three being put to good use.

'On the house! Don't you *love* it?' Sim said, as she messily, rapidly poured a glass of champagne for Lily.

'What she means,' said Grace, a tall, lithe brunette who had the deepest, richest, most breathtaking olive skin, and the lightest green-blue eyes Lily had ever seen, 'is that Ed, the guy who runs the joint, is totally smits with Skye, and he'll be sending over bubbly all night so she'll finally blow him.'

Lily nodded, shooting a knowing smile to Skye, who was grinning with a 'What can you do?' expression on her gorgeous little pixie face.

As the four girls laughed, and Grace smoked, and Skye and Simone bopped to the house music that dominated the venue, Lily could imagine how it might feel hanging backstage at a Victoria's Secret show, only with a pub full of men's lascivious glances and outright stares added to the mix. She'd be a reporter, or dressing-gown hanger-uperer, obviously.

She could hold her own with these girls, Lily thought, puffing up her chest ever so slightly and painting a huge smile on her face. She might not be a model, but she looked okay in her little dress. And anyway, she wasn't looking for male attention, she reminded herself. She was just here to have fun and, as Simone said, be young and cute and single.

8

When Lily woke up the next morning, head heavier than her entire body and mouth feeling as though it was filled with a handful of dust, Simone was nowhere to be seen, heard or smelled. Lily recalled leaving the girls on the dance floor, a wild, sweaty, mess of people, with stabby pointed fingers and warnings of doom if Simone acted on any of the several million advances she'd had from men during the night.

'I'm FINE, Lil! Don'worry, I know! Not evena *kiss* or a *phone numba* or even a tex'message!'

'*I'll* kiss you, babe!' Grace had yelled, before giving Simone a big open-mouth kiss. Sim returned it theatrically, of course, because that's what margaritas, cocaine and champagne mixed with a penchant for exhibitionism leads to. Two models enjoying a bit of showy girl-on-girl action was immediately noticed by the ring of men (pretending not to deliberately position themselves) around the girls, and a chorus of cheers and whistles and no doubt boners exploded. This only encouraged them to keep going.

As Lily had made to leave, the girls finally broke apart and laughed hysterically, dancing. Grace was approached by a dishy young guy in some serious denim-on-denim, whom she kissed on the lips as a hello before going in for some R'n'B-style grinding with him. Lily knew where their night was headed, and that Grace's boyfriend was about to have his idea of monogamy challenged yet again.

Lily had waved to Skye, who was rolling her eyes, and as she walked out of the pulsing hotel into the warm summer air, she felt the first twinge of missing men. It would be nice to have a little dance-floor pash, she thought to herself as she looked for a cab. Or to be going home with some gorgeous guy for some fooling around. She sighed heavily and jogged towards a cab with its light on. She could do this, she confirmed to herself. She was just drunk and toey. The man-detox was the Right Thing to be doing.

In the harsh morning light, Lily was feeling far less invincible. She looked at her phone through glazed eyes. There were three missed calls from Mimi. Why? Lily thought. It's Sunday morning. That's not when your mum calls. Not once and not three times.

Collapsing on the couch with the movie channel on and a fizzing Berocca in hand, Lily checked Facebook on her phone. She wondered if Pete had written anything to her or on his wall after their spat last night – it was very like him to post a dramatic, cryptic status update, the kind favoured by hormonal teenage girls, when he was angry at the world. But she couldn't get into his page. She refreshed and tried again. And then it dawned on her: he'd unfriended her. She dropped her phone on her lap and shook her head. He was a complete child, Lily thought. It had all happened for a reason, she realised, sipping the revolting, cloudy orange soup in her hand. She was meant to sleep with him and be let down by him so she could move on, and stop thinking about him as though they might have a possible future. A blessing can come in many different forms, Simone constantly said.

It was liberating, Lily realised. She could do whatever she

wanted, and didn't have to worry about guys. Not running into one she liked, not seeing one she didn't like, not even Facebook stalking was an option any more. How marvellously freeing. She hit call on her phone.

'*There* she is!'

'Mimi, do you know what day and time it is?'

A laugh and then, 'Better than you, I think. Today's the day we booked our Italian cooking class.'

'Oh, *shit*, oh God, I totally forgot. I'm so sorry, what time does it start?'

'In twenty minutes. I was calling to see if you wanted me to pick you up but it's too late now.' Mimi wasn't one of those mollycoddling mums. She'd do her best then leave you to your own devices. Suffer, baby, suffer and all that jazz.

'You sound a bit rough darling . . . Big night?' she asked.

'Accidental. Sim bullied me into it.'

'Are you still up for this? I was about to ask Denis, which might be best if you'd rather stay at home and wallow in your hangover —'

Denis was Mimi's gay best friend. Ever since Lily's parents had split the two of them had been joined at the hip, and they loved nothing more than cooking and decorating together like an old married couple, just without the sex and romance.

'No, I can do this. A big greasy pasta is just what I need. Okay, I might be a bit late but I'll get there as fast as I can.' The class was being held in a huge Italian warehouse, complete with cooking school, restaurant, provedore and gelateria. Lily had been there for work once; she could vaguely picture the street it was on.

'All right, darling. Drive safely, please. Strong coffee and no speeding.'

Lily skolled the remnants of her drink and tore upstairs to shower. What a shithead she was – she'd bought this for Mimi for her birthday, she *knew* how excited her mum was about it, and now Lily had almost ruined it. Bad daughter. Today the idea of being delightful and fully present and learny and cooking a three-course Italian meal was her idea of hell, but she was going to do it, and she was going to do it convincingly, or so may her house be filled with rotting meatballs forever more.

'I must say I *was* happy with my sardines —'

'OUR sardines, thank you,' Lily corrected Mimi cheekily, the life flowing back into her thanks to the huge bowl of pasta she'd all but polished off. And her third Chinotto. Mimi, on the other hand, was beside herself to have discovered a bottle of barolo was part of the package, and was slurping away at it with intense enjoyment. Lily could do no more than a token glass, which was a real shame, as it was prohibitively expensive and extremely tasty.

'Yes, *whatever* would I have done if you weren't here to chop the parsley. But weren't the sardines lovely? I would never have thought to add walnuts.'

'We're still getting some gelati on the way out, right?' Low-blood-sugar Lily had been disappointed to learn that three courses did not include dessert, but rather antipasto, entrée and then main.

'Would you stop thinking ahead for one moment, greedy-guts? We put a lot of love and time into this meal . . . You're always so fidgety, Bean. Drives me up the wall.'

Bean had been Lily's nickname since she was in the womb.

'I didn't even check my phone once! Even though my flatmate could be dead or missing, for all I know.'

'She'll ruin those stunning looks of hers if she's not careful,' Mimi said, elegantly placing the final pieces of her pasta into her mouth and savouring the taste as she dabbed her mouth with her napkin.

'Impossible.' Sim had won the genetic jackpot at birth, and still had plenty of winnings in the bank.

'I'd actually like to do a bit of shopping in the provedore, too . . . Closest I can get to feeling like I'm in Italy until I'm actually over there in a few months,' Mimi finished off her glass of wine and corked the bottle to take with her. She had started taking herself off on international holidays ten years ago under the guise of 'research' for her homewares store, but in truth she was addicted to travel. In Europe especially.

Lily collected her bag and checked her phone – nothing from Sim. She'd be fine, Lily reassured herself. She'd be somewhere safe and warm, fast asleep.

Fifteen minutes later, Lily could no longer stand her mother's snail-pace browsing and took herself off for a Ferrero Rocher gelato from the adorable little hole-in-the-wall gelateria. She waited in line, and upon finally getting her waffle cone and bulbous gelato, went to find Mimi. As she walked through the fresh produce she saw her mother chatting to someone in the pasta section. Just before reaching them, she recognised who Mimi was with. *Jack Winters.* Her heart rate picked up, and she immediately smoothed her mess of a ponytail, as if that would somehow undo all the other physical mess. What was *he* doing here, Lily wondered; although being a chef, and this being one of Sydney's wankiest food provedores, it wasn't that far a stretch. Jack looked up and saw her standing there like a dork, licking her gigantic ice-cream. A small smile – a smirk? – crossed his face, then he went back to speaking to her mother. Lily looked down at her light-blue shirt, smattered with oil and tomato flecks, and her Converse and her jeans, and realised the best option here was to retreat. Casually turning around, pretending to look at the tinned legumes, Lily headed back towards the flower section, which, with its wild greenery, would conceal her until he'd left.

She waited five minutes, and seeing her mother, now thankfully solo, head towards the register, wire basket brimming with cheeses and pasta, Lily binned the last of her gelato and walked towards her, wiping her hands on her bum as she did so.

'You've got something on your shoe.'

Lily stopped dead, registering the voice, and looked down at her shoe, which was indeed giving a free ride to a long piece of wax paper.

She bent down and ripped it off, chucking it aside before spinning around to face Jack, whom she most definitely did not want to turn around and face. He was wearing a white T-shirt, dark jeans and a plain navy cap.

'*Thanks*, Jack,' Lily said, wondering how Jack got so far in life when he was so rude. He didn't even say hello, for God's sake.

'And something on your face.' He wiped his own face as an indicator, that same smile-smirk painted on his stupid face.

Lily blushed, her hands flying up to her mouth and chin, wiping frantically. She couldn't decide if she were more annoyed at looking like such a mess, or at Jack's lack of politeness in pointing out her numerous flaws.

'Anything else?' she asked, more petulantly than she had intended.

'Just trying to help,' he said, a cheeky smile on his face.

' 'Kay, well, thanks. See you tomorrow. Get a good night's sleep, it's gonna be a big one.'

She couldn't resist, knowing how nervous he was already.

He looked like he was about to say something but Lily began walking towards Mimi, fuming with something – embarrassment? incredulity? She couldn't place it.

'*There* you are! Oh, Bean, I met *such* a divine man in the pasta section, he was so knowledgeable and so helpful, and he doesn't even work here. Just a regular Joe, shopping like me. Tell you what,' she lowered her voice mischievously, 'he was a *beautiful*-looking fella. If I were thirty years younger . . .'

Lily smiled at her mother, who was flushed with joy at her moment with Jack. If only Lily could say the same – but generally when *she* had an interlude with Jack, she walked away filled with disbelief at how rude he was. Maybe it was just her. Maybe he didn't like her. Oh well, she thought, I don't like him either.

Lily didn't mention she knew Jack, and worked with him. She didn't have the energy, but also, she was pissed off that Jack, who was so rude to her, had managed to make her mother's *year* with his soliloquy on fettuccine. She was over him already and they hadn't even technically started working together.

9

Lily returned home, desperate for a few hours of trashy TV and an early night to be ready for the first live show tomorrow. Instead, she heard squeals and music and laughter and, if her ears did not deceive her, splashing water.

She gingerly set her keys and bag on the kitchen bench on her way upstairs. There was a shriek from Simone. There was laughter from Skye. And there was a male voice too. Lily almost didn't want to know what she'd find when she got up to the second landing.

The bathroom door was open, and Lily walked towards it, wishing for once she had a normal flatmate who'd be watching *The X-Factor* in her pyjamas on a Sunday evening as opposed to orchestrating what sounded like a mini-spring break.

'Uh, Sim?' Lily called out, trying to make herself heard over Salt-N-Pepa.

'SIM?' she called again, this time with more determination and irritation.

Nothing. Fine, she was going in. She stuck her head around the corner and saw the inspiration behind a million pornos, and some of the more edgy fashion magazines: Skye and Simone were topless in

65

the daggy '80s style corner bath, drinking champagne and splashing each other. There was a very hot, young guy standing in his boxers and a trucker cap laughing, dancing and geeing the girls up, smoking and taking photos on his phone and drinking champagne, all at once, which actually would have been quite impressive if it weren't so disgusting. An iPhone was docked into Simone's little travel speaker on the vanity, but it didn't quite fit, and was hanging on a precarious angle. Not only were the overhead lights on, but the heat lights were on too, making it less 'sexy, swinging spa party' and more 'bathtime then bed'. The whole scene was extraordinarily wrong.

'LIL! Lil's home, my girl's home. Ho, ho, hey-ho, where's my girl been at, oh wheeeeeeere's my girl been at!' Simone grinned at Lily, swaying her head to the tinny music and her singsong greeting. She was off her face. So much so that it was questionable whether she had ever been *on* her face. Her glazed, dilated eyes told a sorry story, one involving no sleep for thirty-six hours, far too much booze and a *lot* of drugs.

'I'm not with him!' Simone suddenly yelled, realising how it might look to Lily to see her 'men cleanse' buddy topless with a guy in the bathroom.

'NOTHING has happened at *all*. I'm a *good* girl, tell her, Kane, tell her nothing has happened and I'magoodgirl. Hezafriend, and I have had no man touches and I'magoodgirl.'

He looked up at Lily.

'She's not into me, babe, swear.'

Lily believed them. He was not her type at all, far too young and broke-looking.

'Lily, come *in*!' squealed Skye, clapping her hands as best she could while holding a flute of champagne. 'We're having our own pool party!'

Skye became more infantile the more messed up she got, which was a lethal combination for men, especially when paired with partial nudity. Lily turned to the guy, still trying to make sense of it all. He was texting, but when he looked up and saw her looking at him, chucked his phone down onto the sink and bounded over and took her hand, jumping around and singing, trying to get her to bounce along with him. He could not have been older than twenty-one. His left arm was heaving with tattoos, and they all looked about two days old.

'This is like, the *best* song ever,' he said, sincerely. 'Like, old-school cool. Just, you know, how it *used* to be.'

Lily wondered if this boy had even been alive when Salt-N-Pepa were big, let alone old enough to comment on it being 'old school'. She shook her hand free, smiling so as not to cause offence, and edged back to the door, mindful of the floor being covered in water.

There didn't *seem* to be a threesome vibe, which was a relief, more just three good-looking gumbies having a bathroom party. But still, Lily wanted them out: they were so loud, and so not going to sleep for a long time, and so blissfully ignorant of the Sunday night Flatmate Consideration Code.

'You guys go ahead, I'm feeling pretty wrecked, and it's my first show tomorrow morning, so I might just head to bed.'

'Party pooooper!' Skye said, with her bottom lip dropped in faux sadness, missing the several undisguised hints in Lily's sentence.

'We'll be soooooooo quiet,' Simone said earnestly. 'We'll be real good for my Lil.' But then the manchild pulled down his undies, and with not a lick of shame or modesty, stepped into the bath, and awkwardly clambered down so that he was sitting under the water. This, of course led to even louder shrieking and laughter and splashing, which Lily took as her cue to leave.

As she walked out and down the hallway to her room, she heard Simone call her name.

'Babe, would you, do you miiiiiind, is it possible for you to maaaaaybe bring up another bottle of champs? Is that okay? Have some! Have some with us!'

'You should come in!' Skye squealed with excitement, as if she'd not just thought of that idea a few minutes ago.

Lily decided there was no point trying to quash this mess, and, sighing, slunk downstairs to the fridge.

Arriving at work the next day with the dregs of a double latte clasped in her hand, feeling like an elf had snuck in during the night and slipped her a handful of sleeping pills, Lily couldn't believe she was expected to function. She put this down to her topless flatmate and simple friends having carried on until three a.m. before finally taking whatever it was they took to sleep and crashing out in the lounge room, with several candles burning and loud music playing.

Lily was surprised to see Dale and Jack chatting by Dale's desk. Mostly because 'chatting' to Dale was harder than putting toothpaste back in its tube, but also because Jack really did seem to be the world's friendliest man to everyone except her. Today, she did not care. She had a job to do. As did he, more importantly.

Eliza was doing her usual thing of not a lot, sitting in her office for a few minutes, then coming into the green room to graciously fawn over the talent, then retreating again. This made her look both busy *and* important, neither of which was very accurate. Sasha, on the other hand, was locked away in the production room, making sure every second of the show would be the very best it could. She was barely seen until after the show, unless she liked what had been cooked in Lily's segment, in which case she would be first on set to claim.

'You got hayfever, Lily Woo? I've got tablets for that. They make you feel like Alice in Wonderland, it's fucking *glorious*,' Alice said, walking past Lily with a tray of coffee for her talent, an adorable brother-sister interior-design duo from Brisbane.

'No?' Lily said, confused. 'Oh . . . I get it. I look like shit. Simone had a bender, I got zero sleep.'

'Did she break your stupid bet?' Alice asked, clearly thrilled at the idea.

'No, well, not that I *know* of. She and Skye *did* bring a male model home with them, but he seemed more interested in dancing with his own reflection in the mirror.'

Alice laughed.

'Hey, get this,' said Lily. 'I ran into Jack yesterday at Delugi Brothers. He was so rude, didn't even say hello, just told me I had something on my shoe, and then something on my face.'

'Well, did you?' Alice asked seriously.

'Yeah, but, who does that?'

'Was he supposed to *not* say something?'

'Well, *I* thought it was rude. He's rude and abrupt and weird and rude.'

Alice cocked her head to one side, a sly smile spreading over her face. 'I smell a crush. A filthy big sex crush.'

Lily rolled her eyes. 'You think everyone has a crush on everyone. You thought I had a crush on bloody Dale, for God's sake. I can tell you in no uncertain terms that I do NOT have a crush on Jack, because not only is that predictable, but he is consistently offensive.'

'We only get angry with those we have feelings for. Didn't your earth-mother tart of a flatmate teach you that?' And Alice began to walk off, winking at Lily as she did.

IO

Lily walked onto set and felt the familiar combo of excitement, nerves and adrenalin sprint through her veins: it was go time, the first live show of the year. All the planning and meeting and spreadsheets took a back seat and, finally, she started to remember why she loved her job.

She watched Jack read over his script on set and had to admit he looked pretty good. Even in his stupid apron. His thick hair sat scruffily, perfectly messy on his head, the dark blond mingling with the brown in a way that women pay hundreds of dollars for at the hairdressers, and styled to look as though he'd just woken up. And he had the perfect amount of stubble, two-day growth at most. The mums at home were going to lose it when they met Jack Winters.

Eliza had made sure there'd been some press for him over the weekend, including a lame photo shoot with him fake-barbecuing for the gossip pages, which Alice and Lily had found highly amusing. He certainly appeared to be *The Daily*'s new favourite toy. The fact that the market was already saturated with charismatic, handsome chefs didn't seem to matter.

Jack looked up as Lily walked onto the dark 'floorboards' of the trendy fake kitchen.

'Hey,' he said, nodding. Oh, God. He was completely petrified. His eyes were wide and distracted as his brain clearly tried to make all of the words in his script stick. The set, as deconstructed and hip as it was, was still swimming in bright TV lights.

'How you doing there? Got all you need? Everything good to go?' Lily felt weird doing the 'checking on you' thing, but it was her job. He obviously needed someone to calm him down, and, dammit, producers and talent were meant to be close, working together, a team.

'Yep, yep, all good.' He nodded quickly. Well, thought Lily, maybe he doesn't need my help after all. Or maybe he just needs a bit of time alone. She began to walk away when she heard a familiar voice.

'Ummmm, *hi*! I'm Nikkii, I'm the entertainment and celeb producer, SO nice to meet you finally! I've heard *such* amazing things about you, Jack Winters.'

Lily swivelled around to see Nikkii, all heavy bronzer and twelve-centimetre heels, swoop over to kiss Jack on the cheek, because *that* was super appropriate and all. The scent of her thick, syrupy, undoubtedly celebrity fragrance invaded the entire set. It was indecent at this hour. *She* was indecent.

'Hi, nice to meet you – Nikki, is it?' Jack was polite but clearly overwhelmed by her general Nikkii-ness.

Here it comes, thought Lily.

'Yep, two "k"s, three "i"s.'

One hand slid up to run over her perfectly uniform curls. She never had any other hairstyle. Just the same middle-part, the same extensions, the same toffee highlights over a chestnut base and the same unconvincing curls from tip to ears, leaving the top flat.

'So I just realised we need to *haze* you! We're having drinks Friday night at this bar, like, literally two streets away; you should come. They do the BEST mojitos, ohmygod, I *die*. You *have* to come!'

Lily started walking away again when she heard Jack call out.

'Actually, Lily?'

She stopped and turned back to Jack, who, on top of being attack-invited by Nikkii to what would be the worst Friday night drinks since Fridays were invented, was now being dabbed aggressively with a powder puff by a make-up artist.

He continued quickly, 'Can I check a few things?'

Aha, Lily thought. He's not so tough after all. 'Sure, what's up?' she said.

Nikkii turned and aimed.

'Lil! Can't believe you've already been here working and I've been slacking off til today . . . I'm *so* bad. Did you have a good one? I went to Bali with my girls, and we stayed in this heaven villa. It was NUTS, like, literally reality-TV-show nuts.'

'Sounds fun,' Lily said with as much enthusiasm as she could muster for a woman who was consistently trying to make the workplace as tacky and insincere as possible. Alice disliked Nikkii equally, but conceded she was a good presenter, which, in Lily's more generous moments she agreed with. No one could engage the camera quite like Nikkii. When she was on, she was *on*. All those pretentious media courses had paid off, evidently. It was Nikkii's lazy producing and vast ego Lily took issue with.

'Hey, we go on in a few minutes. I just need to sort this out with Jack. Do you mind?'

There was a flash of annoyance in Nikkii's eyes. How dare the boring cooking girl get to hang out with the new chef hunk.

'No probs, I am totally snowed anyway; we have Delta Goodrem on tomorrow so there's SO much to do.' She turned back to her prey. '*Soooo* good to meet you Jack, you're going to kill it, I can tell. Toodles!' And with an over-exaggerated smile to Lily, she stalked off.

Jack held up his script – more of a recipe with comments, really – visibly confused and slightly amused by the whirlwind that was Nikkii. 'It is vital I stick to this word by word?'

'No, no, it's just meant to act as a loose run sheet for the segment . . . Look, you do need to *roughly* follow it, because it's the step-by-step for the recipe and Rob uses it as his autocue, and when he or Mel are on here with you – and they won't always be, remember, there'll be plenty of time for you to get creative when it's just you – they'll rely on it, just like in the rehearsal last week.

'And remember that today we have two three and a half minute segments with an ad break in between, so the camera crew will need you to stay within the allocated time . . . Jack, are you okay?'

Jack looked like he was in danger of self-implosion. His eyes were the size of golf balls and were darting frantically from left to right, trying to make sense of what Lily was saying. Oh God, Lily suddenly thought. He's dyslexic. He's about to break down and tell me he can't read a single fucking word.

'Jack?'

She watched his Adam's apple slide up and then back down as he gulped.

He cleared his throat, 'It's just that I'm really more of an ad-lib guy, you know, so, say when I'm cooking the prawns, I'm probably best off talking about it as I go, instead of doing the lines . . .'

Lily was torn. On one hand she felt for this poor guy, who was clearly way out of his comfort zone, plucked from the country and thrust into the big smoke, hurled in front of a national audience. On the other hand, he'd waited until it was a LIVE TV SITUATION to tell her he was struggling.

'Yes, no, we definitely want that, it's all about you having a chat, and talking us through what you're doing, connecting with the viewers, all of which I'm sure Eliza went over with you —'

'She didn't really go over any of that stuff,' he said, looking to Lily with panicked eyes. She marvelled at the change in him – from the cocky, abrupt man she'd seen yesterday, to this scared little boy.

'It's fine. It's simple, I promise. You chose this recipe, you know it back to front, and Rob will be there with you, asking questions and guiding the segment. All you have to do is cook the meal, and tell the camera – and him – what you're doing in as simple terms as you can . . . Assume the viewer has never turned on a stove in their life. Be conversational, like they're your friends, and you're just explaining the dish as you cook it, in your own, very well-lit kitchen.'

Lily tried to give Jack her widest, most comforting smile. Whether he was a pig or not, and she was sensing that perhaps he was not, it was her job to make sure he felt comfortable, and not like he should quickly re-appropriate his deveining knife. When the segment went well Eliza nicked the credit, but when they fell flat, or the talent was hopeless, Lily copped the blame. It was in her best interest that he feel good.

He exhaled and closed his eyes for a few seconds, a smile coming over his face.

'Thanks. Yeah, that's what I thought it was, but with all the cameras and being on set and with the clock counting down . . .'

Lily smiled again, this time genuinely. How attractive he was when he was vulnerable, she thought perversely. Perhaps they would get along after all.

'Totally normal. You will be great. I promise. And remember, I'm here to help: need a coffee? Water? Shot of Bundy rum? That's what you cowboys drink, isn't it?'

He smiled broadly as he looked at her, shaking his head for no. Just as he did so, the full set lights came up, and Lily faintly heard the sound of harps and angels gently shaking their gilded locks. Oh, my, she thought as she bathed in his luminosity. So *this* is why Eliza chose him.

She nodded and walk-ran off the set to find Dale, tweet a backstage pic of Jack as a teaser, and find a Red Bull.

The segment was a success. Rob and Jack's chemistry was great, the set looked unreal, and the entire female population of Twitter, including Sophie J, a pretty and famous singer/DJ with 145000 followers, had panted and lusted obscenely over Jack, which pleased Sasha very much.

Despite the fact Jack had wigged out pre-show, and had a pretty shocking rehearsal, he'd been deceptively confident in front of the camera today. He began a little shaky, but as soon as he and Rob started bantering, he was off. Lily was amazed that he seemed incapable of holding a human conversation in real life, and yet on live TV, he was suddenly the world's most charming man.

'*Told* you he'd be fantastic!' Eliza whispered excitedly to Lily as she helped Dale clean up the set. She was giddy with relief.

'Yeah, he did well,' Lily said, smiling enthusiastically.

'Rob talked over him – when *doesn't* he? – but he held his own, and what about that bit where he barrelled the camera and smiled? I mean, I nearly *collapsed*.'

'Mmm, it was pretty great,' Lily agreed.

'Did you think it worked?' Lily asked Dale when they were alone. 'Honestly, guys' perspective?'

Dale thought for a second. 'Yes.' And he walked off to the real kitchen with a stack of dirty pans.

Lily was glad that Dale thought Jack did a good job. Dale might be socially dyslexic, but he was a good nuts-and-bolts guy, and had a strong understanding of what was successful and what sucked. Plus, he was male, and therefore not influenced by Jack's physical radiance. Lily had promised herself she would not be granting Jack any concessions just because he was a dreamboat, but thankfully, she might not even need to.

11

Lily drove home, weary and impatiently scarfing chips from the bag of takeaway she'd picked up as a treat for a good first show. She couldn't get Jack out of her head, or from underneath her skin. She couldn't very well talk to Simone about it, because even though Lily knew there was definitely no crush, Simone would be on the same Mills & Boon page as Alice, and accuse her of falling for him. And that would be a clear violation of the man-detox. Even though *Sim* was the one who had been in the bathtub topless with Zoolander last night. Which reminded her of the mess Lily might be walking into tonight, if Simone hadn't yet located her brain, or was still asleep to make up for the sleep 'fast' she'd been on since Saturday.

Opening the front door, she called out to her flatmate. No response. But Simone had clearly been awake. She'd been expressly awake, in fact, judging by the sparkling kitchen, the fresh bunch of pink oriental lilies – Lily's favourite – on the coffee table and the smell of expensive fig candles in the air. Lily dumped her handbag and takeaway on the bench and read the handwritten note propped against the vase.

Lil . . . I am so SO sorry for last night and my behaviour in

the bathroom (!!!) and just all of it. I hope I didn't ruin your
day too much. Let me take you for dinner this week to say
sorry, please, babe! I have dinner with Dad who's in town
tonight but will see you if you're still awake when I get home.
Sorry, sorry.
LOTS OF LOVE AND APOLS XOXOXOXOXO

Lily could've predicted this exact scenario, because every time
Simone had a bender, it was the same: intense guilt, manic cleaning and apology flowers. At least Sim wasn't on suicide watch,
which was how she jokingly referred to the day-after downer. Lily
shook her head and wondered how much longer she could live with
Simone. Lately she'd been fantasising about living on her own.
Maybe turning thirty this year was the kick up the arse she needed
to finally do it. Not that Sim was a terrible flatmate by any means,
but these benders did Lily's head in, and sometimes just the sheer
presence of another person in the house was enough to irritate Lily
after a long day at work.

Mimi had always said a woman must live on her own at least
once in her life, before 'the husband and children' claimed all
available space and time, and Lily kind of agreed. She wasn't going
to use Bathgate as her impetus, though; that was unfair. Simone
was an excellent flatmate most of the time, even if she had an
unnecessary and unwarranted vendetta against cow's milk and soft
drinks; plus she charged Lily embarrassingly low rent. Nonetheless, it wouldn't be the worst thing in the world to sniff out what
was available in terms of non-prohibitively expensive one-bedroom
apartments in the area. Ideally Lily would buy one, but with only
five grand saved up – another thing she had to work on – that was
as likely as Simone gnawing on a T-bone.

In a pitiable attempt at being a grown-up, Lily dumped her

burger and the remainder of her chips onto a dinner plate before settling on the sofa to watch *The Big Bang Theory*. It was the most delicious portion of her day by a long stretch, and only a Snickers ice-cream bar would've made it better. Lily heard the keys in the front door. A smile crept onto her lips; Simone would be very sheepish after last night, and it was always fun to laugh at her in her depleted state.

But if she was either of these things, she didn't show it: she walked in wearing a short pink dress and long silver and orange earrings, her hair loose and flowing. She looked fresh and pretty, like the girls in tampon ads who rode horses and frolicked on the beach, no matter how bloated and crampy they supposedly were.

'Do you just not get hangovers?' Lily said as she took in her flatmate.

Simone looked as though she didn't understand why Lily would say such a thing.

'Are you serious? I felt *so* gross all day! I just had a casting this arvo, that's all. Took several Sudafed to wake me up, don't you worry.' She flipped her keys back and forth in her hand and looked anxiously at Lily.

'Babe, I am *so* sorry for last night. What you saw was disgusting. I'm . . . we just got caught up in the mood, and we clearly didn't know when to stop.' She placed the keys on the dresser and walked over to the couch, perching on the arm.

'Yeah, I figured that when I got home on a Sunday evening to find you having a spa party.' Lily smiled.

Simone smacked her hands over her face in embarrassment, a muffled 'ohmygod' slipping between the fingers.

Suddenly she ripped her hands off and stared straight at Lily, eyes wide.

'I didn't do a THING with Kane, by the way. He's a friend of

Skye's – well, they hook up, but sometimes he has a boyfriend too – so, you know, but anyway: point is I know how that would've looked, but I did NOT break our pact, babe, trust me.'

'Hmm,' Lily said, playing unconvinced, opening her laptop to fire off a few emails before bed.

'*Lil!* It would take a HELL of a lot more drugs to get me to do anything with him – *so* not my type, and anyway, have a little faith in your girl! I can party without hooking up, you know.'

Lily raised one eyebrow.

'SKYE was with him! Not me, I was dancing!'

Lily broke into laughter. 'I didn't say a thing! You're on your own here.'

Simone tossed a cushion at Lily. 'Anyway, it won't happen again.'

The memory of how bad Lily had felt that morning sharply reminded her that she was not in the mood for playing Lady Gullible tonight.

'Sim, it will, and you and I both know it. But it's your house, and you're allowed to do as you please. I should've just stayed at Mimi's. Was my own fault.'

A look of hurt crossed Simone's cherubic face. Lily had ruminated and analysed it all so intently – most of it at one a.m. this morning in a fit of fury – that she'd forgotten that to Simone, hearing it at 'conclusion' point, it sounded pretty harsh.

'Babe, you live here too. It's OUR home, our sanctuary. I'm sorry I did that; will you forgive me? Please? I hate when you're all cranky with me.'

'I was definitely pissed at you this morning, but I'm over it now. I'm just tired. It was first show back today.'

Simone's left hand flew up to cover her mouth. 'Oh NOOOO! And you didn't get any sleep!'

Lily gave her freakishly fresh-looking friend a weak smile. She would not have managed it ten hours ago. 'It's fine, Sim. The new chef was surprisingly good, which is a relief.'

'Guy or girl? I can't remember, sorry.'

You can't remember because I didn't tell you, Lily thought to herself. There was no point introducing the idea of a hunky chef at the workplace during a man-detox, it would just make Simone suss and annoying. And she *never* watched the show, so Lily's secret was safe.

'A guy. He's nice enough, quiet country lad.'

Simone eyed up her flatmate. 'Is he hot?'

'If you like Ken dolls. Not my type.'

'You won't get a crush on him, by any chance, will you, babe? We're not even a month into this thing and —'

'You're already sharing baths with nude men I *know*! It's a disgrace.'

Simone giggled and poured herself a glass of water from the filtered, alkaline water jug in the kitchen, which Lily never bothered with because she was too lazy to refill it. She poured one for Lily and placed it next to the evidence of her burger on the coffee table. She didn't say a word about Lily eating takeaway, which Lily knew meant she was *really* trying to behave herself.

'So how's your dad?' Lily asked with her eyes on her screen checking if she'd missed anything in the final script for tomorrow's show.

'Oh, fine. Usual distracted self. Babe, I'm beat, I'll see you in the morning.'

On her way upstairs, Simone called out, 'Are you free for dinner anytime this week? I thought we could try the new Mexican place on Victoria Street?'

'Sold!' Lily yelled back, then hit send on the email to Dale with the script. She decided she'd get in before her usual six a.m. start tomorrow so she had a chance to go over it with Jack before the segment, and make sure he was completely comfortable with it. Then maybe they could finally just be regular workmates instead of him being a weird, anxious guy with a stunning jawline and great hair.

She closed her laptop with a flourish and dragged her feet up to bed to not think about Jack.

12

Sasha was in a very good mood. The first two weeks of ratings were excellent. They had beaten *The Jenny Show* three times, which was a big deal, since last year they had beaten her that many times in as many months.

'All comes down to the Adonis in the kitchen, I'd say. Have you seen what women are saying about him on social media? He was all over Twitter on Friday, just because his white T-shirt got wet. I've never seen anything quite like it, to be honest.' Sasha shook her head, her bright lipstick immaculate, her haircut crisp and sharp.

Eliza nodded like a robot at everything Sasha said, mmm-ing enthusiastically. Her grey knee-length skirt was clinging to her in an unnatural and unsightly fashion, as though she were meat in a sausage, albeit a very tiny, thin one. She was missing an earring, Lily noted.

'Well, I mean, I think we've had a *reeeally* strong line up of guests, too.' Nikkii butted in, leaning forward to assert her presence, in case her lurid aqua top didn't do the job. 'Miranda Kerr certainly helped, and don't forget we were up again—'

'It's Jack,' Sasha interrupted, looking down at her phone as she spoke. 'He is our golden goose, and we need to make sure we keep him top of mind. I'd like some more publicity for him too, Siobhan – he hasn't quite got the profile we need yet. There's no reality TV background, no cookbook to speak of, no high-profile dolly on his arm – do what you can to put a bit more wind in that sail, would you? Perhaps *The Night Show* can get him on every now and again, and let's have him do some more radio, too.' Sasha stood up, collecting her iPad and phone, and fluffing her deep-violet scarf lightly with one hand.

'But well done, is my headline. Let's keep it going.' She smiled at the team and walked out, her assistant scrambling after her.

Nikkii assumed the role of Most Powerful Person in the Room the second Sasha was gone, leaning forward and placing her palms on the table, before asking Siobhan earnestly if she needed any help with media contacts, because she was on *amazing* terms with a lot of people in the media, and more than happy to assist. As Nikkii commenced one of the most feverish name-drop storms Lily had ever witnessed, Eliza nodded and mmm-ed even more furiously, and Lily doodled absently on her notebook. Alice appeared to be falling asleep. Poor darling: she always peaked around ten a.m., then crashed after lunch, a five-year-old in the depths of fatigue after a dizzying sugar high.

Lily closed her notebook and gently interrupted. 'Sorry, guys, uh, do you need us any more?' She used the most inoffensive, sweet tone she could. They could have this boring, self-aggrandising chat alone; she had recipes to type out and a new apron to source for Jack. 'White is far too drab,' Sasha had said. 'He should be in something dashing. Something to highlight those eyes.'

Nikkii looked at Lily with her usual mix of condescension and pretend affection. 'Lil, we're just sorting these contacts out. It's actually quite important?'

So much passive aggression, so few words to convey it. And always that unnecessary upwards inflection at the end.

Lily smiled, shooting rolled eyes at Alice the second Nikkii went back to her bullshit rave to Siobhan, who, as a *publicist*, already knew everyone worth knowing anyway.

'Alrighty then!' Eliza said, finally, still thinking it was a funny thing to say almost twenty years after *Ace Ventura*. 'That will probably do us til next week.'

As everyone stood up, she said, 'Lily, can I have a quick word?' Alice shot Lily a look of surprise. The hairs on the back of Lily's neck stood up. She felt like she was back at school. Or busted shoplifting, which had happened only once, because she had only ever shoplifted once, and was clearly horrible at it. All ridiculous thoughts, since Eliza was probably just going to ask her what she thought about adding some magnets to the on-set fridge.

Once the room was cleared, Eliza closed the door in an over-the-top manner and then perched on the table, a move she'd probably seen on TV and wanted to try for herself.

'Lily, I'm not sure if you've heard, but there are some changes happening across the station and also here at *The Daily*.'

Oh, sweet Jesus, Lily thought. She was being fired. Or some-thinged.

'No?' Lily said honestly, her heart racing.

'Just a few *small* changes, movement, promotions and new positions and whatnot, you know, normal restructuring stuff . . .'

Lily swallowed.

'Anyway, there's a series producer role coming up . . . within the station, and I thought you'd like to know. I know you're probably wanting to move up by now, and I don't blame you.' She smiled as though she had just presented Lily with a brand new Aston Martin.

Lily's heart instantly flicked gears, from terrified to excited.

'Wow, really? Do you know which show?'

Cue a smile that definitely *did* know, from a person who was almost definitely benefitting from this news on some level.

'Mmm, I really can't say any more, sorry, Lil. But I did want to give you a bit of a heads-up, because it's all so exciting and I think you should consider finding out more when that information becomes available. Don't you agree?'

Oh well, thought Lily. It was pretty useless info for now, but at least Eliza was alerting her to the possibility of a promotion. This could be a game-changer. She felt exhilaration flow through her veins. All she wanted this year was a promotion and now one was possible. Destiny, you cheeky old fox . . .

'Thanks so much for letting me know, Eliza.'

'Oh, you know I love helping out!' she said, full-stopping with a giggle. She was far too excited about all this, which meant she was almost certainly being promoted – although to what Lily had no idea; in the big scheme of things Eliza was about as useful as the fake on-set sink.

Lily headed to the kitchen with her head in a swirl of possibilities. Maybe this was *finally* her time. Maybe this was the year she became a grown-up, which she'd been positive was a myth created by health insurance companies. She would have a proper, impressive job, and she could maybe even move out on her own. She flinched a bit when she realised that the missing element to this glorious new life was love, which seemed to be further away than it ever had been. And with this man-detox making Lily a complete workaholic – and a pent-up one at that – things weren't exactly shimmering with hope in that area. Was it too much to ask for a guy to present himself who wasn't a nob or an alcoholic or a loser?

Simone was cruising through this detox, Lily conceded. She was cheerful and had found no reason to stop being her usual gregarious, good-time self, if her partying was anything to go by. Maybe she got a thrill from having all the boys throw themselves at her, and then telling them that she was awfully sorry, but she was not-allowedsies at the moment, and they should stop sending so many long-stemmed roses and diamond earrings. That, or she was secretly seeing Michael again, which she'd done before, to her immense emotional detriment and Lily's chagrin. As far as *Lily* knew, the last time Simone and Michael had seen each other was just before Christmas at a wedding. Simone had looked heavenly and refrained from drinking so she didn't make any stupid mistakes, and this strength clearly acted as a powerful aphrodisiac, with Michael basically proposing to her outside the women's toilets after following her there. To Lily's delight (and surprise) Simone knocked him back and left the wedding.

Lily was beginning to wonder whether there was any point going out if you couldn't pick up, or be chatted up, or hook up. It was the gilded excitement of the unknown, the lure of spontaneity, the thrill of not knowing where your night might end up, or with whom, that gave her the energy to go out . . . not the idea of drinking til she was unintelligible, and sucking down kebabs and hot chips at four a.m., delicious as they were.

She leaned against one of the chairs and waited for her kettle to boil, so deep in thought she didn't see Jack enter the kitchen. He leaned over to where the kettle was and looked at Lily, his hand hovering over the power point.

'Can I take this?' he said, brows raised.

Lily snapped to attention when she realised what he was about to do. It had been weeks since he'd last done it but she was just as territorial of her kettle.

'*Hey!* I'm using tha—' And she stopped herself, realising how impolite she was being to her golden goose.

'Just messing with you, Woodward,' he said in a way that made her feel stupid. Lily pretended not to notice that he'd changed from this morning, and was now wearing a polo and shorts, and that he had excellent legs. Very casual for the office, she thought, throwing stones in her jeans, sandals and T-shirt.

'Well, you know, you *do* have a tendency for nicking it, so it's not crazy to think you might do it again,' she grumbled, pouring the precious hot water into her mug and over her teabag. She quite liked that he'd called her Woodward. It felt familiar. Like he was the popular guy at school giving her some crude form of recognition

'I reckon you need a biscuit for that,' he said suddenly, eyes dipping to her tea. Before she could answer, he'd darted off. He was like a mad scientist in that test kitchen; once he had finished the show he'd go straight in there til late afternoon, when, after being briefed on the following day's show, he left for the day.

A few minutes later, just as Lily was weighing up whether it was rude to head back to her desk or not, he flew back into the kitchen, holding out two lumpy golden cookies on a paper towel.

'What are *these*?' Lily asked, her mouth gently coating itself in anticipatory saliva.

'Peanut butter, salted caramel and white chocolate.'

'No WAY,' Lily exclaimed, in ecstatic disbelief at the flavours presented to her in biscuit form.

'PB is my favourite thing in the universe; I put it on everything. I can't think of one thing that isn't improved by it. Have you tried it in porridge with banana and honey? It's the *best*.'

Jack smiled, his eyes sparkled and there was a gentle warmth in his gaze. It was a bit much to have all of that focused on you, Lily realised. How ever did his girlfriends cope? She asked that not knowing whether he had one – not that the entire female population of the station hadn't done their best to find out. He was too

88

understated, too much of a cookie-baking savant to talk about his personal life. It drove Siobhan crazy: she needed a hook for the gossip ravens. Lily was quietly impressed he'd held out. She took one of the cookies.

'Take both, I ate half the cookie mix,' he said sheepishly.

Lily took the paper towel politely from Jack, their fingers touching ever so quickly as she did so.

'Thanks, Jack, that's very nice of you,' she said, wondering what she was supposed to do now, because he was still standing in front of her, blocking the doorway, a goofy grin on his face.

'Well, go on,' he said, looking expectantly at her.

Feeling awkward, Lily set her mug and notebook back on the counter so she didn't drop them *and* the biscuits and mess up this whole heightened Movie Moment.

She bit into one of the cookies. It was the perfect blend of crunchy and chewy, and as each of the flavours elegantly shouted for attention in her mouth, she closed her eyes and savoured it.

'Sweet baby Jesus. That is SO good,' she said, mouth still full of cookie, eyes wide with sugar and delight.

'Not too peanutty?' His eyes were clouded in genuine concern. He was like a Stepford wife trying to perfect his recipe for a stern, unappreciative husband.

'Well,' she said, wiping the crumbs from her mouth with the back of her free hand, realising how gross it was only after the act, 'that's a stupid question to ask a PB maniac, isn't it.' And she took another bite, all thoughts of being ladylike suddenly extinct.

'True.' He watched her enjoy the cookie, smiling, until Lily felt awkward and picked up her mug and notebook carefully, to head back to her desk.

'Thanks again,' she said. 'I'm always open for business when it comes to cookie tasting.'

'And friands?' he said playfully.

Lily blushed slightly. 'Sorry, but they were gross. They were and you know it.'

'Meh, it happens sometimes,' he said cheerfully before leaving, presumably back to the test kitchen. As Lily strolled to her desk, she couldn't help wondering if he'd offered Nikkii or Eliza or even Alice some of his cookies, or if she was The Special One. The realisation that he had specially brought her cookies, hand-delivered and with feedback eagerly anticipated, had her lolling around in the sunshine of her mind.

13

Yes, still on man-ban. No, not in love with Jack. Tho he did bring
me some just-made cookies to eat with my tea the other day . . .

Lily hit send on her text to Mimi, smiling at the memory, aware
that she was giving her mother ammunition in her quest to make
Lily pursue Jack, but not really caring. She'd told Mimi all about
him – the good and the bad – over dinner on the weekend, and now
Mimi was convinced she'd found her daughter's future husband. It
wasn't the first time.

Men don't just bring women cookies willy-nilly ox

Mimi wrote.

They do when you're producing their cooking segment.

Lily hit back without skipping a beat. But maybe she's right,
Lily thought, a gentle momentum building in her. Maybe a
little crush on Jack *was* worth exploring. Hell, maybe he was

even worth detox-breaking.

Taking her mother's advice to be young, free and social, and finally feeling like she had the energy for it, Lily finally decided to call Simone on her dinner offer, and they made a plan to eat at the trendy Mexican joint. Of course, when Lily tried to book, there were no tables for a fortnight, but Simone assured her it would be fine, and sure enough, as soon as the pair arrived, the girl on the door recognised Simone and, in a flurry of air kisses and 'babes' and 'you look *hot*' and '*amazing* dress', they were straight inside.

Simone looked the part with her mini-dress and gold heels, even if that part was slightly reminiscent of a certain role played by Julia Roberts in a certain film starring Richard Gere; while Lily, wearing a simple black dress and wooden wedges, looked like she was there to clear the plates. Sensing this was not optimal for potential ego-boosting man-attracting-then-dismissing, Lily immediately pulled her long hair out of her high topknot and shook it loose.

'HOT,' Simone said, nodding seriously. 'Always hotter out. *Always*.'

'Speaking of, this place is an oven, would it kill them to turn the aircon on?'

'No way. Hotter is sexier.'

'What about this menu? Is this sexy, would you say, or is it hot?' Lily asked, picking up the drinks menu – housed in a Mexican children's book – and shaking it in front of her friend's face playfully.

'That's cool. Different.'

'Aha.'

'Babe, it's so fun to go out, just the two of us. Why don't we do this ever? Remember the fun we used to have at Pelicans? Ohmygod those Pimms jugs were the *worst* but it was so *fun*!' Simone said, clapping her hands together excitedly.

'Because I'm overworked, and you travel a lot.'

'I haven't been travelling much lately, actually,' Simone said, thoughtfully. 'I've really just been trying to centre, you know? Get grounded. I went to this amazing talk on transcendental meditation the other day; I'm going to learn how to do it. There's a retreat in Bali next month. I want to locate my inner bliss. By the pool.'

'Sure there's no secret man bringing you bliss I should know about? You're not home much at the moment . . .'

Simone shook her head quickly, tightly, a frown forming over her fresh, pretty, make-up-free eyes. 'I've just had some late shoots and Grace's boyfriend moved out, so I stayed there last weekend because she was a *total* mess and —'

'I'm *kidding*. I know the reason you don't have a boyfriend is cos you're ugly and mean, but we also have a pact, and we don't break pacts.' As Lily said it, she thought of Jack and felt a shiver of shame trickle down her back like icy water.

'Can we grab two tobacco margaritas, please?' Simone called out to a waiter who had stopped for a second near them. He looked up at the voice, prepared to be pissed off, but one look at Simone's dazzling smile and he simply nodded and walked off to perform his duties for the new Queen of Mexico.

'Well, *they* sound disgusting,' Lily said.

'They're the signature drink. Grace said they're gorge. Anyway, you're a cooking person, you should be game to try weird stuff.'

'I'll have *one*. Can't get too pissed tonight, I need my brain tomorrow.'

'Couple won't hurt,' Sim said, with the syrupy coercion of a seasoned enabler. 'Oh, there's that douche Sean I saw for a bit. Owns that pilates studio in Paddington and cracks on to all his clients.'

'Sounds like a great guy, why'd you let him go?'

'He's the exact reason we're ignoring men,' she said, waving manically at someone across the bar – probably Sean – then blowing them a kiss.

'I'm not exactly fighting them off with a stick.'

'One jug of tobacco margaritas,' the young waiter announced, setting down a '70s-style plastic water jug and two plastic tumblers more appropriate in a preschool than a restaurant. 'On the house,' he said, blushing at Simone and scarpering away.

'What a little honey,' Sim said, as she poured out two drinks. 'To us!' she exclaimed.

'To whatever this gross drink is!' Lily added, taking a sip of the strangest, strongest cocktail she'd ever made the mistake of drinking.

Three hours and the wrong amount of margaritas later, Lily and Simone were with Grace at Bahama. Skye turned up, fresh from a house party, with her energy sitting at approximately 185 out of 10.

'*Woooooooh!*' Grace squealed, hand in the air as Calvin Harris pumped through the enormous speakers on the wall. She was chatting to a very, very beautiful man with a shaved head and no regard for the wedding finger on his left hand, and Simone was telling Lily in no uncertain terms Lily had to stay.

'So *what* if you're abi'tired tomorrow, the show will go on!'

'The show! Must! Go! On!' Skye contributed, marching like a soldier, her hand flipping in and out in a salute in time with the music.

Lily shook her head. She actually felt quite unsteady on her feet. A whisper of ceviche, some fish tacos and one thousand cocktails will do that, she realised.

'No. No, no, *no*, issnot like that, I HAVE to be there and make sure everything is smooth and running smoothly.'

'IS THE HUNK COMING?' Skye yelled directly into Simone's

ear. She really was quite the rubbish drunk. Simone cupped her hand over Skye's mouth and said, '*Shhhhh.*'

'Who?' Lily demanded, sensing she was missing something. Something important.

'No one!' Simone said, grabbing Lily's hand and kissing it messily.

'You sure?' Lily was now on high alert. Simone nodded resolutely, her eyes glazed and wide.

'Lil, why you wanna leave all the time? One more drink? Pleeeease?' Simone was doing her sexy-baby-get-what-she-wantsy voice, which might work on everyone else, but Lily wasn't swayed.

'No, no, no, I'm out, youguyss have fun, and hey, whyno'go to Skye or Grace's house if you decide to have a spa party, why don'you?' She may have been drunk, but she still knew she wasn't interested in another drug-soaked trash fest on home turf. She fumbled around on the bench for her tiny red bag, underneath the mammoth Alexander Wang and Balenciaga sacks belonging to Skye and Grace.

'Promise,' said Simone. 'I'll have a Xanny and all you'll hear is my head slapping the pillow.'

Lily shook her head. 'Thass *dangerous* after drinking, you know that, right?'

'*Who's* famous?' Simone yelled, as the music hit a crescendo.

It was definitely, definitely time to leave, Lily thought. She walked out of the tiny bar, clutching her bag tightly to her body so as to avoid a shower of drunk-gesticulating-person beverages raining down on it. Not *one* guy had shown interest in her tonight, she realised sadly. Although to be fair, it would be hard to see past the trio of hair and legs and breasts that were Sim, Skye and Grace. Why did she do this to herself? Who was she trying to fool? She wasn't a young, sassy, sexy model who could afford to get written off on a school night; she was a (pretty much) thirty-year-old producer trying to secure a promotion on the number-one morning show for women aged 25–54. She was angry at herself for thinking she needed to go out and prove herself, she was upset that no one had even tried to chat her up, let alone get to a point where she could knock them back, and she was incredibly focused on finding a takeaway shop.

14

'Tim, can you *please* move that stand off set, we go live in minutes and I need it off, now.'

Lily cleared her throat. She was so thirsty. So, so thirsty. Not even two Diet Cokes and a Hydralyte and 1.5 litres of water had helped quench the desert in her mouth.

'I'll do it,' Jack piped up, and quickly lifted the heavy metal stand out of shot.

Lily didn't have the energy to fawn or overthink every little thing he did today. She just needed to get through the day.

'Thanks, Jack. Tim only hears things that don't involve WORK.'

'I heard that!' Tim piped up from behind, grinning.

'See?' Lily raised her eyebrows at Jack, who was smiling.

'Everything all right, Lil?' Jack asked.

'I'm fine, just. Probably drank a little more than I needed to last night.'

'Thought so. Eyes gave you away.'

'Gee, thanks.'

'Hangovers don't get my sympathy, sorry.' Gross, thought Lily. He was being one of those self-satisfied hangover-hating people.

'I'll remember that next time you have one,' she said.

'You'll be waiting a while.'

'I *knew* you were a non-drinker. No one who drinks would ever be so mean to the fragile and depleted.'

'I had my time, believe me.'

'I don't drink often, I just – it was a close friend's birthday.' Lily wasn't sure why she felt she should lie, or play it down, or defend her actions. But Jack made her feel somehow . . . inadequate.

Jack laughed. 'You don't need to justify anything to me.'

He meant it, but Lily still felt a veil of shame wash over her. That was it. She was NOT coming into work with a hangover again. It wasn't worth it; it *definitely* wasn't worth it. Alice's mantra of having hangovers on work's time rather than your own had *seemed* like a sound philosophy, but Lily needed her brain a bit more these days. Especially if she wanted that promotion. Which she did.

'So Rob *and* Mel are in this segment with you, and I need you to mention Rob's horrible effort at a birthday cake for Mel, because that leads into —'

'The surprise party,' he interrupted.

'And the —'

'Birthday cake, I know. I made it, remember, Lil?'

She smiled at him in defeat, and he smiled back. She felt her eyes twinkling, despite their bleariness, and his eyes processed and enjoyed that cute little twinkle, and everything just shut up for one beautiful second: Lily's headache and her stressful inner monologue, and the sound of cameramen and floor crew being clowns.

'Sorry to break up this romantic moment but forty seconds to go.' Grimmo's voice rudely interrupted, editorialising in the extremely inappropriate way only he could do. He loved teasing Lily, said she reminded him of his daughter.

Lily swung her head to him. '*Grimmo!* Jesus . . .' And before Jack could see her blush, she walked over to the sofa to accompany the hosts to the 'kitchen', seeing as they were having too much fun chatting and seemed to have forgotten where they were required.

Lily watched the three get into position. First few shows aside, Jack was now calm and prepared before his segment, and charming and good at explaining things during filming, and just the right mix of educational and playful, too. He was proving to be a bit of a find, she had to give Eliza that.

The segment was a wild success, even if it wasn't for the right reasons. Mel was so shocked and terrified when the streamers dropped and the balloons launched and the birthday music played that she'd yelled 'Fuck!' and then ducked and dropped her mug of tea on the floor and as she bent down to get it, so did Jack, and they knocked heads, and then, just as the gods in slapstick heaven applauded their magnificent handiwork, Jack slipped on the wet floor and fell on his arse. And it was all caught on glorious live TV.

Sasha was thrilled to her Issey Miyake collar. She wanted authenticity and fun to be the cornerstones of the show, and the circus in the kitchen had delivered just that. Once Lily had stopped laughing, at and with the crew, and made sure her stars were okay, especially Jack, which they were, albeit embarrassed, she immediately told Siobhan to get a cut of the scene to put on the website and on social media. It was too funny not to. Lily herself watched it twelve times.

'Hey, since we're still here at eight p.m., we've earned a wine – got any?'

Alice, all blazing red curls and wearing what genuinely looked like a purple painting smock and may well have been, had walk-rolled her chair over to Lily's desk while spearing a plastic fork into a horrible-looking noodle cup, probably in the hope of finding something in there other than MSG and water.

'You can. I've been masking a huge hangover all —'

'Oh yeah, you really "masked" it, toots. Everyone knew you were hung as.'

A wave of panic rippled through Lily.

'Everyone? Like, Sasha and Eliza?'

'Dunno about them, but crew, definitely. Problem is you're too pretty in real life, so when you look a mess, it shows. Hey, your seg today . . . I couldn't get my eyes and brain around what was happening.'

'Fuck!' Lily's lack of sleep and heavy head and fatigue had all finally caught up with each other, and she was not coping. She felt teary and histrionic.

'Chill, Lil, it's fine, we've all been there . . . Remember the time I had to vomit into a shopping bag in the foyer so Sasha didn't see? Don't be sad . . .' Alice looked at her friend with kind eyes.

'I just, it's not the time to be dropping the ball, is all.' Lily wondered whether to reveal her knowledge about the series producer role to Alice. They were both segment producers; they were both eligible. Alice might use the information to outshine Lily. Although, to be fair, while Alice was good at her job, she was by no means as accomplished as Lily. Lily felt horrible admitting that about her friend, but ultimately, this was business, and she had to look out for herself. Her co-workers were not going to help her; she had to help herself.

'Hey, how's . . . Jim? Bob? Dingus? I can't keep up.'

'Nick. Went overseas for six weeks on Saturday but I'm ending it anyway. He was way too fuckin' clingy. Would text and email me constantly, those shitty emoticons splattered all over the place . . .

He even tried to come when I went to get a *wax*. How can I be attracted to a man who has nothing better to do on a weekend than accompany me while I have my vagina groomed?'

'You think *all* guys are clingy because you frustrate and confuse them by being so independent.'

The look on Alice's face indicated that this had in fact occurred to her, but it wasn't the point.

'So you and Jack are right old bezzies these days, huh? His face certainly lights up when you're around . . . *I* reckon that maybe your crush is mutual . . .'

'You're a goose. Take your noodles and roll off, I need to finish this so I can go home and feel like I had *some* kind of life before seeing your head back in here at six a.m.'

'We are suuuuuuuuuuch looooooooooooosers . . .' Alice sang as she walk-rolled like a crab back to her desk, weaving through desks in the empty office, snooping along the way.

Lily turned back to her screen but the words blurred before her. Alice was an idiot. Jack would *never* think of her like that. If anything, they were just morphing into mates, almost a brother-sister dynamic, complete with teasing and ribbing. Lily was quite sure he was not the kind of guy who would stay single for long and that soon she wouldn't even have the luxury of maybe-possibly-in-another-universe dreaming of him noticing her, because he would have some annoyingly perfect girlfriend who was *way* more on his level. She shook her head to physically remove this idea. Jack Winters was not her type, and she was not his, and just because they were getting along well didn't mean shit. This was strictly business, she said quietly, because it was the kind of cool sentence you never got to actually say in Real Life, and this might be her only chance.

15

Simone was padding around the kitchen in a singlet and undies, and boiling the kettle when Lily got home, starving and thinking of little else but the macaroni and cheese she was about to make.

'Hey, dancing queen, how you feeling?' Lily noticed Simone had make-up on, which meant she hadn't spent the day sleeping off her big night, an impressive feat given her state last night.

'Hi, babe! *Good!* Came up with this incredible new smoothie today which *totally* reboots your system after a big one . . . banana and kale and flaxseed and chia and almond milk and cashew butter, you should have one next time you're hungover. I put the recipe on my blog. It's worth it, trust me. Got, like, 5000 likes on Instagram, too.' Lily always found it wildly hypocritical that Mrs Health Fanatic Sim thought nothing of depositing copious amounts of cocaine and booze into her body. Not even a pilates-bikram double and a kale, spinach and parsley cold-pressed juice could undo that shit, no matter what Sim chanted to herself as she meditated.

'Mmm,' Lily said distractedly. She was urgently looking for cheese in the fridge – not sheep's milk cheese, not soy cheese, not goat's milk feta, just CHEESE, for fuck's sake. It was looking dire. She'd even settle for Alice's noodles at this point, even though MSG gave her the sweats, jitters, nightmares and *day*mares.

'Annoyingly I slept til two, which isn't great. I'll have to be back in bed soon as I'm due on set at five a.m. tomorrow for a shoot, but at least my skin will look well rested.'

'I'm sure you'll just pop a Valium or five and you'll be off with the sleep fairies,' Lily said with no malice in her voice, although she had noticed Simone had been more fond than usual of her beloved 'tranqs' lately.

'I use *Xannies* for sleep, silly . . . Jesus, what *are* you looking for?' Simone sipped on her all-organic, all-biodynamic, made-from-Buddha's-actual-DNA tea, the perfect entrée to a dinner of prescription drugs, and frowned at her housemate's frenzied kitchen search.

'Look, I know it's my fault for never shopping, but there's nothing but healthy stuff in here, and I was *trying* to be good and not get Maccas on the way home, but now I really, really wish I had, because I am so hungry, and so hungover and so unhappy at the idea of packet miso soup and celery sticks.'

Simone smiled angelically, pityingly. 'Have some of the frittata I made yesterday. You can drench it in tommy sauce if you must.'

'*Yyyyes*. Yes, please.'

'Bottom shelf, under the foil. How fun was last night, huh?'

'Those girls are mental, Sim.' Lily sliced a huge wedge of colourful frittata and popped it in the microwave, or 'cancer box', as Simone called it.

'Do you know what's funny is that we've never all been single at the same time?'

'But you're *not* single . . . you're man-detoxing. Different.'

Simone smiled with her mouth closed.

'What is that smile? *What* did you *do*? Did you cheat on me?'

'LIL! No. Check my Facebook, I haven't even been flirting on it.

Check my phone even! Here!' She picked it up from the bench and held it out, its glittery pink case shimmering under the kitchen lights.

Lily pulled her steaming-hot plate out of the microwave, and immediately sprinkled salt and then poured tomato sauce on the meal.

'You could at least try it before you butcher it,' Simone muttered, like she always did. 'I'm gonna hit the sack, hey – you around tomorrow night?'

Simone had that look in her eyes like when she wanted to have a house chat about Lily always leaving the door unlocked, or forgetting to pay the cleaner.

'Yeah, probably work late, though. Did I tell you there's a promotion up for grabs? I really want it, Sim. A lot. Maybe *then* I can actually move out and live like a grown-up woman by myself,' Lily said, doing that thing, as usual, where she blurted out something she'd had time to process, but shocking anyone who didn't reside in her mind.

'What do you mean, move out? Are you not happy here?' Simone's voice sounded panicky and Lily realised that there was a cat in the room that was no longer in its bag.

'Of *course* I am, I love this place —'

'Did I do something wrong?' Simone looked like a scared little girl. All the sass and the sexiness and party-girl bravado was in a heap on the floor. She was in many ways more confident and successful and worldly than Lily, but she looked up to her friend, and relied on her to stay grounded and maintain some semblance of normality. Lily knew she'd tried living with other models, and it had led to one of the worst, most drug-addicted, unhappy and unhealthy periods of her life. She'd developed a full-blown eating disorder, and a slew of bad habits. Then came Michael, and that whole mess, which she was still healing from. But with Lily, Simone said she felt like she had a home, and a sister of sorts. She was healthy and looked after herself here. She was in a good place now.

'No. Of course not, Sim,' Lily said, reassuringly. 'It was just a throwaway comment. I love living with you.'

'I know I have been partying a bit lately, but I can totally put a lid on it. I want you to love living here . . . It's our little temple. Are you sure?'

'Of course I'm sure,' Lily said, only forty per cent of her lying.

''Kay . . . Just always be honest with me, please, babe?' Simone said. 'If you pack your stuff and leave in the night you're in deep and steaming shit, I swear to God.'

'Promise I won't. And you promise not to take too many sleepers and overdose on me, Lindsay Lohan.'

Simone, sipping her tea, gave the universal sign for okay with her right hand, and walked upstairs and out of sight.

Moving out of here was not going to be easy, thought Lily. Best to get the promotion first *then* deal with it.

Friday's show was ridiculous. It happened occasionally: an energy like the last day of school permeated the entire set, and for a few hours, the viewers were treated to footage of giggling idiots making mistakes and terrible jokes, as though someone had slipped rum into their coffee. The result was a hyper, hysterical, boisterous party that somehow – Lily genuinely had no idea how – worked. Jack had been particularly charming, even signing off with an earnest, 'Cook it, share it, *enjoy* it,' right down the barrel of the camera, which Lily knew Sasha would love. Sasha *loved* a chef with a catchphrase.

Post-show, Jack was in the kitchen pouring himself a glass of water while Lily was quickly scraping together some breakfast, her first miserable piece of food for the day. She noticed that as always after the show, he was out of his fancy TV non-plaid shirt and back in his regular plaid shirt.

'*My* quote would be "buy it, fry it, eat it",' Lily said mischievously as she loaded her Vegemite toast onto what may well have been a serving platter, but was the only plate left.

Jack laughed. 'I believe that. Why do you eat that rubbish, Woodward? You know there's always enough food from set for you, I can easily put some aside.'

'How dare you. This is an Aussie staple.'

'It's crap. That bread is crap. If you're going to eat bread, make it worth it, get some decent sourdough or some soy and linseed.'

'Are you cheffing me?' She turned and peered at him with squinted eyes.

'Yes, I am. Life is too short for shitty bread.'

'Life is too short to track down your fancy precious posh bread, more like it,' Lily said with a guffaw, filling the kettle with water and clicking it on.

'*There* you are!' Eliza interrupted. 'You guys, what on earth was going on today? Your segment was ridiculous, it was like you were all . . . I don't know, high or something!' She was standing in the kitchen doorway wearing a short black dress that was intended for a younger woman with designs on a tacky nightclub. She'd teamed it with high cream heels for a classy morning look. She was trying to morph into Nikkii, Lily realised with internal hilarity.

'I promise I was sober,' Jack said in a friendly tone.

'Fine, but why were you all being so *weird*?'

'It was just a bit high-energy today for some reason. I'm not sure why.' Jack spoke with confidence.

'Lily,' Eliza's eyes settled on Lily with a look generally reserved for disappointed mothers. 'You know it's *your* job to keep things in line. I don't know why you let Mel sing that song when —'

'Trust me, there's nothing Lily could've done in that moment, Eliza. And actually, I thought she handled us perfectly.'

Lily's eyes widened: had Jack just stood up for her? And complimented her?

Eliza was enjoying Jack's assertive defence of Lily about as much as a broken collarbone.

'Well, I'm glad *you* were all having fun, meanwhi—'

'Fun is the name of the game, Eliza. Always.' Sasha's calm, wise voice floated into the room as she walked past the kitchen and continued on her way, like a perfectly timed yogi. How does she *do* that? Lily wondered.

Eliza's head snapped to the left to watch her boss, her eyes wide with humiliation, or at the very least a close cousin.

'I wish you would all learn to control yourselves; you're giving me a flipping heart attack. It's *live TV* for goodness sake,' she said, defeated, before chasing in an undignified fashion after Sasha.

Lily and Jack raised their eyebrows conspiratorially at each other and a wide grin washed over Lily's face. She was still glowing in the memory of his gallant verbal protection.

'How long have you worked here, Lil?' Jack asked, sipping his water, leaning back against the sink like some kind of hunk advertising filter-tap systems.

'Um, almost two years now.'

'Isn't that about the time you Gen Ys start getting fidgety?' he asked, with a knowing smile. He was so warm and chatty today. She basked in it.

'Spoken like a true Gen Xer.'

'Whoa, settle down, I'm only thirty-four. So then, what's the big plan? Where will you be in five years?'

She looked into Jack's blue eyes as she thought about her answer. His skin was a bit tanned, a bit weathered, kind of . . . lived in, she noted. It gave him a touch of *The Man From Snowy River*. Handsome and rugged, they'd call it.

'I'd love to be an EP one day, like Sasha. *Literally* like Sasha – she's so experienced, and talented, and wise, and generous, and so well respected in the industry. First I have to make series producer though.'

'You after Eliza's job?' he asked with a cheeky grin. It was dazzling. Whatever had been slipped into his coffee that day, Lily wanted a cruise liner's worth.

'Noooo . . . No, no, no. Well, kind of. Yeah, I guess. Very much so.'

Jack laughed, the small gap between his front teeth on full show. The excitement in her stomach and her enormous grin indicated to her that perhaps she was a little bit failing this man-detox. But maybe, *maybe* that was the whole point of it, the thing she and Simone had failed to see – that when you stop trying to attract men and stop thinking about them so much, it happens *organically*. Yes. That made perfect bloody sense. Put that in your essential oil burner and light it, Sim.

'Yours for the taking,' Jack said, finishing off his water, and plonking the glass in the dishwasher, like everyone else never did. He looked at her as he closed the dishwasher door.

'You're good at your job, Lil. That was a circus this morning, but you had it under control, you let us know when to rein it in, and you knew when to encourage us. Plus, you know, I'm new to all this, and you've made it a *lot* less nerve-racking. I reckon you definitely have Sasha's perspective on things. It's good.'

With that he walked out of the kitchen.

'Aren't you going to tell me to cook it, share it, *enjoy* it?' she heckled after him.

He popped his head back into the kitchen, his face etched in light humiliation. 'Ease up, Woodward, it just fell out of my mouth.'

'Too bad. It's now your official catchphrase. We'll probably get some T-shirts made.'

'Are you serious?' he asked, eyebrows at risk of punching through the atmosphere.

'Sorry!' she said in a not-at-all sorry voice, turning back to pour her hot water and add her two sugars.

'You will be,' he muttered, before walking off, leaving Lily smiling like a loon. She did a quick mental spreadsheet: Jack could cook like a dream, was fun and charming, was a natural on TV, baked *peanut-butter-based* desserts, was Ken-doll handsome, and was thoughtful, fun, kind and supportive. It was too much. If Lily was being tested, she'd just decided to fail by volition.

Alice walked into the kitchen barefoot, something she was told repeatedly not to do for OH&S reasons, but continually did, for comfort reasons. Dale was behind her, but he simply filled his aluminium water bottle before darting out again, a corduroy-clad fawn in a big scary forest.

'God, Eliza's stink today, isn't she?' said Alice. 'She gave me a serve for not getting a giveaway today, when she knows I'm only supposed to have two a week, and I've already done both this week.'

'Inside voice, Al, inside voice.'

'Sorry, Woo, didn't mean to interrupt your daydreaming about what lurks under Jack's undies.'

'Hilarious!' Lily said boisterously, clapping. 'Please, more of this fantastic comedy!'

'I saw him walk out of here; I know I'm right.' Alice was busy making herself a Milo milkshake, because she was five.

'Oh, well, obviously.'

'Bad news on that front by the way . . . Prince Charming is seeing someone,' Alice continued, stirring her drink furiously with the bottom of a butter knife.

'What?' Lily forgot to play cool.

'According to Siobhan, who knows everything that is pointless, he was at Bondi beach with some blonde bird yesterday afternoon.'

Lily wondered how she could get more information without looking obvious.

'And judging by his buoyant mood today, she mustn't be the treat-'em-mean type, if you know what I mean.' Alice winked lecherously and walked out of the kitchen, her little high-waisted red shorts cutting a line right down her arse.

Lily walked, biting absently into her cold toast, computing this new and horrible information. *Of course he was dating someone!* Jesus, why wouldn't he be? She herself had just compiled a solid list of why he was perfect. Even though Lily knew she was being hyper-optimistic to assume he would ever be interested in *her*, especially if he was dating some blonde slice of heaven, she grew resentful of the man-detox all the same.

It was time to end it, she confirmed. It was fucking useless. It was making no dent whatsoever in Lily's life, except for maybe a small wishful one that involved missing out on a lifetime of happiness and small gaps between teeth and eating homemade cookies in bed. Once at her desk, she picked up her phone and texted Simone.

Wanna get dinner? ☺

An immediate response, which was unusual for Sim.

Yessss! Sakura? Lets say 7 will txt if running late xoxo

Done x

Lily shuffled through the tiny, cramped restaurant to the back where Simone was waiting. She looked like a Bond girl, all tanned with enormous, hot-rollered hair, intense black eye make-up and a denim jacket over a little black dress. Lily knew this was post-shoot hair and make-up, but the other customers may not have. Sim was oblivious.

'Don't *you* look a treat tonight.'

'I couldn't be arsed taking it off,' Sim said, making way for Lily's big brown satchel on the bench next to her. 'I ordered some edamame, I'm *staaaarving.*'

The girls ordered their usual eggplant miso, seaweed salad, teriyaki tofu and a large bottle of warm sake, and Lily couldn't help thinking Sim had something on her mind. Oh God, maybe she was back with Michael. That was it. Of *course* that was it. They had been trying to do cold turkey ever since they'd split, but Simone was rubbish at refraining from drunk texting or calling. She had once even passed out on the steps of his apartment block after a particularly heartbroken mess of a night.

'Babe, so, I actually need to talk to you about something . . .' Simone said, gulping down her teeny cup of sake.

'I knew it! I knew something was up.' Lily's energy was probably a little too frenzied for the situation, but she was starting to feel anxious and wanted Sim to get talking.

'Promise you won't be mad?' Simone seemed as anxious to keep her news locked in her mouth as Lily was for her to spit it out.

'Come on, whatever it is, I'm sure it's fine.'

A deep breath, and then: 'I've met a guy.'

'*Simone!*' Lily sat back in her chair, her mouth gaping. She crossed her arms over her chest and shook her head slowly. Secretly she was thrilled it wasn't about Michael, and even more secretly she was double thrilled because this meant *she* wouldn't have to call the detox off.

'It's not Michael, is it? I *thought* you were *maybe* going to say you were back in touch with him.'

Simone shook her head quickly. 'Nope, haven't spoken to him for ages.'

'Well, who is he?' Lily asked with a tsk-tsk in her voice, a faint smile trying to peek through.

'I *know* the man-detox was my idea, and I promise you I *was* doing it properly, and I haven't kissed this guy or anything, I just . . . I think, well, he might be different.'

'Let the record state that you didn't even last two months.'

'I know! I know.'

'So, you admit I win?'

Simone frowned. 'It wasn't a competition. *I* thought we were doing it so we could reject the all-consuming and dominant male energy and return to our pure and feminine sta—'

'Reject *what*? I didn't have any men to knock back. The detox cursed me.'

'I mean, we *both* agreed this was a good thing to do, and you were tortured over Pete, and it gave you some time out to get your head straight.'

Lily sighed. 'Whatever. It's over now and the important thing is that I won – now, who is he?'

Simone's mouth broke into a wide, gooey smile. 'Well, I don't know *that* much about him, to be honest. He's been coming into the shop for a few weeks, buying all kinds of weird herbs and ingredients, and straight away you notice him, because he is like, incredibly handsome, Lil, like, all tall and chiselled and these amazing blue eyes . . .'

'Don't you usually go for small, shifty types who live on vodka and lies?'

'That's the thing, he's *different* . . . Normal. Anyway, so being on our detox I obviously didn't chat to him beyond small talk, like with everyone else, but he would sometimes linger when he bought a smoothie so it got like, really awkward for me to not talk more.'

Lily laughed. 'Oh, well, you mustn't be rude, Sim. Can't have that.'

'Anyway, last week I had a juice with him, just as friends, just at the cafe, and then, um, we went for a coffee in Bondi yesterday after work —'

'You *shit*! You stood in that kitchen with me last night and didn't say a peep!'

'— and then when he mentioned plans for dinner, THAT' – she increased her volume considerably, seeing Lily open her mouth to harangue her – 'THAT's when I realised that I needed to talk to you, babe, and tell you that I was opting out.'

'It's not a mobile phone contract, Sim, I won't penalise you for breaking your contract early. I do, however, maintain teasing rights.'

'Well, I think he's worth it, so knock yourself out.'

'So when's your dinner with Mr Normal?' Lily asked, popping some soy beans into her mouth and stripping the peas out with her teeth.

'Tomorrow night.' Simone was grinning in the specific way that had seen her escape punishment hundreds of times. 'He is so hot and a total gentleman. Isn't even judgy that I am a cossie model or anyth—'

'What man has *ever* judged you for that, Sim? So what does he do?'

'He's a chef. Lil, can I just say, this is the first time I've felt a proper spark since, well, Michael —'

'Where does he chef?'

'Um, he just moved here from middle of nowhere, Mudgee, I think it's called, where he was at some posh restaurant, and now he's doing some TV stuff . . . actually, you might know him!'

The invisible, cool snake of comprehension slithered down Lily's neck and onto her back. Oh no. Oh no, no, no, no. NO. It was Jack. Her Jack. Of all the people in the fucking world.

'Jack Winters? Tall, stacked, blondy-brown hair, loves checked shirts, drives a ridiculous black ute?'

'Yeah . . . Wow, how did you know all that?' Simone's face was bunched in amused confusion.

'Um, he's my chef at *The Daily,* my new chef who started this year . . .'

'You are KIDDING me. No *way*! Babe! I can't believe this! You *work* together?'

Lily folded her arms against her chest and gave her best 'well, how about that' expression. The deep-fried tofu that Lily had dreamed of all afternoon sat steaming before her, but she'd suddenly lost her appetite. Her heart was working triple time and the pit of her stomach was gurgling unhappily. Simone had managed to find Jack, and woo him with her big-busted sorcery and perfect hair and general loveliness. How perfectly predictable.

Whoa. Lily caught herself. That was unfair. Simone had no idea it was the same guy. And Lily wasn't even into Jack like that . . . was she? Nothing like one of your best friends grabbing the guy first to bring *that* to light, she thought bitterly. At least now Lily knew she'd never even had a chance, if his thing was luscious blonde models.

Simone grinned. 'Anyway, so I think he wants to cook for me tomorrow night.'

'Gosh, straight to home-cooked meals after one date,' Lily said, feigning excitement for her friend against whom she had no right to feel anger or jealousy.

Sim had stopped listening; she was too high on goo. 'I think it's *so* romantic. Don't you think it's romantic? Isn't he such a lovely guy? I bet you two get on great, be hard not to. I love me a country boy. You know . . . I think I manifested him, babe. I wanted a regular guy to go away with on weekends and cook with, and BOOM! Look who walks into my life! Ask, believe, receive . . .'

Lily exhaled. All of this was forcing her to face up to her feelings about Jack, which was making her extremely uncomfortable. She looked over at her friend, eyes glittering in the way only someone who was deeply, irrevocably infatuated did, and smiled.

'He's a really lovely guy. And just think of all the grilled capsicum recipes you two can drive each other mad with . . . I propose a toast to the end of that stupid detox and your potential new beau. I heartily approve.'

Simone grinned and giggled, glowing with excitement, and Lily held up her tiny sake cup and clinked Simone's, not daring to think what all of this might mean.

16

Jack was in a spectacularly good mood at work on Monday. Lily had increased her test kitchen visits by fifty per cent since he'd started at *The Daily*, and was now usually rewarded with a friendly, boisterous chat, allowing her to gauge his moods almost perfectly. It was nice, since during the show it was usually too fast-paced and manic to talk beyond giving instructions or making last-second changes. Sadly, after her chat with Simone the other night Lily now knew the sunny mood came down to her flatmate's existence in his life. She resolved once more that she shouldn't be jealous, or territorial. After all, *she didn't like him like that.*

'Hey Lil,' he said, beaming with good skin, a fresh haircut and, of course, a checked shirt, filling up a water jug with filtered water.

'Hey chef,' she said, stirring sugar through her fourth cup of tea for the day.

'Can you believe my burner blew up? Hope it didn't affect Rob's pasta. I saw you sneak off with a plateful so I'm guessing you'd know?'

Lily had had the idea for Jack to cook each of the on-air talent's favourite dishes. Rob, being a child of the '70s, had chosen fettuccine carbonara.

Lily blushed. 'Mel doesn't eat dairy, wheat, sugar – or food in general – so I didn't want it to go to waste. But yes, it was delicious . . . And I *hate* carbonara.'

'Glad you liked it. Why didn't you get a dish choice? Would've been peanut-butter pancakes or the like, I'm guessing?'

Lily's mind began gorging itself on the visual of him making her pancakes on a lazy Sunday morning . . . She was going mad. Was she really so competitive that as soon as he was someone else's she had to possess him? How embarrassing.

'Might have been foie gras, you'll never know,' she said, walking out of the kitchen and away from the treacherous and unfounded thoughts swimming through her head. She couldn't talk to him when he was in such a good mood and being so adorable.

Nikkii was advancing towards her, doing that bouncy, self-aware strut that Alice loved to mimic when she'd had a few beers. Lily gave her a tight smile and kept her head down but Nikkii had her in her crosshairs.

'*Heyyy*, Lil!' she said, stopping in the hallway and giving her an over-the-top greeting as though it was a Christmas present and Lily should be thankful. Lily knew the fastest way out of this was to talk about the exact thing Nikkii was going to bring up anyway.

'Hey, Nikkii, nice piece with One Direction last week, you seemed to really have fun with them. Nice guys?'

In truth it was a horrible interview; Nikkii was flirty and infantile and the boys gave monosyllabic, bored answers.

She placed her hand on her heart, a good half-centimetre of bare nail between her grown-out red gel polish and her cuticle, and sighed dramatically.

'Oh my *GOD*. They were so . . . *charged*, Lily. Like, they were *literally* on heat; do you know what I mean? It was intense. I had to just take a moment afterwards, to be honest. *All that* male energy

117

directed at you on live TV can be a bit much. Oh, and you'll LOVE this . . .'

She rambled on and on, Lily listening blankly, nodding where appropriate. Of course Nikkii would interpret the interview as being about *her*, not the fact that One Direction were basically walking penises with cute shoes and decent singing voices.

' . . . so it all went *totally* cray-cray after Harry asked for my number, and the piece in *The Telegraph* only made it a thousand times worse, and so I'm like, thanks guys, thanks *so* much, and now I've *literally* been getting death threats and it's just *so full on*. Eliza told me to delete my Twitter account but I am *totally* anti-troll and refuse to give them any power.'

She said this as though she were running for prime minister, and had just delivered her oratory king hit.

'Gosh, that's crazy . . . I had no idea.' Lily had read something about it online, but would never let on that she ever read or thought about Nikkii in a million years.

'It was even on the *Daily Mail*, it went completely worldwide; it's been *really* intense.' Lily could hear the sound of Nikkii's conversational fishing rod plop into the water, but she wasn't about to bite.

'Sorry to hear that, Nikkii, hope things get better.' And with a smile, Lily began to walk off, keen to get back to daydreams about Jack and cake.

'Hey, can I ask you something?'

Lily stopped and turned back to Nikkii. 'Sure, what's up?'

'Weeeeelll, I *actually* wanted to ask your advice. You see, I'm applying for Eliza's series producer role. Of course I am literally *dying* that she's leaving in a month, I will miss her to pieces, but I wondered if you had any ideas for how to make my application super-amazing. You're good at that stuff, aren't you? PowerPoint and whatever?'

Lily blinked a few times as though that might assist her understanding of what she'd just heard. Good things: Eliza *was* leaving. Bad things: the job had already been made public and she hadn't known; Eliza would pretty much hand it to Nikkii in a muffin-lined basket. Hopeful things: for once Nikkii's chronic mis- and overuse of the word 'literally' might be true, and she was actually dying.

'It's been announced, has it?' Lily said, needing Nikkii to know she already knew about it.

'Lize told me about it, she thinks I have a *reeeaally* good chance.'

Of course she fucking does, Lily thought, because she is your number-one fan, and also, she has NO CLUE about what a series producer is or does, despite being one herself.

'Should I do a whole reel for Sasha, do you think, or just, like, a PowerPoint?'

'Series producer is a big role, Nikkii, it might mean you won't get to do all your on-air stuff any more . . .' Without fully realising it, Lily was dissuading Nikkii from the role.

'Lize said they'll make exceptions,' she said swiftly. 'It's a flexible role.'

Lily couldn't tell if Nikkii was deliberately fucking with her, or genuinely didn't know she was being offensive, and that Lily would obviously be going for the role too.

'Um, I'm really not sure, Nikkii. Eliza will be more helpful than me, I'd say.'

'True, 'kay, thanks anyway. Wish me lu-uck!' and with a spin, she bounced off down the hallway, her bum wiggling in just the fashion a bum shouldn't in the workplace.

Lily couldn't even accuse Eliza of colluding with her star staffer to get her a promotion, because she'd told Lily about the role, too. Oh well, Lily sighed, she would just have to dazzle Sasha with her application and her actual, tangible and documented skill set.

There was nothing to worry about, Lily told herself, she was *completely* qualified for this job. It was her time. She deserved it. Bring it on.

Returning to her desk, she saw a missed call and a text from Mimi.

Dinner tonight? New French brasserie near me has opened up and I fancy some snails. (For you there are fries.) Call me. ox

The order of her hugs and kisses (wrong) always brought a smile to Lily's face. And actually, dinner with her mum and a bottle or twelve of red wine sounded like an excellent idea.

Oui! I can be there at 7. Text me address xx

Lily woke up her computer screen, a menacingly empty word document glared back at her. She had decided to create a food tour for Jack, to take the segment out into the country and give all the horny housewives a chance to see him in person, and jam up their Facebook feed with photos of him.

Sasha had agreed to it, but wanted places that already had a 'foodie' slant, so they weren't going to be devoid of an audience, and preferably there would be an existing event in place that they could crash, and borrow all of the equipment and infrastructure. Lily had to give it to Sasha for being so resourceful.

So far, Lily had the crayfish wharves on the south coast, a wine festival in the southern highlands, a cheese fair on the north coast, and a 'condiments' market in the Blue Mountains. And they were all shit. There *had* to be a better way to do things. She'd instructed Dale to get thinking, and was doing the same. This could be her moment to shine, Lily realised; the thing that made Sasha realise she was totally ready for a new role and new responsibilities and a new salary. She had to come up with something cool and fun and unique, and then project-manage the shit out of it.

Alice had walked over and was perched on Lily's desk to chat, scooping out the bottom of a yoghurt tub.

'Can I borrow a tenner? I forgot to go to the ATM at lunch and I lost a bet to Grimmo.'

'Um, yeah, hang on a sec,' Lily was finally deep in work mode and didn't appreciate the distraction.

'Oh *shit*,' Alice yelped. 'I'm meeting Sasha at four, fuck a duck, shit, fuck!' and she dumped the empty yogurt carton in Lily's bin and was gone.

Why was she meeting Sasha? Was it about the role? It had to be; why else would Alice be meeting with the EP? Why wasn't Lily meeting with Sasha? Why was everyone else getting the job she wanted? Fuck! Panic set in. She had to get this role. Life at *The Daily* under one of her co-workers – friend or foe – would be no life at all.

'Why don't I eat this every night? This is the greatest meal ever.' Lily was inhaling her delicious, crispy fries, dipping them into the wine merchant sauce poured generously over her minute steak.

'You'd die of heart disease at forty, darling,' Mimi said as she elegantly chewed on garlic-soaked escargot. 'You're looking so slim, Lil. You look lovely.'

Mimi *loved* skinniness. As she'd been deprived of it for so many years, an early menopause ensured that it was now her holy grail. If Lily were the impressionable type she would have developed an eating disorder young. She was probably a *touch* skinnier than usual at the moment because she was stressed, but there was no point telling Mimi that, she'd just ask where she could buy some.

Lily shook her head and sipped her wine.

'Everything's a bit shit.'

'Really?' Mimi's eyebrows raised. 'That good.'

Lily sighed and rested her knife and fork on her plate for a moment; her stomach could probably do with the breather anyway.

'A series producer role has finally come up, and I want it, and I *deserve* it, but I don't think I'm going to get it.'

'Rubbish. You work harder than anyone else in there, Bean.'

'We all work too hard. Alice is going to apply too. Every dick and his dog is.'

Lily picked up her cutlery and stabbed at her steak. She knew she was being a sook, but she wanted this job so much more than Alice or Nikkii did, she knew she did.

'Don't let this one slip out of your hands because you've convinced yourself someone else beat you to the punch. I taught you better than that.'

Mimi was right. Lily was being theatrical and juvenile.

'Hey, so Simone broke the man-detox pact last night.'

'And thank *God* for that. What a load of nonsense, keeping two gorgeous, trim creatures like you man-free when you're in your prime. There will come a time when it's involuntary, then you'll curse the day you did it willingly, I promise you.'

'She broke it off cos she's seeing Jack. My chef Jack.'

Mimi's hand stopped mid-air on the way to her mouth. '*No*'.

'Yep.' Lily took a long sip of her wine.

'Well. This is *wonderful* news! I'm *thrilled*! What a gorgeous couple. It's about time she ditched the bad boys and went for a nice guy, and we all know they don't come nicer than him.'

Lily cleared her throat. What was she, chopped liver? Her own mother didn't even for one nanosecond think that Jack might be better suited to her own daughter?

'Yeah, well, it's all very new, so who knows,' Lily said quietly, a cardigan of wine-based spite hanging loosely across her shoulders.

'What genetically gifted offspring they'll have. Can you even *imagine*?'

'Whoa, calm the farm, Mimi . . . they've been for like, two dates.'

'Bean, you're not . . . jealous, are you?' Mimi peered at her daughter while stealing a few more of Lily's fries.

Lily took a long sip of water, suddenly remembering she had to drive home, and *might* have enjoyed too much wine.

'Don't be ridiculous. He's not my type. They're much better suited.' Lily ate some more fries, then realised she had already eaten half a kilo's worth, and placed her napkin over the remaining mound to stop herself from eating more.

'Don't you thin—'

Before Mimi could finish, a man in a white shirt and jeans came over to the table. He was in his mid-fifties, tanned, dark hair flecked with grey, with a warm, smiling face.

'Sorry to interrupt, ladies, but I wanted to know if everything was to your liking this evening?' He had a slight accent, but Lily couldn't pick it.

'Oh, yes, it was *marvellous*. The escargot! My goodness, just divine.' Lily was amused to see Mimi pick herself up a little and tuck her hair behind her ears.

The man looked at Lily's napkin covering her plate. 'Was there something terrifying in your meal you cannot bear to look at?'

Lily laughed. 'No, no, just a bit of "out of sight, out of mind" with the fries. I gave them a good nudge, I promise. And the steak was perfect, thank you.'

'I should introduce myself. I am Niko, and I am *not* French, I am Croatian, but I prefer French food. This is my restaurant, we're new and anxious to please, so I like to make sure everyone is enjoying their food, and then butter them up with some free sweets. Which I will return with shortly. Excellent choice of wine, by the way, Vacqueyras is the perfect pairing for escargot.' He gave a dazzling smile to Mimi, and disappeared back into the kitchen.

'*Well*. That doesn't happen every day, does it?' Mimi said, blushing slightly, pulling out her make-up mirror and checking her teeth, and fixing up her curly brown hair and applying some dusky-pink lipstick.

'No ring, I noticed.'

'Oh, stop it,' Mimi said, but her grin gave her away. 'He had a terrific smile, didn't he? Probably gay. This is where they thrive, after all. Denis's boyfriend lives a block away.'

Lily's heart was warmed, seeing her mother fluff and primp for the handsome devil from the kitchen. What was it with the Woodward women and chefs?

17

Simone had either been chewing through her Benzo stash, or she was caught up in the lust bubble. All Lily received when she asked how things were going with Jack on a dull Tuesday morning was:

He is heaven . . . ☺ ☺ ☺ xoxo

Her description of their latest date when she and Lily finally caught up a few days later was not much better. It was peppered with swooning and smiles and sighs and more gushing than a broken dam. She and Jack already had their next date planned: a trip to the grower's market, naturally, and after 'J' – Simone was an enormous fan of calling people by their first initial – had commented positively on Simone's freckles, Simone, all giggles and smiles, admitted she had now ditched foundation on her cheeks so that they could better peek through. Lily listened to all of this with a fresh, steely resolve to be happy for them both, and not be weird about it, and see it as a blessing, because Simone might finally kick her Michael thing once and for all, and the beautiful twinset could only be good publicity for the show. That Lily *also* had freckles was entirely irrelevant.

Lily walked over to Alice's desk where she sat working away, chewing on a pen, hair wild, humming loudly.

'Come to the snack machine?'

Alice turned and saw Lily's grim facial expression.

'Whoa, *stormy* lady . . . Did your little red secret arrive? I thought we were in sync, mine came last wee—'

'No, no. Come on, come,' and she turned and walked.

'Hey, will you go for Eliza's job, do you reckon?' Lily said once they reached the hallway, trying to play cool, indifferent, no-big-dealsy.

'Rather eat my own vom. But YOU should go for it. Man, I would fucking love being your slave.'

Lily turned to look at her friend's huge eyes and wanted to hug her.

'Thanks, Al. I'd give you a million-dollar raise immediately. But sadly I fear Eliza will hand-deliver it to you-know-who.'

'Then we'll both leave and open a strip club.'

Lily exhaled, nodding. She stared at the snack machine, which, being wedged between two old printers at the far end of the corridor, was the perfect place for gossip and the secret shame of drinking Fanta.

'Also, Jack's blonde? Simone.' Alice had been on site so much lately, Lily hadn't even had the chance to spill the news.

Alice's mouth broke into an enormous O.

'You're *fucking kidding me.*' Alice smacked her right hand up to her mouth, her eyes huge and sparkling with excitement and disbelief.

'Simone broke our man-detox for it. He's already had her over for a home-cooked meal.' Lily tried to keep any bitterness from her tone.

Alice's arms crossed in front of her with suspicion. 'Does he know you know?'

'Assume she told him, but I haven't mentioned it. It's his personal life, you know?'

'Jeeeez. Small fucking world, isn't it. What are the chances? Are you weirding out?'

'Why would I be?' Lily asked, a bit too quickly.

Alice's head flopped to one side, her expression one of disbelief.

'Still pretending you don't have a crush on him, huh?'

'You think I have a crush on everyone. Even Trent the soundo, for God's sake.'

'You just *know* he's the biggest masturbator in the southern hemisphere, don't you? I bet you could crack his bedsheets . . .' Alice shuddered.

Lily turned and quickly punched in her favourite code, B22, and slid in two two-dollar coins one after the other.

'I don't have a thing for Jack, and his going for Simone indicates his type of girl is several postcodes from me, so you can drop that idea now, I reckon.' She bent over and claimed her salt and vinegar chips and then stood up with a flourish, flicking her long hair as she did so.

As Lily began walking, urgently opening her chips and jamming a handful in her mouth, Alice deep in thought behind her, Jack walked out of Sasha's office and towards the girls.

'Mind, here comes your non-crush . . .' Alice said in a whisper.

'Salt and vinegar, the flavour of kings', Jack said cheerfully as he passed the girls, with a doff of his head to Lily's chips, and a large smile, and kept walking.

Alice said, once he was gone, 'That is called *flirting*, Woo.'

'Al, that's not flirting. That's Jack in a good mood because of his hot new girlfriend.'

'You're such a wet sock,' Alice mumbled.

'Blanket,' Lily corrected, rounding the corner and moving towards her desk.

'Whatever.'

As Lily sat down in her chair, she looked at the spreadsheet on her screen, and a shiver of excitement whizzed through her body. Sometimes, with so much stress and so many morons taking precedence much of the time, she forgot how much she loved her job. Jesus, she was getting her jollies from Excel; she really needed some action. But as Lily read over what she'd created, she couldn't help the small hum of delight from creeping back in. She'd come up with a Big New Idea for the food tour, and was now channelling all of her energy and time into it in the hope that Sasha would see how much more creative and invested in the show she was than someone like Nikkii, who essentially used the show as fodder for her multiple social-media accounts. Also, Lily figured if she worked this hard for the next month the whole Jack and Simone thing would become so normalised that any feelings of unrest would kick a tyre, have a sulk and eventually leave.

The Big Idea involved touring in a retro-style food truck. She'd read about one in the US that travelled for a whole month and got all kinds of national press; people were following the truck in their cars and camping alongside it. It sounded so incredibly cool. *Far* too cool for *The Daily*, but she could tailor it. She had sourced an old newspaper truck they could do up and brand. The idea was that for a fortnight they would take Jack around to rural areas, hosting the segment from the truck. Each meal would be themed according to what the area was known for, be that berries or cheese or lamb or bloody lemon butter, so they'd be keeping Sasha happy. The idea was almost finished: she had six very strong shows complete and three fairly strong backups, although heading to Bundanoon to make haggis edible might be a stretch. Eliza would nod vaguely and sweetly, unable to comprehend the idea but willing to assume some form of ownership over it if Sasha liked it, but Sasha was Lily's first stop. She wasn't going to let this one slip away.

Dale suddenly appeared from behind her with a folder full of printouts. He seemed nervous, as usual, and kept his eyes facing down lest the floor suddenly started cracking and rippling, and the demons from hell started climbing up, and he needed to make a quick exit.

'Found a woman in Coffs Harbour who claims to be a descendent of the Russian royal family and is in possession of the original pavlova recipe. She's open to a visit. I have a meeting with Sasha now, so I could be late for production.'

And he walked away.

Dale.

Dale was being considered for the job. Dale, the lowly assistant producer, admin monkey and onion-chopper? The last – only! – decent idea *he'd* come up with on this set was the one to cut off his stinky, greasy long hair. Lily slammed the folder down on to her desk and clicked angrily on her mouse to let off some steam. Shit was getting *completely* out of hand.

18

'What's all this about?' Lily asked, arriving home to find her flat-mate tearing around the house manically, polishing and wiping. Lily knew the answer already and hated it. They had a cleaner, who came every week. Someone 'special' must be coming over. Some-one Lily would rather not see on her home turf, majestic land of tracksuit pants, no bra and reruns of *Veep*.

Simone looked up at Lily, her pupils dilated. 'Hi, babe! J is com-ing over tomorrow and I'm shooting all day, and so I am making the house *perfect* tonight.'

Lily immediately confirmed to herself she would be out tomor-row night.

Simone peered at her friend. 'Will you be around tomorrow night?'

'Plans,' Lily said, smiling. 'You'll have the place all to your per-fect selves.'

'Babes, don't be silly! I was going to ask if you wanted to *join* us!' Sim's pupils were the size of raisins. She was definitely high.

'I'm seeing a movie with Alice, but thanks anyway . . . You seem *awfully* awake, Sim; been making Sudafed smoothies, have we?'

Even in her hyper state, that clearly cut. Simone frowned and rested her hands on her hips. 'Well, that was bitchy. What's with you today?'

Lily shook her head, feeling like an arsehole. 'Nothing, I'm sorry. I just – work is a bit shit right now. Everyone seems to be getting an interview for this promotion except for me.'

Simone was quiet for a moment.

'Okay, I did take some Codral, but *only* because I was feeling *so* tired and needed some extra motivation to clean.'

It was getting out of control again. Simone was back to upping or downing as soon as she felt herself vary from perfectly normal. Failed to mention *that* on her holier-than-thou blog, didn't she, Lily thought bitchily. No, no, it was all green juice and spirulina with activated almond sprinkles if you needed energy in blog land.

'Do you think they might be spacing the interviews out or something? Maybe on Monday you'll know?'

Lily unpacked her Indian takeaway and took a fork out of the top drawer.

'Maybe. I *am* working on a project that will blow the EP out of the water, so I guess some extra time wouldn't be the worst thing.' Lily took her plastic container and fork and walked to the table, where she pulled out a chair and collapsed in it dramatically.

'Do you *really* want this job?' Simone asked.

'Yes! I've been segment producer for two years now; I've done my time. I'm good at what I do and I —'

'I wasn't saying you aren't, I just think if you're serious you might need to, well . . .' She stopped and looked at Lily, 'You might want to maybe change . . . *this.*' She pointed at Lily's outfit. 'Y'know, just to show you're the right person in *every* way.'

'How does what I look like have anything to do with my competence?' Lily asked irritably.

'Have you ever heard about wearing clothes for the job you want, not the one you've got?' Simone said, only slightly butchering a perfectly decent adage.

Lily looked down at her outfit: black jeans and an old chambray button-down with her trusty black ballet flats. Her hair was shoved back in a long plait and her face hadn't seen make-up for days. Her instinct was to be defensive and carry on whenever Simone chided her for her sartorial choices, but maybe she had a point this time. Maybe *this* was the problem. Maybe she wasn't showing the world she should be taken seriously.

She exhaled, her body slumping as she did. 'You're probably right.'

Simone squealed, her blonde ponytail bobbing, 'Does this mean we can go shopping?'

'This is not going to turn into some lame montage sequence from a sitcom, so forget it. I'm seeing Mimi Saturday, I'll pick up some stuff with her.'

'*Mimi!* You're going to shop with Mimi? You'll come back looking like a bloody jazz singer! Let me take you, babe, please?' Simone did the cute, pleading face that had sunk a million men.

'No, no, it's fine. I only need a few things.'

'Fine. Well, can you at least read my new *Vogue* and *Elle* for inspo?' She pointed them out on the coffee table. 'Take them to bed and study them. You're nearly thirty, so start dressing like it.' This, coming from the twenty-six-year-old currently dressed like a fourteen-year-old cheerleader.

'Okay, okay . . . So, what are you cooking for Jack? How intimidating. *Definitely* don't cook lamb, he's the king of lamb, and also he does incredible risotto, so I wouldn't challenge that either, his fish is —'

'Well, it will be vego, obviously, duh. Something with loads of tofu, since he doesn't reckon it's possible to make it tasty and filling.' Simone cut Lily's ramble off and gave a blissful, confident smile. Was it annoying for Simone that Lily already knew Jack so well? Lily wondered. Nah, Simone was too lovely to care about shit like that. And Lily had to give it to Sim for not grilling her on every detail she knew about him.

'Proud of me for finding a nice guy for once?' Simone said, as she went back to her cleaning.

Lily spoke with her mouth half full of curry. 'Indeed. Specially since it means disgusting Michael is finally out of the picture.'

Simone went quiet.

'*What!*'

'No, no, nothing . . . I just, I was feeling calm and in my power, so I wrote him an email saying I forgave him and wished him all the best. I think it was a good thing to do.'

Lily peered at her friend. 'Did you mean it?'

'I really think I did. Babe, I can't keep dragging this chain around forever. Anger makes *you* sick, not the object of your anger. He's getting on with his life, why shouldn't I? I know the break-up messed me up, and I've had a few slip-ups, and maybe it's because now I've met a GOOD guy that I'm feeling stronger, but I just felt like I needed to make contact and get some closure.'

Lily had watched Simone try and 'get some closure' with Michael for almost a year now. Emails, visits, catch-up coffees, drunken Facebook rants . . . But it never worked because Simone's self-confidence still hadn't fully returned, and she still wasn't completely over Michael. Lily decided the lecturing threshold had already been reached for tonight and let it slide.

'Well, good for you.'

*

Mimi was suffering from the kind of happy shock that required a stiff drink: she had finally been asked to go Grown-Up Shopping with her recalcitrant tomboy daughter. She was in such a tornado of delight that she 'accidentally' closed the shop early, even though it was Saturday, her best trading day. She even wore her best walking shoes – 'they look like old-lady shoes but they feel like soufflé'.

Lily had made her agree that it was Lily's shop choice and her say was final, and that no further discussion would be entered into. Mimi immediately contravened this by suggesting they pop into an atrocious formalwear shop targeted at misguided teens and bridesmaids. From there on she was relegated to sit silently in the boyfriend chair until her opinion was requested.

Lily had studied the magazines, and knew she was in need of at least: black cigarette pants, dark skinny jeans, a simple black blazer, a good white shirt and some heels. Simple, pointed-toe ones in nude seemed to be the go. Or black. She tried to stop herself from always defaulting to black, but it was who she was. She just didn't care for looking like a tropical fish, all decked out in yellows and pinks and with garish necklaces. She tried to think about what Laura wore, the stylist who was a guest on the show each week; she had great style. She wore a lot of leather, Lily had noted, but also jeans. Yet she made them look *fancy* . . . How? HOW did she make them look fancy? Lily wondered as she removed another horrible dress in the cramped changing room. Dressy tops, she realised. Dressy tops and good hair.

HAIR. That was it! Lily thought. She would get a haircut. Isn't that what women did when they wanted to show the world they were sophisticated and stuff?

Lily popped her head out from behind the change room curtain. 'I'm going to cut my hair off!'

Mimi removed her glasses to hear her daughter better.

'Oh, Lil, I don't think that's why we're here today, is it?' There was fear in her voice. Just as Mimi lived through Lily's slim figure, she also lived through her lovely long hair, which Mimi had always had until her sixtieth birthday, when she had begrudgingly cut it short.

'We're here to make me look like a professional woman, and professional women don't have hair this long. Young actresses and schoolgirls, yes, but not women who want to be taken seriously at work.'

Mimi shook her head. 'Did you break up with someone I don't know about? Why the sudden changes?'

'I want this promotion!' Lily said and closed the curtain with a flourish. She wondered if Jack would notice all of this on Monday, the high heels and swishy silky tops. She wondered what he would think, or say . . . Maybe he might see her a little differently, no longer as just his daggy producer. Immediately she chastised herself for her thoughts. He was Simone's boyfriend. What he thought of her appearance was inconsequential.

19

'Holy shit, *look at your HAIR!*'

Alice had arrived to the production meeting late and minus her sense of meeting etiquette. She took her seat, her eyes never once leaving her friend's hair, an enormous grin on her face.

Lily blushed and dropped her head. 'Stop it, Al!'

'Oh! I was *wondering* what was different,' Eliza said, trademark confused expression on her face. 'It looks fantastic, Lily!'

'It does look great.' Siobhan said excitedly, touching her own hair. 'You might have inspired me to do the same.'

Simone had just about choked on her carrots and hummus when she saw Lily's hair, and had declared her the most beautiful she had ever looked, and that she must never, ever not have her hair this length again, which was a lot of double negatives in one sentence, but Lily understood. And she was chuffed to have Simone's blessing. It was always nice having the pretty, popular girl pat you on the head for giving it your best shot.

Dale was looking down at the table, and Sasha was busy on the phone. Lily hadn't realised cutting her hair was such a big deal, especially since she'd made the decision in less than three seconds.

Who cared? It was just hair and it gave her the shits half the time anyway. Now it was all one length and sat swishing about just below her chin. She wasn't one to think of herself as attractive, but even Lily could concede it accentuated her jawline and cheekbones, and seemed to make her lips and eyes stand out more.

Even Mimi, President of the Long Hair Party, thought it looked terrific. 'My little girl's all grown up,' she kept saying on Saturday night, as though Lily had just bought her first bra. Lily had texted Simone Saturday afternoon after the shopping/hair trip, telling her she was crashing at Mimi's and she and Jack would have the house to themselves til tomorrow. She did this despite feeling unsettled knowing Jack would be in her home, on her couch.

'Right, where were we?' Sasha said, placing her iPhone gently back on the table.

'Lil got a haircut!' Alice said, in the cute, fruity way that only she could and not sound insipid.

Sasha looked at Lily and smiled warmly. 'Very becoming. Like the jacket, too. It's all working. Siobhan, how are we doing with numbers for the Circular Quay show, please? And did *The Night Show* confirm when Jack is going on?'

'Almost full and yes,' Siobhan said confidently.

Lily sat radiating in Sasha's compliments. Precisely the desired effect.

'Siobhan, those photos of him in the trash mags today, what are they about? I haven't seen them.'

'It's him and some girl in a cap at the markets. She's skinny. Gorgeous. He might not be single any more.'

'Is she known?'

Lily gulped quietly.

'Um, it just said, "gorgeous mystery friend" in the caption and I didn't recognise her, but I'm working on it.'

Alice shot Lily a look. Lily shot one back, with a micro-shrug and tiny brow-raise thrown in. What was she supposed to do, throw Sim to the gossip wolves? No.

'Don't worry too much, and don't bring it up with him just yet,' said Sasha. 'Any pap shots are good pap shots at this stage. Now, what's the story with our beauty and health expert, have we settled on someone regular yet?

When the meeting was over, and everyone began to file out, Lily heard Sasha call her name. She turned, hoping she'd heard right. Sasha's face was smiling and she beckoned her to hold back.

'Lily, would you mind popping by my office after lunch? Say, three?'

Oh, yes, yes, a million goddamn times yes, Lily thought, her heart racing.

'Yes, of course. Do I need to bring anything?'

'Just yourself,' Sasha said serenely.

Lily walked calmly to the kitchen, trying not to fall off the ray of sunshine under her feet. She finally had her meeting. *Finally!* Jesus, she'd need to make sure her food-truck pitch was tight before then. One cup of tea and maybe a Kingston or two, and then to work.

Someone walked into the kitchen as she was pouring hot water into her mug, then she heard a polite 'Sorry' as a hand reached over her to grab a mug. It was a Jack hand. She turned to face him.

'Well, *you're* being very polite,' she said with a smile.

'Woodward!' he cried, a friendly smile on his face. He had the effervescence of a man who'd recently started sleeping with a swimsuit model. It was revolting.

'You look so . . . different!' He gave her a polite once-over, taking in her subtle new sartorial direction. She was wearing her pointy-toe heels, jeans and a white T-shirt under a blazer. Baby steps. But! She'd put it together all by herself.

'Job interview?' he asked gently, obviously confused at her new appearance.

Well, pretty much, she thought . . .

'Nope, just wanted to change things up a bi—'

'Hair! *That's* what it is!' He reached over and felt the ends of her hair, as a friend might do, and Lily's body tensed up at his hand being so close to her face, touching her *actual hair*. How ridiculous, she chided herself. Get a grip.

'Guys are terrible at noticing hair, sorry. Really suits you, Woodward. All of it. You look great.' He nodded his approval, leaning back against the table to take her in. She blushed furiously, turning quickly to the fridge so he wouldn't see.

He was the one who looked great, Lily noted. He was wearing a dark-blue V-neck sweater, the kind only boys who went to private schools knew how to carry off, and it was doing a dreadful job of hiding what kind of body was underneath.

'It's just what we girls do, I suppose.' Because Lily would know, obviously.

This morning Jack had cooked crumbed lamb cutlets and the whole studio, no, *station* now smelled of them. The finished product was *delicious*, something Lily knew because the hosts were not interested in eating anything fried; whereas for Lily that basically qualified as a food group, especially with homemade dijonnaise and mustard-seed potato mash. Even at nine a.m. *Especially* at nine a.m.

'So, been having fun at my house?' Hoping her face was no longer the colour of tomato sauce, Lily turned back to Jack, stirring her tea, looking at him with a playful smile. This was the first time she'd acknowledged him and Simone, but what, was she supposed to play dumb forever?

He grinned sheepishly. 'Lovely place you girls have. I went through all your drawers, obviously.' He moved to the sink and filled his mug with water.

'I'll know if any of my dirty magazines are missing,' she said, surprising even herself with her bawdiness. Who had this hair turned her into?

He laughed, tipping his head back.

'You banana. No, it was lovely, and as you no doubt know, Simone can really cook. Anyone who can make *tofu* taste good is impressive.'

'When she saturates it in tamari and fries it, it can actually be okay.'

Jack looked at her as though she'd read his diary. 'That's exactly what we ate!'

Lily pushed the visual of them making out on the sofa out of her mind.

'Next time you're over I'll have to cook some of my famous Heinz spaghetti on toast.'

'Remind me to never come over when you're cooking,' and he was gone. Lily imagined what a home-cooked meal in her house with Jack might be like, and then, remembering he was already doing that with her friend, shook her head quickly. She did not have a thing for Jack, and she was happy for Simone. He was good-looking and nice, but so were lots of guys. Whatever.

She walked back to her desk to prepare for her meeting; she would blow Sasha out of the water today. Her makeover couldn't have come at a better time. How prescient, how utterly fortuitous, she mused, a confident smile playing on her lips. *This was her moment.*

Lily emerged from her meeting with Sasha unsettled. It felt a bit . . . obligatory, like she had to give Lily a meeting, because she had to give everyone one. On the plus side, Eliza was definitely leaving, which was good news no matter which way you looked at it. Sasha seemed *kind of* impressed with Lily's food-truck idea, but she was pretty economical with praise in general. Lily tried not to get flustered. Maybe she was just having a bad day, Lily told herself. We all have them. The important thing was that Lily had made the best of her time in there, perched on one of Sasha's uncomfortable Eames chairs, eyes constantly gliding to the bright red and yellow Bellenger print on the wall behind Sasha. Lily felt confident she had made it very clear as to why she was the right candidate for the role, and how ready she was, and how this was just the challenge she was looking for. Surely her new hair and outfit and Big Idea made that clear? Sasha was no fool. She knew Lily was capable. She liked her, too. That counted. Right? *Right?*

Alice popped up above her computer screen across the office like a meerkat and mouthed the word 'Well?' when Lily walked back to her seat. Lily shrugged and screwed up her mouth to one side. She honestly didn't know. At least she knew Alice wasn't competition since she didn't even want the gig. She looked over to Dale, who was adding another colour-coded sticky to his wall of perfectly organised stickies, deep in thought. Surely *he* wasn't going to be the boss? He was an *assistant*! He could barely look Jack in the eye! He was a planner and a researcher and a food preparer! Not a leader and delegator and ideas-generator!

Lily wasn't sure she could wait out the next couple of weeks, knowing it might not be her who got this role. All she could really do was ensure she did, she decided, waking up her computer and getting straight to work. She wasn't alone. The office was humming with the sound of typing; everyone was hard at work for once. This could be put down to the fact that *The Jenny Show* had started doing titanic, Oprah-style giveaways, and *The Daily* had dropped in ratings as a result. Because of this everyone was being forced to produce 'magic' on every segment every day. Plus, the station as a whole was now third, after years of being number one, and the money guys were not super-thrilled about that, so EPs like Sasha were under inordinate amounts of pressure. This obviously filtered down, which was why the usually nebulous Eliza was now a fidgety maniac. Lily tried to imagine herself in that position, to see how she'd handle it when/if she got the role, and visualised herself as a calm genius who helped alleviate the stress with brilliant, bold ideas and an excellent array of sugary, 'keep up the great work' treats.

Her phone vibrated on the desk; it was Mimi. She really shouldn't answer, but she'd screened her mum's last couple of calls and felt bad.

'You'll never guess who I'm having a coffee date with on Sunday,' Mimi singsonged as soon as Lily answered.

'So tell me then.'

'Gosh! Tough day, Bean?'

Lily felt bad for sabotaging the happy moment. She smiled, hoping it would come through in her voice.

'Yes, but who cares. Who's the lucky man?'

'It's *Niko*, the man who came and said toot-toot at the end of the meal and brought us sweets!' There was pure joy in Mimi's voice. Lily suddenly felt strangely protective. If this guy played her mother, or hurt her in any way, she would personally see to it that his bistro was set on fire.

'Look at *you*, dating the handsome boss of the hot new restaurant . . .'

'He asked me today, I popped in to get a coffee and —'

'Bit far from work to "pop in", isn't it?'

'So we got to chatting, and, of course, because I was wearing my space fat-suckers and my busty red dress, I was looking dishy, and he asked me to go for a coffee on the weekend. Now I'll have to wear those bloody things every time I see him . . .'

Mimi's space fat-suckers were knee-to-shoulder shapewear

she'd bought off the TV late at night that claimed to burn fat as you wore them, and were developed by the same people who made gear for the NASA astronauts or canteen staff or something. They made her itch and caused her circulation to stop, but she felt thin in them, so they were treated with extreme reverence.

'I can't wait to hear how it goes.'

'Would you come over and help me with what to wear? I'll make pancakes?'

'Of course. I'll bring you some of Sim's Valium; keep you calm.'

'Might bloody need it too. Do you know how long it's been? Jesus, Elvis and Buddha, don't let me stuff this one up . . .'

'You will be your usual, gorgeous self, and he will adore you.'

'I'm a bit nervous, is all. Not every day this old bird gets a look-in. Okay, see you Sunday darling. Love you! And chin up. Life is wonderful!'

The next morning, as Jack expertly explained the key to making risotto, Siobhan sidled up to Lily as she watched from the side of the set.

'Um, so I heard Jack's new girlfriend is your *flatmate*? Is that right?'

Lily seized up a little, wondering how that morsel got out. But then, everything got out around here.

'She's a bikini model, right?' Siobhan pressed.

Lily smiled but remained looking at the set. Why Siobhan was interrupting during Lily's most intense four minutes and forty seconds of the day was unclear.

'Yes, and she's one of my best friends, and that's all you'll get from me.'

Siobhan laughed. 'Oh, come on, Lil. Page Ten is running a story on them and asked if I had any inside info.'

'Which you don't, so just say you don't.'

Lily could feel Siobhan staring at her. She turned to see her looking at Lily as if she had just given her a nipple cripple.

Lily just shrugged. She wasn't budging.

Siobhan sighed and crossed her arms, looking at Lily with a blend of pity and disappointment. Lily knew exactly her thought pattern, having heard her vocalise it a million times: why couldn't someone for once appreciate what her job was, and how crucial it was that everyone pitched in to help her?

'Lil, it's my job to create publicity for the show, and this kind of story – star chef dates a hot model – will get far more ink than some piece on Mel's stupid new charity. Trust me.'

'Why don't you ask Jack? I reckon he *might* know more than me.' And Lily dropped her head back down to her run sheet.

A sigh. 'He gets all funny. Says it's not up for discussion, can you believe it? I thought Sasha explained to him how much we need these personal stories out there; I shouldn't have to beg for one bloody quote. Does Sabrina have Facebook? Maybe I'll contact her, models usually love the attention.'

'Her name is *SIMONE*. And she's not that kind of model, she's smart and funny and successful and actually has a very popular alternative-health blog. That feta, quinoa and pomegranate salad that you loved last week? It was one of *her* recipes.'

Siobhan was shocked at Lily's outburst, but Lily didn't care. She might not be completely in love with the fact that Jack and Simone were a couple, but she'd protect their right to privacy.

'Fine, I'll go check it out. Sorry if I offended you, Lil. I'm just trying to do my job.'

Lily offered a tight smile and pulled her head back down to her notes, which Siobhan seemed to finally understand as her cue to leave.

20

Lily parked illegally outside her favourite pizza bar and ran in to pick up a margherita with pineapple. These goddamn heels were the worst to run in, she thought, as she almost flipped onto her back racing to the door. As she yanked the door open, it was pushed from the other side, making her almost lose her footing again.

'Fuck!' she yelled instinctively, clutching at the door handle to steady herself, her left hand spinning wildly like she was impersonating a bird or doing interpretive aerobics or was impersonating a bird doing aerobics.

She steadied herself and looked up at the man who was asking if she was okay. He was backlit, and she couldn't make out his face, but he looked homeless, from what she could make out. All beard and long, shaggy brown hair.

'Yeah, fine. Thanks,' she said, opening the door back so he could step out. Which is when she saw that he was actually quite a lovely-looking young man indeed. He smiled, his perfect teeth contrasting with his hobo facial hair, his brown eyes warm and inviting, and walked past her.

Her pizza wasn't quite ready, which was a shame because it

meant small talk with Sam, the slimy owner, but she simply pulled up a stool, flicked through a *Cosmo* from four years ago and did her usual routine: 'No, I'm not married yet, no I'm not looking, no, Sam, I don't think your wife would like that, ha ha ha.'

She heard the bell at the door, but didn't look up. She was thinking about Nikkii, who had been banging on excitedly about Eliza's fare-well drinks in the kitchen today, and how she'd organised a special live music act who were 'soooo amazing, and you won't believe who they are, it was really hard to get them, I'm so amazing, my shoes are so expensive, blah blah blah'.

'Sammy, you forgot my garlic bread, you snake in the grass.'

It was beard guy. He was a ready-made member of a folk band, with his tight jeans and scuffed boots and shirt done up to his neck. All that was missing was a hat and a banjo.

He smiled at Lily, a dazzling, excited, nervous smile and, grasp-ing his hot bread, slowly turned his body towards her and took a step in.

'Do you, have you got a boyfriend?' he asked shyly.

Lily, taken back by the forwardness, answered honestly. 'No.'

'Cool, cool. So, I know this is really forward, but I think you're, um, very, very pretty, so I thought, I just had a vibe, and I thought I would ask if I could maybe get your number?'

He pulled out his phone slowly, at about the same rate his eye-brows were raising.

Why not, Lily thought. She hadn't been asked out or on a date or even had a kiss for about a decade. He was kind of cute, what harm could it do? Might take the edge off the whole Jack thing nicely. A good distraction.

'Why not?'

He jabbed her number into his phone and looked up at Lily with an infectious grin.

'It's Byron, by the way. I'll call you. Or hang on, are you a text girl? I don't want to do the wrong one.'

'Text is fine.' She gave him her best smile, feeling her confidence quadruple at his interest. 'And my name is Lily.'

'Oh man, what a loser, I didn't even ask. Sorry, Lily. Hey, I like that name . . . *Lily*.'

Lily stood up to collect and pay, and Byron took the hint.

' 'Kay. Have a fun night, Lily.'

'Bye,' she said, smiling and unzipping her wallet to pay. Byron walked out and Lily turned to Sam, who was being particularly vile, but Lily barely noticed, because she'd just been chatted up by a cute guy who was going to text her.

Two hours, one pizza and just shy of one bottle of red wine later, Lily was floating happily. Just her and the lounge tonight – heaven. Simone hadn't mentioned anything about being home, so Lily assumed she was with Jack. Simone had been staying over at Jack's place quite a lot, Lily noted. Things must be going *very* well. Oh well, good for them. May the beautiful people forever enjoy their beautiful lives.

Lily had removed her bra, kicked off her heels and jeans and was wearing her House Pants – Mimi's old business-class pyjamas – with her white T-shirt. Each time she went to the kitchen she saw her boobs through her flimsy T-shirt on the mirrored splashback and cringed. She hated her boobs without a bra; they were so pointy and prepubescent. Simone, on the other hand, rarely wore a bra, partly because her silicone-filled buddies were so perky, and partly because she thought nipples were hot/sexy/cool.

A Rihanna song came on the music channel as Lily flicked through the stations, and she turned it up and started dancing. She tucked her T-shirt back onto itself like she used to do at primary school to reveal her tummy and attempted to do some of the sexier moves she'd never quite mastered but hoped to be able to pull off one day to much male appreciation. Overheating in her house pants, she kicked them off, and started swinging her hips around the lounge room. She dropped to the floor and did a bit of 'sexy', stripper-esque floor work, assuming the moves of a Beyoncé film clip from about seven years ago she'd always considered the pinnacle of sexy ground dancing, which was a strange category, but one that female pop stars seemed to excel in.

Of course, at this exact moment the key turned in the front door, and, unbeknown to a pissed and gyrating Lily, with the TV up full bore, Simone and Jack walked in.

'OHMYGOD!' Simone squealed, her hand flying to her mouth at the sight of a near naked Lily rolling around on the floor, one half of her undies wedged up her arse, hair swishing, hands out in front of her like a demented, frenzied tigress. She pushed Jack back out – 'Baby, I don't think you need to see this' – trying not to laugh, and she closed the door quickly, an act Lily, even in her haze, could see was extremely thoughtful, though Jack had definitely already seen too much.

Lily screamed and crawled quickly behind the sofa, panting and trying to make herself as small as possible, pulling her T-shirt over her knees to cover as much as she could.

'WHAT ARE YOU *DOING* HERE?' she yelled, holding back with the might of the Hoover Dam the realisation of what had been witnessed, and focusing instead on being not so nude.

'I live here, you freak!' Simone was laughing now. She grabbed the remote and turned down the TV, still laughing. A lot. She also seemed to have accidentally worn a singlet instead of a dress with her knee-high boots.

'I have to be upstairs before you let him in,' Lily hissed, needing this to not be happening, doubly needing to be invisible and triply needing to be dressed and far, far away from this horrible, horrible scene.

'Of course I won't let him in yet, chill, hun.' Simone's enormous smile was doing a pitiful job of concealing just how amused she was.

Lily leaped out from behind the couch and darted up the stairs like Gollum chasing his Precious.

She closed her bedroom door and went limp. She was exhausted – from the dancing, from the wine, but mostly the adrenalin and panic. The ONE night she cuts loose, the ONE night she goes a bit wild, fucking Simone brings Jack over. Thanks for the notice, she thought bitterly. Although to be fair, Lily was usually out, or innocently lying on the sofa watching TV when Simone came home. Sim wasn't to know Shakira had recently moved in.

Lily took a few breaths. She needed to normalise. And put a bra on. Knowing Simone, a huge fan of barging into bedrooms unannounced, the night wasn't over. Lily grabbed her jeans from the floor and jammed them back on. Just as she clipped on a new bra – she had left her old one downstairs – sure enough, Simone barged in, at least having the decency to close the door behind her and lean against it. She looked at Lily in dead seriousness.

'Okay. Which pills did you take from my bedside drawer – were they the small yellow ones? The large oval blue ones?'

'No! Nothing! Just wine. Red wine. Jesus . . .'

'Oh, thank God, I was worried for a second there. Yeah, actually, your teeth *are* all red and gross . . .'

'Cheers.'

'Okay, so where has THIS Lily been hiding? I love it, babes! More, please!' Simone clapped gaily.

'Think I needed to let off some steam.'

'Now, will you come play with me and Jack already?' She opened the door and grabbed for Lily's hand as she did so.

'No!' Lily said, panicking. 'I'm a mess, my teeth, the dancing, the boobs, no, not now, come on, no.'

Simone laughed. 'Brush your teeth then come down.' And she was gone. Fucking bully, Lily thought. She sighed and looked at herself in the mirror, trying to fix her hair. It didn't look *too* bad all mussed up, she had to admit.

Five minutes later Lily gingerly stepped out of her bedroom and ducked into the bathroom to brush her teeth. It was no big deal. Some girls put photos on Instagram that were more naked than he'd seen her just now. It was fine.

Taking a deep breath to magically sober up, she walked out into the hallway and down the stairs.

21

'All the way from Alabama, I present Candy, our newest addition to Showgirls!' Simone said, giggling, as Lily clomped reluctantly downstairs. Jack was leaning with both elbows on the breakfast bar and doing a horrendous job of containing his laughter. It was at once strange and familiar seeing him in her home. She resented how together and handsome he looked, and how pretty and confident and smug Simone looked, while she was the at-home-on-a-Friday night loser flatmate.

'Hey Jack . . . Was just rehearsing for Monday's show, I'm opening with a dance number.' She had practised the line upstairs. She had to make light of it or she would never be able to look him in the eyes again.

'Good one. Sasha might want you to wear some pants though.'

'*All* right. That'll do.'

Simone smiled. 'I *totally forgot* how chummy you two would be cos of the show,' she said to Jack, kissing him on the lips as she took his hand and led him to the table, where they each sat down with a herbal tea. Of course. Poor Jack was probably hoping for a strong espresso and he gets rooibos and rose petals.

'Hey, we're cooking a huge paella tomorrow night. Grace and Skye are coming over too, then we're going out – are you around?' Simone asked, moving her chair closer to Jack's.

'Are we?' Jack said, smiling but clearly puzzled.

'Yeah, to that new club my friend Jason owns. It's opening night and I promised.'

'I'm not really into clubs. You girls should go though.'

A flicker of irritation crossed Simone's face.

'You can't *always* wiggle out of going out, Grandpa!' She jabbed him lightly on the chest and kissed him.

'Um, I have plans, sorry, guys.' Lily interrupted to save Jack. Personally she could not think of a worse evening. Problem was she *didn't* have plans and would now – again – have to find some. This was becoming tedious.

'Also I despise nightclubs, you know that.'

'*God*, you two are as boring as each other! You should just stay here and play Scrabble all night while I go cut up the DF.'

'My paella is pretty good, Woodward, you would really be missing out,' Jack said, turning to face Lily as she paused at the bottom of the stairs, ready to make a getaway.

'OUR paella, thank you!' Simone added playfully.

'I'm sure it will be sensational but I'm busy . . . Gosh, you know, all that dancing seems to have taken it out of me. Enjoy your night, guys, I'm out.'

She wanted to yell 'DO NOT HAVE LOUD SEX OR I WILL SLEEP IN THE CAR AND SO GOD HELP ME, I WILL,' and wondered where her earplugs might be.

'Night, Lil,' they chimed together, all cute and couple-like and gross, before returning to the conversation about tomorrow night. Lily stomped up the stairs, annoyed that somewhere down there her shitty old bra was lying, winking, waiting for Jack to see it.

' . . . I get that, but the club is supposed to be AMAZING, can't you just come for one drink?' she heard Simone saying before she closed the door to her room, and, closing her eyes, leaned back against it for a moment. On one hand, she was relieved that meeting Jack for the first time in her home was over, as unbearably embarrassing as it had been. On the other, she couldn't help feeling a little . . . crushed? seeing Jack and Simone kissing, together, in her home. Knowing it was going to be a more and more regular thing only compacted the blow.

Why it bothered Lily quite so much vexed her.

The next morning Lily waited and waited, listening for noises of people in the house before getting up, lest her favourite couple be in the kitchen, and Jack catch her with morning hair and sporting the breath of an ox. You've really created a whole new level of stress for me, Sim, she thought angrily. Any other guy and Lily wouldn't have given a burp; she would barely even bother to learn their name, and would slop around the house as usual, but this was *Jack*. She needed to be . . . professional? Pretty? Something. Just not her usual slob self, moosing down toast in her trackies and ugg boots. And that was annoying. *All* of it was annoying.

She opened her door and, hearing silence, walked out gingerly and leaped into the bathroom to clean her face. She saw a rugged, expensive-looking male watch on the vanity and picked it up. Jack's watch. The watch he wore every day. In her hands. Realising what a creep she was being, she gently placed it back, applied some tinted moisturiser and brushed her teeth. Then sprayed some perfume. Why not? Her hair was tousled and messy, but she was starting to prefer it that way with the new length. It was far cooler than she was, and she needed all the help she could get when it came to looking cool.

Walking out into the hallway she cocked an ear, but they'd

definitely gone. She walked downstairs, wondering how it had come to pass that the only chap she'd felt something for in a while had decided to fall for one of her best friends. It really was quite remarkable. Her phone buzzed in her hand.

It was a number she didn't recognise.

How was your pizza?

Who was that? Lily wondered.

It's Byron, by the way! Pizza shop guy.

Bless him, Lily thought. How many Byrons could any one person possibly know or meet in their life? He was actually, when she thought about it, more Alice's type. Which wasn't the best thought to have when you're supposed to be interested in getting to know a guy.

It was lovely, thank you . . . and yours?

How boring. She really needed to get better at this. And the ellipsis; how predictable. She never used them in real life, just when texting boys.

Too many beers but it's just the way Friday night goes, isn't it. So, are you busy tonight?

So forward! Lily kind of liked it. She hoped it wasn't just because it had been so long since a guy had shown interest. Or because seeing Jack and Simone together had ignited something strange and covetous within her.

I am, yes. But don't have plans this afternoon . . .

She had always been rubbish at playing hard to get.

Would I be able to take you for a drink? I'd say coffee but I don't drink it and don't want to give you an impression that I'm sophisticated.

She texted back,

We could both have a coke spider?

There was a pause. Lily's heart was racing with the fun of it all, and the anticipation of a drink with a guy who *had* said she was 'very, very pretty'.

Would you think less of me if I had creaming soda?

She laughed.

Maybe a little.

Lily congratulated herself for passing Flirting Basics, Level 1.

Can I pick you up, or is that a weird thing to ask a girl these days and we should meet somewhere? Is 4 okay?

A pick up would be lovely. My address is 34a Green St, North Bondi.

Why don't you give him your pin number and blood type while

you're at it, she could hear Mimi hissing in her head. Oh well. He seemed nice enough.

See you at 4. B

Lily chucked her phone down and flopped back onto the sofa. What an odd twenty-four hours it had been.

22

The following Monday morning Lily stood watching anxiously as one of Melbourne's top chefs, Tony Agnositi, performed a barbecue cook-off with Jack. Despite having never met before, and Tony being at least twice Jack's age and four times his experience, the two men were having quite a laugh. Jack wore a snug T-shirt under his denim apron, photos of which Siobhan made sure she plastered all over social media for the online pervs. It was entirely sexist, but Jack didn't seem to mind or even notice.

Once Mel had controversially announced Tony as the winner, and the ad break had kicked in, Lily moved on-set to help clear up the bench, which was covered in herbs and drips and splodges. Jack was chatting and farewelling Tony, his new best friend by the looks of things, and Eliza, never one to miss a celebrity visit, was standing on set too, laughing uproariously at everything that was said and indiscreetly putting a large portion of steak aside for herself.

As she cleaned the filthy set with Dale, Lily was unable to miss the fact that *she* hadn't had a chance to try the steak. Typical. They were bloody vultures around here. Finally Eliza left, and so did Tony, and when Dale scarpered off to replenish stocks for tomorrow, only Lily and Jack remained.

Jack had started scrubbing the grill they'd brought in specially for the show, which Lily appreciated since it was a job she enjoyed about as much as a deep knife cut. Lily could tell he wanted to say something.

'Everything all right there, soldier?' she said. 'Is that a tear I see? You're sad because you didn't win the cook-off, aren't you?'

He laughed, shaking his head.

'Devastated. I almost think you chose him specifically because you knew he'd smash me.'

'How dare you.'

'You know Mel and he are old mates, right? I was never winning that one.'

'Well, be better at cooking and maybe you will.'

She grinned widely at him, thrilled to be back in the throes of their silly banter. He didn't return the smile. In fact, he suddenly looked very unsmiley indeed.

'Hey, I did want to ask you something, actually.' His voice dropped and he started fiddling with a tea towel. 'Was Simone home last night?'

Lily swallowed. Bloody Simone. She'd known this moment would come.

'You know, I'm not really sure,' she said vaguely and with about as much conviction as a pissed teenager feigning sobriety.

He frowned. He should do that more, Lily thought. His smile was lovely, but his frown was magnificent. Brooding suited him.

'Was she home this morning?' he asked, confusion rising in his voice.

'Um —'

'Look, I don't want to be That Guy, Lil. She's a grown-up and I know she's probably fine, but she hasn't answered her phone since

Saturday arvo and, well, I've got two younger sisters and I guess I overthink things . . .'

'Hang on, what about paella on Saturday night and all of that?'

'It didn't happen in the end, she went out with Skye and Grace . . .'

'They would've gone out and had a bit too much to drink and she would've stayed at one of their places.' Lily smiled in a closed-book-that's-that fashion. Better he knew Simone *was* a trashbag than thought she was *in* a trashbag.

Lily cleared her throat. She wondered how to best put this.

'I didn't *see* her this morning, per se. But she was probably sleeping.'

Jack's brow furrowed.

'She's fine. You know she doesn't mind a big night every now and then. Dancing and carrying on, you know.'

He looked at her in a way she felt sure his little sisters were very familiar with.

'When you say, likes to party . . . I'm assuming you mean *party*, party?'

Lily bunched her mouth over to one side in neither admission nor denial, pulling the dishcloth in her hand over and over between her fingers.

'This happens pretty frequently, Lil. Is there something I should know? Do you ever worry if anything . . . you know, bad has happened to her?'

Lily felt horrible. She knew her loyalty should be with Simone, but she felt sick for poor Jack, whose guts were tied into knots thinking his gorgeous new girlfriend had been drink-spiked and was now passed out, minus her kidneys and purse, in a dingy apartment somewhere.

She took a deep breath and put the dishcloth down. She would have to deal with Simone later, but served her right for being a cocaine-fuelled, pharmaceutical-loving shit who didn't answer her phone when her handsome, perfect boyfriend called.

'She'll wake up later and call you, and be totally fine. She just goes a bit feral when she's out with those two, they can go all weekend, and half the next day. It would be impressive if it weren't so gross.'

Jack exhaled and unfolded his arms. He seemed happy enough with that. He'd want to be; she'd just ratted out her friend.

'You know she'll kill me if she finds out I said any of this to you, right?'

He nodded. 'Yes. And thank you. I've seen her put away a fair amount of booze, but I'm assuming it's more than booze that's keeping her out for two days straight.'

'It's a gorgeous-young-model thing. Par for the course.'

Lily wondered as she said this whether she believed it.

'I feel a bit like an anxious dad . . . '

'Know the feeling. I feel like her older sister sometimes . . . but I *am* technically older, so that's not so weird.'

Jack smiled. 'How old are you, if you don't mind me asking?'

'Thirty next month. It sucks. I haven't done *half* the stuff I wanted to. Don't even own a dog, let alone my own apartment. And I always told myself I was allowed to have a dog by twenty-eight, because that's grown up.'

He laughed. 'I have three dogs back home; you can have one of them. I think you'd like Rocky. He's not that good at being bossed around but you could give it a go.'

'You saying I'm bossy?' She recognised the distinct tone of flirting but seemed unable to stop.

'You're *meant* to be bossy, otherwise clowns like me wouldn't know what to do.'

'Hmm.' Lily raised her brows, loving the banter, but also feeling bad for loving the banter.

'I prefer my thirties. I was a mess in my twenties. Simone and I would have got along famously back then . . . You don't know who you are, so you just kind of stumble through, following everyone else, putting pressure on yourself to do things, and have things and be things before a certain age. But once you get there, you realise it's not about that. It's about enjoying the journey. Being happy in yourself. All that jazz.'

Lily couldn't help thinking this was what people in their thirties always said to make themselves feel better about being in their thirties, plus, it was fine for Jack, he was a top chef and TV-star hunk with a stunning model girlfriend – *Lily* was the one falling behind on every level, personally and professionally.

Jack knew he'd lost her.

'Hey, thanks again. I won't rat you out. Promise.' He locked eyes with her and after a few seconds Lily had to look down at the bench. *Shit*. She wanted to hold that gaze for about a week. That wasn't a good sign for their totally and completely platonic work relationship.

'Don't worry about Sim. She'll call soon,' Lily muttered nonchalantly as she finished up.

She smiled at Jack as he turned and walked away, wondering if she had betrayed or helped Simone by giving Jack an insight into her ways. Who knows, maybe he would be her saviour, her one-man intervention, and he and Simone would go live on a farm somewhere making perfect little humans with terrific cooking skills and gorgeous hair. Lily felt depressed visualising that, even though it didn't seem very likely. Sim loved travelling and beaches and clubs and knowing the right people on the door too much. How could their relationship possibly last? she found herself asking. Sim would surely get bored of Mr Chilled Out eventually.

23

'He's nice, but I just couldn't be bothered with a second date to be honest. I haven't written back to his text yet. He sent it on Wednesday.'

'Nice. We both know what *that* means.' Alice looked at Lily with one eyebrow raised and a smug smile.

They were walking through a modern art exhibition in a huge warehouse, on a small island on the Harbour, and with all of their chatter, had barely noticed a thing. Alice had liked the chandelier made from toasters, but that was an opinion mostly formed by hunger.

'No, no, you're putting words into my mouth —'

'Speaking of which, can we get a coffee or nuts or . . . *anything* really? I am about to eat that fat little girl's arm.'

'Yes, you lead . . . Byron is fine, it's just that —'

'*Fine!* That's even worse than nice! Imagine if he could hear the horrible things you're saying behind his back.'

'We had a nice date and he's a cute guy. I can't give you much more than that.'

'The problem is that he isn't Jack. *That's* the problem.'

'Here we go.'

Alice, whose eyes were scanning the great expanse of cavern-ous warehouse for any sign of sustenance, seemed happy enough with that.

'Don't waste time on "nice" guys, Woo. If there's no spark, it's just a waste of time, and you're better off alone or with another guy.'

'*You'd* know . . .' Lily couldn't resist making a dig at Alice.

'It's fun. You should try it. Even sex, you should just try some sex.' Spying a small coffee cart, Alice darted off, grabbing Lily's hand as she went. She had such a freeness and spirit about her, Lily mused, with a small amount of jealousy.

As they waited in line, Alice hoarding two giant muffins in her tiny hands, Lily thought about her date with Byron. She was reluc-tant to concede defeat – especially to Alice in bloody Wonderland, who was never short of a suitor – because Byron was cute and they *did* have a nice time, but nice wasn't the adjective one should be using after a first date. Or any date, really. He did all the right things, he picked her up, he took her to a cool bar with an ivy-walled courtyard, he asked all about her, he worked as a sound engineer at concerts, he was friendly and had a lovely smile. But, as Alice pointed out, he was no Jack.

'Remember how much you hated Jack at the start?' Alice asked, a told-you-so ready to leap from her lips.

'He was *such* a dick,' Lily remembered how furious he'd made her with his arrogance and kettle-thieving.

'That's sexy. Nice guys are . . . *nice.*' She shrugged and raised her brows.

'*You* date nice guys! Matt was THE nicest guy! He would make you breakfast to take to work!'

'And where is Matt now?'

'You broke his heart. You're making all the nice guys out there messed up, you know. Ruining it for girls like me.'

163

'They're better when they're a bit fucked up. Angry at the world. Nursing some big secret or out to revenge their father's death.'

'You're a sicko.'

'I just like intriguing men.'

'You spent Christmas with a couple of barely legal German backpackers. How intriguing could they have been?'

'They were *hot*. Trust me.' It was Alice's turn in the line. 'Just these and a double latte, please. Do you do flavours?'

'Just coffee flavour,' the guy serving said.

'Do you know I haven't had sex or even a kiss since filthy Pete?' said Lily. 'Are you okay, do you want a hand?' Alice was about to drop some or all things.

'Mmm.' Alice bit into her muffin with an enormous, gaping mouth, teeth bared and eyes wide open. Then, with a mouthful of food mumbled indistinctly, 'Well, that's your fault, really.'

'Show me a decent man in Sydney and I will show you my penis.'

'They're everywhere! If you came out with me occasionally you'd see.'

'Why does everyone keep saying that? I *do* go out!'

Alice looked at Lily dead in the eyes, her furious chewing suspended for a moment.

'You *used* to with Pete, but all you do is work now —'

'Do you know I didn't get home before nine p.m. this whole week?' Lily conceded. The week had flown. She hadn't even had a chance to carefully suss the Simone going AWOL situation.

'— Or hang with your mum, and I love the shit out of Mimi, but come on: do you think you're gonna get laid hanging with a woman in her sixties every weekend?'

Before Lily became defensive, she considered what she was being accused of. It was true. She was incredibly boring.

'Ohmygod. I'm *Dale*.'

Alice laughed so hard she had to cover her mouth to stop stray bits of cake shooting out.

'He needs a shag as much as you do, why don't you both —'

'*Don't*. This isn't funny. I'm about to leave my twenties as a total loser. HOW, Alice, HOW is it going to get any better in my thirties, huh? There is no magical fairy that comes and bloody spits magic dust on your head on your thirtieth birthday . . . It's just going to get harder!'

Lily flopped dramatically onto some wide, wooden steps and shook her head. How did this happen? She was the Girl Most Likely all through school, the hero of uni, head of the fun squad in her early twenties, and now, she'd just become a dull, lonely workaholic whose best friend was her mum.

Alice stood directly in front of her friend with a look of concern and, finally, satiated hunger. She bent down so that she was at eye level, one hand on Lily's left knee for balance.

'Listen, idiot. When the world looks at you they see a sexy, Eurasian babe with a killer smile. Foxy hair. Great arse. House in Bondi with all the trendy wankers. A job that everyone wants, working on a TV show everyone watches, with awesome workmates like me. Hot rig, funny and a total world-beater. You've got *everything*, Lil. It's all in place. Now you just need to *enjoy* it. The boys will come; trust me. The more I live my life how I want, and do what I love to do, the more guys I meet. You just gotta unclench your sphincter a bit.'

Lily looked up at Alice and gave a closed-lip smile of agreement.

'You're right. Everything is in place but I keep thinking something is missing.'

'Best way to waste a life,' Alice said earnestly as she stood up and took a long slurp of her dull, caramel-free coffee. 'See it *all* the time.' She sounded like a cop talking about what drugs do to people, but to her credit, for her twenty-five years, she had lived a lot.

'Should we go out tonight, Al?' Lily asked with a mischievous sparkle in her eyes, anticipating the next ten hours morphing into a mosaic of getting ready together, drinking cocktails, dancing and nightclub floor pashes.

'*Oh*, I'm sorry Lil,' Alice said with a pained expression, scrunching up her muffin wrapper into a small ball and then lobbing it into a nearby bin, which she missed entirely.

'Sven's cooking and it'd be rude to cancel now.'

'Sven?'

'Sven, you know: monstrously tall, works at the port, *breathtaking* head of hair.'

'I've never heard of Sven,' Lily said definitively, trying not to feel deflated that they wouldn't be heading out for a night of fun and being fun and embracing fun and drinking fun-flavoured cocktails.

'He is just as a Sven should be. Gives *great* massages and when he goes down on me he does this thing where he —'

'All right, all right, I get it.' Lily stood up and sighed. It was fitting, she supposed, that the very same person lecturing her on not having enough fun or dating enough boys was too busy having fun and dating boys to hang out with her tonight. She needed to change things. And with Eliza's replacement being announced next week, she had a feeling change was about to arrive, whether she was ready for it or not.

24

Lily put down the remainder of her tart – Jack's latest pastry triumph, a creamy roasted coconut custard – and stared at her computer screen in disbelief. She read the offending paragraph once more, trying to make the words sink in.

> ...*The Daily* is pleased and excited to announce that Eliza's replacement is Nikkii Steadman, long-time reporter with the show and valuable team member. Nikkii's move into a senior role will not inhibit her famous rapport with celebrities or diminish her huge fan base, however. Her title will be Series Producer and Entertainment Executive.

What the *fuck?!*

Everything about this email was wrong. First of all, it was Wednesday afternoon, and the announcement wasn't due until Friday. Lily was utterly unprepared for this news. Second, why didn't Sasha or Eliza tell Lily or any of the candidates that they hadn't got the role? And finally, NIKKII? Nikkii, who cared more about her fucking pedicure than her scripts? Nikkii, who made the work experience kids and runners type up her web content? Nikkii, who had the *News at Six* hair and make-up girls touch her up before she left the office of a night in case she got papped? *She* was now going to be whom Lily reported to? And Alice? And Dale? Laura? Gabby? All of them? How the fuck had this happened?

Lily urgently popped her head up over her partition to see Alice, but she wasn't there. Nor was Dale. It was lunchtime; the office was skeletal.

She sat back down, forehead creased in confusion, heart pounding, skin tingling in rage, and read the email from start to end again. She was shattered. Not only had Lily *not* received the promotion, but she had been passed over for a twit with the management intelligence of a pinecone. It was so, so unfair! It was hard enough dealing with Eliza's ineffective dithering, but having to put up with Nikkii's ego and inexperience: that was unthinkable.

Lily *had* to speak to Sasha about this. She was hazardously close to quitting her job, today, this very afternoon, and needed someone to talk her off the ledge, and explain to her WHY and HOW Nikkii was given this role over her, and make her see the sense of it. If Sasha honestly thought Nikkii was more talented and capable than Lily, then Lily needed to hear it for herself. And *then* quit. She'd thought about it, she wasn't afraid to do it. She'd work in Mimi's shop if she had to. Get into event management. Sell lemonade in the street. There were four million things she could think of that were better than staying here under the watch of Nikkii's heavily lined eye.

The protocol with Sasha, and any EP, Lily imagined, was to email for a meeting, but this was an entirely different circumstance. This was life-changing stuff, deal-breaking gear. Dammit, *where was Alice?* Lily called her mobile from her desk phone but there was no answer. She was probably on location shooting, she realised, with her phone on silent.

But Lily knew Alice wouldn't give her the reaction she wanted. She would just shake her head, make a joke about Nikkii changing the name of the show to the *The Daily, Literally*, and then get on with life. Plus, she was young, she could afford to loll around in an assistant producer role for a couple more years. But Lily; Lily needed to move onwards and upwards.

She stood up, tucked her navy-blue collared shirt into her jeans, and pulled her hair back into a low ponytail so she looked more serious and impressive.

She inhaled, pushed her chair in, cursed Alice, *double* cursed Nikkii while simultaneously praying she wouldn't run into her, and began the walk to Sasha's office, up the hallway and past the kitchen. She glanced in there and saw Dale eating his usual home-made sandwich from a brown paper bag and stopped.

'So . . .' Lily said, a knowing look on her face. 'Big news, huh?'

Dale looked up at Lily in confusion, mostly because someone was actually talking to him, she presumed. He finished his mouthful and rested his large brown eyes on Lily's face.

'What news?'

'Oh, you didn't see Sasha's email yet?'

His face indicated he had not.

'It's about Eliza's replacement.'

'Oh,' Dale said, seemingly already knowing it wasn't him, but not interested enough in the situation or conversation to probe further.

'Do you want to know who got it?' Lily asked, slightly irritated he hadn't asked, and annoyed that he clearly knew it wasn't her, and probably never thought she was a chance.

'Okay,' he said vaguely, one hand suspended in the air with half a sandwich in it. It was Vegemite and cheese, from the look of it.

His mum probably made it for him.

'Nikkii. Nikkii got the role.'

'Oh.'

'Don't you think tha—' but Lily was distracted by the sight of Sasha walking past the kitchen towards her office.

'Gotta go,' she said and darted after her. Waiting a moment until Sasha had disappeared into her office, she gingerly knocked on her door.

Sasha looked up, mild surprise on her face. Her lips were flaming red, and she looked to have had a kind of undercut; her top layer of hair fell forward and over her left eye, like she was Rihanna, but thirty years down the track, and with an impressive Dinosaur Designs necklace collection.

'Lily, hi, what's up?'

Lily paused. She hadn't actually got as far as this part in her brilliant plan of interrogating the EP. Facing Sasha, looking all composed and cheerful and completely oblivious to what Lily might want to chat about, simultaneously incensed and intimidated her.

'Do you, could we chat for a moment, if you have time?'

'Of course, pull up a chair. And close the door behind you.'

Lily did so, taking deep, secret breaths as quietly as she could. She needed to be a professional, not petulant, she reminded herself. *Be cool.*

'I just read your email about, uh, Eliza's replacement.'

'Yes, it was quite the highly contested role in the end.'

'I, I just thought that maybe . . .'

'Yes?'

Lily grappled for something that didn't sound whiney.

'That maybe, well, those who didn't get the role would be informed before, you know, the announcement.'

Sasha read between the lines.

'I'm sorry you missed out, Lily.' Her eyes were kind, her voice consolatory.

Lily was horrified to feel tears begin to well in her eyes. She immediately pretended to gaze around the office, while thinking of what she was going to say next. She hated anyone being kind to her when she was angry, as it almost always produced tears, tears that were pointless and embarrassing. Lily wasn't a crier. She was tougher than that.

'Can I ask, if it's not too rude, why I didn't make the cut? Just, so, you know, I know which areas I can improve and where I lack skills and what I can do so that I can move up in the company?' And have a solid reason to slide my resignation under your door this Friday, she thought as a silent full stop.

Sasha looked at Lily with interest, even curiosity.

'I've never had anyone ask that, you know,' she said, and Lily instantly regretted speaking. Who did she think she was, barging into her EP's office and demanding answers as to why she didn't get the job? What a little snot.

'But it's a good idea, because it can only help you in the long term. Also, obviously, it can help assuage any feelings of disappointment you might be experiencing.'

She took a breath.

'Lily, I gave the role to Nikkii for a few reasons. One is that she has more experience; she's worked on two other shows within the station and is a regular on *The Night Show*. She understands various teams and formats. The other reason is probably more relevant, though, and it's because *The Daily* is changing direction. It's come from above, it wasn't my initiative' – she seemed mildly disenchanted, Lily noted – 'but it's become apparent we need more celebrity content, more gossip, more flash, more trash . . . We're competing with so much more these days, not even just websites or blogs, but social media and all of it. So, it's been determined that in order to stay relevant and exciting, we need to have content that is *instantly* enticing, and generally, that's the celeb stuff. We'll be more *E! News* and less *Today* show, put it that way. Almost everything will change in some way, and some segments will sadly make their way to TV heaven. Obviously, as celebrity and immediacy is Nikkii's world, it makes sense that she leads the charge. And that's also why she retained her entertainment title. She's good at that stuff, Lily.'

As Sasha described the changes, Lily could tell there was a hint of defeat in her voice. It was strangely comforting. But still, Lily could head up that shit, surely. It wasn't like she was a die-hard foodie, she just wanted to produce. *What* she produced wasn't really even of consequence.

'I like entertainment stuff . . . I could do more of that, if you liked.' Lily was frustrated at her inability to express herself. She shifted uncomfortably in her chair.

'Lily, what I need you to do is what you do, because you do it so well. The food segment is excellent. Your production is exceptional. In the big discussions about this change, it was unanimously agreed that yours was the one genuinely strong segment on the show. Jack's work, Jack the personality, who you've helped him become, is so vital to the success of *The Daily*. I can't express that enough. Your food-truck idea is absolutely inspired, and we are spending extra cash to support it, I should let you know.'

She looked at Lily as though she expected a thank you. Lily gave nothing.

'Lily, I couldn't take you off food, because we need you there, and we want to support your talent. You're doing great things, and to bring in someone new to food and move you into what is essentially a glorified personality-management role didn't seem right.'

Lily sank a little into her chair, letting Sasha's words wash over her. She was pleased to know her segment was a success, but a few compliments weren't going to change the fact that she would now be reporting to Nikkii with two k's and three i's. Eliza was appallingly ineffective, but Nikkii was pure megalomaniac.

'Does that makes sense, Lily? A linear promotion isn't always a step up, and that's worth remembering. Better to be on the bottom of the right ladder, than the top of the wrong one.' She smiled with lips closed and made to pick up her phone, indicating her time with Lily was at a close.

Lily took in a deep breath and exhaled as she stood up. It did kind of make sense, actually. But it was still humiliating.

'Thanks, Sasha. That's very helpful. And I'm sorry to barge in.' Lily smiled a sheepish grin and turned to walk out.

'You're on the right ladder, Lily. I assure you,' Sasha said as she began tapping away on her phone.

Lily turned to face her but she didn't look up, so Lily walked out into the hallway, thinking about what that meant. Was she destined to stay a lowly segment producer forever? Or was she genuinely talented in food, and it would be silly to give it up for a more impressive title somewhere else? Oh God, it was all a bit much. She needed a beer.

Walking back to her desk, Lily saw the flame of red hair. Alice was back. Good. They were going to the Pig and Barrow for a drink. *Now*.

25

'Jeez, who died?' Simone said, on seeing Lily walk in the front door.

'Didn't get the promotion.'

Simone's expression softened but her high, swingy ponytail and tiny pink singlet and shorts somewhat countered her earnest expression.

'Oh, babe . . . I'm sorry . . .'

'Nikkii, the goose who does all the entertainment stuff, she got the job. The EP reckons the show's moving in a more celebrity, gossipy direction and told me I wouldn't want the job anyway. They want me to stay in food, grooming your boyfriend for world domination.'

'Ooh, please do! You two are so great together. I watch the clips online all the time now. *Love* the new denim apron by the way.'

'Thanks, Sim,' Lily said, reminding herself to read Simone's blog more often, or ever. She noticed the table heaving with fresh flowers and several thousand candles. Jack must be coming over. Wonderful.

'Well, you know what they say about one door closing, hun . . .' A textbook sunny/useless Simone response.

'Maybe. Alice is going to be let go though, which bites. You know, I'm seriously considering leaving.'

That was the thing Lily was most upset about: Alice had been told that morning they were cutting her segment, and as she wasn't interested in switching to producing all of the online video – not only the wrong ladder but the lowest weak and wobbling rung of it – she was almost certainly going to be leaving. She didn't mind; she saw it as exciting. 'Might change career altogether. Become a baker. Sell artisan vodka. Invent a new balloon shape.' Lily had half a mind to join her.

She pulled off her shoes and kicked them towards the stairs, forgetting that Sim had clearly just vacuumed and mopped the sparkling floor til she'd busted a sweat. Not a regular-person sweat, of course, more the kind that appears on models in men's magazines. It was grossly unfair that Simone got sexier as she did housework, Lily thought.

'Babe, you're *so* far from a failure, and you know it. You've been given a chance from the universe to find your right path, that's all. Change and confusion *always* leads to clarity. It's a *gift*. Total gift.'

'Mmm,' Lily said, pouring herself a glass of water to temper the two beers she'd skolled with Alice.

'It's all good, babe. It's meant to be. Whenever I've been knocked back from a job, or a guy I ju—'

'When have you *ever* been knocked back by a guy?' Lily asked cynically.

'Whenever I am knocked back,' she continued, ignoring Lily, 'It's always because something better is waiting and that door *had* to be closed so I wouldn't accidentally go through it and lose the opportunity waiting just around the corner. Plus, Venus is in retrograde, it's the perfect time to make empowered decisions of the head and heart. You should listen to this podcast by this woman Carrie

Faith I'm into, she is *amaze*.'

Lily nodded, already forgetting the woman's name.

'So here's to whatever awesome, beautiful and perfect thing awaits you, babes.'

She smiled sincerely at Lily then bent down and popped some gluten-free naan in the oven to warm.

'You're here for dinner, yes?'

'Love to,' Lily said, starving as usual. She wasn't so sure about Simone's theory – right now it felt like Alice was moving on, Nikkii was moving up, and Lily was going to be left trotting out pesto linguine for all eternity.

'Hey, did Jack say something to you about me being AWOL the other weekend?' Simone asked as she stood back up.

'Just asked if I had seen you,' Lily said nonchalantly, cursing Jack with multiple swearwords in her head.

Simone nodded. 'Lil, he was *so* pissed at me. It was as if I was his *daughter* or something.'

'Well, you *did* not answer your phone for like, two days.'

Simone's face changed from righteous indignation to defensive. Lily wondered if she had been too quick to take sides.

'It was my friend Abby, she owns the promo agency I do work for sometimes, it was her birthday lunch, and it got messy so I cancelled paella night, which Jack didn't seem to mind at all; and then my battery died and then we all went out that night and I don't know, then we all went back to Grace's afterwards and you know how it gets. I didn't realise I had to bloody check in.'

Lily wondered how many women over the years had heard their boyfriends feed them an almost identical tale. It irritated her that Simone couldn't grasp that Jack was not the kind of guy you messed around like this. He was a *keeper*. One of the good ones. She didn't say anything, and Simone resumed chopping up herbs.

'*Owww*, please stop being so judgy, I feel bad enough already!'

'I'm not judging . . . I just kind of get where Jack's coming from.'

'I just, it was a bit of a bender, they happen sometimes! And Michael was there, and it was all a bit of a headfuck, to be honest . . .'

Lily looked at her friend, her eyes squinting involuntarily in disapproval.

'Is that so.'

'Had some young twig with him, and, I kid you not, she was a fucking preschooler. They were making us all sick so we left, but then he came to Dawn without her, and found me, and was off his head and started being *really* in my face, and so I got upset and left and, yeah, same old story, really.'

Lily bit her tongue hard.

'What? I can't help it if he follows me round like a bad smell!'

Lily considered suggesting that Simone avoid the places Michael frequented but knew better.

'I know Jack deserves better than an MIA party girl. But I'm just . . . I'm *me*, you know? I'm ten years younger than him, I love going out, and having fun, and he's not into that. Doesn't get it at all. Our vibrations are on such different levels sometimes. We're different. Maybe we're *too* different . . .' She shook her head slowly.

Lily sipped on her drink and found herself silently agreeing. She flopped on the sofa, spilling water on her jeans as she did so, like a true lady. There was a gentle knock at the door. Lily's eyes shot up to Simone.

'Oh, Jack's coming for dinner. Did I not mention?' Simone breathed deeply, closed her eyes for a moment, then smiled. She skipped over to the door and threw it open, planting a huge kiss on Jack's lips. Lily marvelled at her rapid mood change. And the fact she didn't bother to change into Actual Clothes before he arrived.

They hadn't been together that long, had they? To be essentially in undies for dinner?

'*Hi,* sexy. Oh, you brought wine! Nawww, that's so sweet, *thank* you . . .' Taking it from him, she gave him another kiss then walked back to the stove to stir something, placing the bottle on the bench.

'Woodward, it's been what, hours?,' he said, placing his coat on the hook by the door which Lily had never noticed until now. He looked freshly washed and shaved and cosy in jeans and a bottle-green long-sleeved polo. Unable to help himself, he wandered straight over to the kitchen to oversee the carrots Simone had chopped and see what she was up to.

'Whoa, whoa, where's your muscle tank?' Lily said, sitting up straight on the sofa.

His head flopped to one side and his lips formed a straight line that wordlessly expressed: Oh, very funny.

'That was *wardrobe's* fault, not mine.'

'Hey, it's fine. You work hard for your body and you want to show it off, I get it.'

He crossed his arms and shook his head at Lily, smiling.

'You know Jacqui is always trying to make me look like the cover of a Gold's Gym magazine, what am I supposed to do? I bring my own shirts which disappear from my office and are replaced with these . . .these . . .'

'Gun wraps.'

'What are you two ON about?' Simone interrupted, obviously feeling left out. She had arranged the naan in a small bowl and was now finishing off her homemade yoghurt sauce at the bench, bustling Jack out of the way as she did so. He moved to the side of the bench, leaning against it as he often did in the fake kitchen at work.

'Your boyfriend insists on wearing one-size-too-small tight T-shirts under his apron. He's trying to broaden his appeal, I think.'

'You SHOULD be wearing tight tops, babe, your body is heaven . . . Lil, we went to this incredible new CrossFit gym in Paddo last week, you should come one time.'

'That might mean she'd have to put down her salt and vinegar chips, and I can't see that happening,' Jack teased Lily, grinning at her widely.

'*Excuse* me, they were Alice's.'

Lily saw a flicker of annoyance in Simone's eyes and realised that maybe she and Jack *were* carrying on a bit much. She stood up and walked over to the table to start setting it.

'Anyway, I'd rather drink metho than do exercise. That's why *you* two are such a great match, because you can bore each other stupid with fitness facts and nutrition chat.'

'She's right, hun, we're perfectly boring and perfectly suited.' Simone leaned over to kiss Jack on the cheek and beamed her famous smile at him. This from a girl who had just declared how different they were, and how much she adored clubbing. Lily happened to look at Jack's face just as he was being kiss-attacked and saw he was looking directly at her. She immediately dropped her head and focused on laying out placemats, napkins and plates.

'Oh, shit. I left the thyme in the car.'

Simone rustled through her handbag looking for her keys. Finding them, she headed out the door, hollering that she'd be back in a second.

'Can I help?' asked Jack. 'Come on, don't treat me like one of those useless guests whose expertise ends at grating cheese.' He grabbed a pile of cutlery that Simone had already pulled out, laying them out next to the three settings Lily had created. She got the jug of filtered water out of the fridge, bringing it and three fancy glass tumblers back to the table. Of course, as was bound to happen, one of the glasses slipped and smashed on the floor.

'*Shit*,' she said, shaking her head and carefully unloading the other two onto the table. Jack immediately came around, bent down and started picking up the shards.

'I'll do that. Stop, stop it.' She bent down to take over.

'You're too clumsy to be handling *unbroken* glass, let alone smashed glass,' Jack said in a friendly tone. As he spoke, a large jab of pain shot through Lily's index finger.

'Ow! *FUCK!*' She dropped the glass fragment and turned over her finger, which was already red with fresh blood.

'See! Woodward, what did I tell you?' Jack snatched a paper napkin from the table and, after a quick inspection, grabbed her hand, pressing the napkin onto the cut tightly.

Lily could smell his aftershave, his skin, his hair, all of it, and whether from the shock of the cut or the fact Jack was holding her hand, her heart rate started hammering and her breath quickened. This kind of intense personal space was reserved for wrestlers, family or lovers, she noted, trying desperately not to notice it.

'What are we gonna do with you, Woodward.' His voice was soft, and Lily's eyes looked up to meet Jack's. He gazed down at her, his face just centimetres away, a caring, affectionate expression on his face. Neither dropped their gaze.

The door swung open and Simone barrelled in bellowing, 'I'm ba-ack!'

Her eyes immediately flew down to the two people crouched on the floor looking into each other's eyes. Lily snatched her hand away from Jack and quickly stood up, but she did it too fast and her head swam with dizziness. She reached out for one of the dining chairs to steady herself, and Jack shot up and grabbed both her shoulders.

'Jesus, take it easy, you look like you're about to faint.'

'What's going on?' Simone asked in a tone tinged with

suspicion, her forehead creased in confusion. She'd stopped dead in her tracks, keys and herbs in her hands, the door still open.

'Your housemate almost cut her finger off on a piece of glass,' Jack said, pulling the chair out gently and easing Lily down onto it.

Simone's eyes raked over the scene. Seemingly satisfied with the evidence, she kicked the door shut and walked over to the kitchen. There was an awkward silence while every person unknowingly processed the same question: did something just happen between Lily and Jack?

'I'll get you a bandage, you poor sausage.' Simone dumped the thyme on the bench and headed upstairs to the bathroom.

Lily kept her head down for fear of locking eyes with Jack again. It was far too risky.

'It's bleeding through, keep that pressure on it.' His voice its usual loud, cheerful tenor. He finished picking up the glass and walked to the kitchen to dispose of it. And just like that, everything was back to normal.

26

Lily rubbed her eyes with her hands. She had been in this fucking food-tour meeting for two hours and was hungry, exhausted and flirting dangerously with delirium. Nikkii had cancelled at the last moment – via text – because she was at a lunch that had run over and had to stay. Lily, obviously, was devastated.

Dale was his usual chatty self, speaking up every forty-five minutes or so when he had a fact to contribute or a made-up Lily fact to correct; otherwise he focused on typing up the confirmed call-and spreadsheet as they locked down the final itinerary. Jack, who had insisted on attending the meeting, was yammering away about the country fair they'd be going to as their closing stop, which happened to be very close to his hometown. He'd been going to that fair since he was a kid, and his grandma used to win the scone-baking contest year after year. In Jack's three years of trying, he had never even cracked the bronze. To say he was determined this year was like saying Dubai was warm. Lily thought his exuberance and energy regarding scones was, quite frankly, preposterous; although she had to concede she liked the idea of seeing where he'd lived and grown up, and which restaurant he'd worked in. Should they have time. Which they definitely would not.

Planning the tour, getting the appropriate budget for it, dealing with pedantic small-town councils for approval and organising transport and accommodation had all been incredibly stressful, but it *did* feel like they were about to head off on school camp. On the road together, travelling around, staying in a selection of Australia's tackiest, most suicidal motels from Monday through to Friday before returning to Sydney to assume some semblance of a normal life over the weekend before the tour resumed for the second and final week.

As Lily listened to Jack discuss the meal he had planned for their last event, she found herself daydreaming about the two of them, cruising down the highway in the wonky old truck, singing along to Fleetwood Mac, him glancing over at her with a smile every so often . . .

In reality, there was a team of six *Daily* staff schlepping to each location, along with the truck, which was to be driven carefully and painstakingly slowly by Grimmo, lest it suddenly blow up or putter out and die. And while technically Lily *would* be in a car (minivan packed to its roof with *The Daily* promotional material) cruising down the highway each day, she would be with a carsick Dale and an incessantly-on-the-phone Siobhan. The crew and gear would fill another two vans and a truck, and Jack would drive his ute.

Lily snapped herself back to attention by standing up and announcing she needed a tea, and would anyone else like one.

'I'm good,' Jack said, as he wrote something down. She hadn't seen him this excited about anything, ever. He was *extremely* pumped to be out of the studio, on the road, being hands-on in the truck and going to parts of the state he'd never been before. Dale shook his head almost imperceptively, so Lily walked out to the kitchen.

Returning five minutes later, she found a Dale-free zone.

'Where's Dale?' she asked Jack, who was still scribbling madly. God forbid he just type his notes directly into a laptop. Lily wasn't even sure he had one.

'Had to go, picking up his mum from work, I think he said.'

Lily stifled a giggle and Jack looked up.

'Don't be mean.'

'I didn't say a thing,' she said, sitting down and wishing there was red wine in her mug, not Earl Grey.

'We're pretty much done now, anyway, right? I said he was fine to go.'

'True. I just need to make sure all these T-shirts and banners are sorted, and that the burners in the truck are full of gas . . . actually you don't need to be here, either.'

'Would be a real shame if there was no gas. I could always just make some ham sangas, I guess.'

'Oh, hey, I emailed Sim and told her she should drive down to the South Coast next Friday so you guys could spend the weekend down there, or at least a night?' Lily said, feeling quietly pleased with her wonderful and encouraging support of their relationship. 'It's *beautiful*. Have you been to Jervis Bay?'

'Mmm, she'll be away, I'm pretty sure,' he said, writing again. 'She's pretty flat chat at the moment.'

'Ah, shit, you're right. Hawaii or something.'

He finally full-stopped his work and closed his notepad, capping his pen as he looked up at Lily. He was flaunting a three-day growth and it looked tremendous. Especially with his black-rimmed spectacles, which Lily had never seen him wear before, but which made him look like he should be wearing a three-piece suit and striding purposefully through the city streets.

'Hey, Lil, do you reckon you could give us a hand when we do the pancakes on day four? Dale says he can't cook, but I'll need help, I reckon, just for speed, and apparently that's the one day the intern isn't around.'

'Sure. I may be a shit cook, but I know how to pour maple syrup.'

'You're not a shit cook, you're just a lazy one who has never tried.'

She prickled.

'I'm happy to teach you, you know,' Jack continued. 'You've got everything in place except the actual cooking part. You're great at choosing recipes and all the prep —'

'And eating.'

'And eating. Now I just have to get you to turn the oven on.'

'Good luck with that. If my own mother can't get me cooking, I doubt *you* can.'

'You'd be surprised at what I can make people do,' he said, standing up and pushing his chair in. A rash of heat spread over the back of Lily's neck. She stared at the bottom of her mug and took a huge sip of tea.

'See ya, Woodward. Have a good night.' And he walked out of the boardroom.

27

'You're looking very trim in that pic you texted, are you on that lemon juice cleanse thingy?'

'Really? Oh, I was *dying* for you to notice! I have lost three whole kilos. *Three kilos!* Unheard of. I almost need new jeans.'

'Well, you're looking great, Mimi. So, any hanky-panky yet? Actually, gross. Forget I said that.'

Lily was treacherously overtired and two energy drinks off seeing small twinkling fairies somersault through the air. She was surprised she'd even managed to remember to call her mother back. Sitting on the ground, in the dirt, she felt exhaustion in every cell of her body. It had been almost two weeks of fourteen-hour days travelling around the state doing the segment live on location, and serving up food and Jack to delighted fans (women) and confused locals (men), but it was being referred to as the 'wildly successful' *Daily* Food Truck Tour by Sasha and 'Eliza's legacy' by stupid Nikkii, but that was to be expected.

'I haven't wanted to call you because I know how busy you are, but I've been gasping to chat, Bean. He is such a *gentleman*: car doors, pulling out chairs, all of those ridiculous things I never thought I cared about . . . I honestly cannot remember the last time I felt this way . . .' Mimi's voice started to tremble slightly. In Lily's exhausted state, a tear quickly welled in her eye.

'You so deserve it . . .' Lily's voice was equally unsteady. She needed sleep. Urgently. She'd become emotional seeing a three-legged dog hop along today; things were dire. Lily wiped her eye and pushed her hair behind her ear. It really was very dusty down here on the ground. And dirty. Why the fuck was she sitting here?

'He's even talking about flying over to join me on my trip . . . Speaking of which, there's something I need to tell you . . . Bean, I've decided to shout you an airfare to Greece for your birthday!'

'No! You can't afford that, Mimi. You're mad!'

A couple of rogue tears snuck down Lily's cheek; it was all too much right now.

'I'm flying on points, and that's none of your business anyway. So: will you come? Oh, it will be magic! Soaking up the sun, drinking wine, just the two of us . . . May is hot, but not oppressively so, and all the tourists haven't started flooding in yet . . . It's the ideal time to go, really.'

Lily failed to think of one decent objection. Why *shouldn't* she go to Greece for her thirtieth? she thought. What thing could be so great back here that could stack up? A party where Simone and Jack would be all over each other? A night out with Alice at a feral pub? It wasn't like there was anything she'd be missing out on.

Lily screwed her mouth over to one side, exhilaration starting to fizz and bubble in her stomach. Yes. *Yes!* She *would* go to Europe. Mimi had been desperate for Lily to join her on her adventures for years, and Lily had always had an excuse. But this time, none came to mind. She might even quit *The Daily*, and take a month off to consider her next move. Who knew. The food-truck tour could kind of act as her swan song.

Yes. She would go. Even if she did stay on at the show, she was going. She had about sixty years of leave owing anyway. Greece would give her thinking time.

'Do you know what, Mimi? I would love to join you.'

Lily wanted to kick Dale. Or, better still, one of the interfering old ducks running the fair, who repeatedly reminded Lily that they needed to move the truck because it was on the 'good grass'; that and they didn't have permission to park it there, and it should be over on the designated 'parking grass'. She'd happily kick anyone, in fact. She was tired, and so shitty, and scratchy from all the cele-bratory wine at last night's final dinner, before the tour ended today. To top it off, someone had forgotten all of the gift bags, so she was now faced with a gathering mass of people who wanted their much-hyped, over-promised goodie bags, and there weren't any.

Lily noticed with absolutely no surprise that ninety per cent of the crowd were young women with far too much perfume, make-up and cleavage for a Sunday country fair. At least it was sunny. Lily took a second to look at the brilliant blue sky as she made her way back to the 'set', which went on forever with not one cloud to punc-ture it. Jack must have had a beautiful childhood out here in the middle of nowhere with his big family and numerous dogs. How different to Lily's urban, single-mother, security-building apart-ment upbringing.

He'd been in terrific form all morning, whipping up gourmet, local-produce-only bacon and egg rolls with caramelised onions and aioli at lightning speed for the salivating, frenzied, mob. Not even running out of gas had fazed him. Lily had tried to get more from some of the other food tents, but they completely ignored her. After all, the *hide* of the Big City girl sabotaging their chance of making some coin that day, after already dishing up free food, a show, and all-day hunk-viewing to their potential customers.

'Mackenzie, can you please find something, *anything*, in the van or truck to give these people waiting for their goodie bag? Or . . . failing that, get Dale's camera and take proper photos of them with Jack and the truck and their email addresses, and tell them we will email them the professional photo, as if we'd meant it all along. And then, tomorrow, do it. I'm sorry . . .'

Originally Lily had unfairly picked Mackenzie to be a Nikkii clone due to her pretentious name and passion for very tight leather-look jeans and dizzying heels; she was, in fact, an incredibly hardworking, clever and intuitive intern. Lily wished she could swap her for Dale. And Nikkii.

'I think all we have in the van are bumper stickers, will they do?'

'Great. Grab them. Bumper stickers and photos it is. Whoever said *The Daily* was cheap?'

Lily took a quick call from Sasha, who had called to wish them luck for the final show and reiterate how fantastic the tour had been. She also gave Lily and the team tomorrow off, which Lily had been hoping for with aggressively pre-emptive resentment, since they had worked all weekend. She noted with chagrin that Sasha shouldn't be calling to check up on and congratulate them, *Nikkii* should. Both Lily and Sasha knew it, but Nikkii was in LA doing a film junket and wouldn't have a clue what Lily was up to, save for the fact it involved food, a truck and Jack, the guy who had rebuffed her advances, wasn't on Facebook and was therefore dead to her.

Lily wondered if she could really quit. Whether it was exhaustion, or the Nikkii factor, or the lack of Alice, or just the clarity that came from being away from the studio, she felt she very much could. Sasha would be disappointed. Would Jack? Was she leaving him high and dry? Jack was inside the truck, leaning with his back against the counter, gulping down a bottle of water. The eventing crew had finally roped off the area to give the guy a rest, but that didn't stop the teenage girls milling around, yelling at Jack, taking photos, and giggling when he looked over and smiled.

'Boy oh boy, Bacon Billy, that was some show you put on today.' Lily peered up at him from the ground.

He immediately turned to face her, a happy grin on his face. He was *so* happy to be back on home turf, she could tell. He fit in here, she noted. The sky, the mountains and grass, the many, many utes and men in checked shirts; it all made so much sense now.

'You *just* missed Mum. She was here but had to go because my sister needed an urgent babysitter, but I wanted you to meet her.'

'Well, heck, I didn't know you brought the whole dang clan down. Do they live on the next farm?'

He smiled wanly. Behind him one of the runners, Felicity, a complete luxury since the budget for Lily's runners had been cut last year, was lazily cleaning his cooking bench and stove, stopping to read from her phone every few minutes. Jack didn't seem to notice or even be irritated by it. He was always so calm, Lily realised. It was very soothing. Maybe that's why she'd been a better producer this year – because her talent was consistent, and talented and fun, and kept a lid on her usual manic panic.

'Funny. No, they're a good half an hour from here. But we came every year. Oh, and that big scone bake-off Nan used to win? It's in a couple of hours, and I'm about to start on my first-prize scones.'

Lily laughed. 'Don't you think scones are a bit . . . old-fashioned for a hunky young TV chef?'

He folded his arms and pulled a stern face.

'This is a family legacy I'm trying to restore here, Lily. Important stuff. Important scone stuff.'

'Right, yes, of course.'

'I *have* to win. I've entered the competition the last three years and lost each time to Marg Milton, who must be bribing the committee, because I'm certain mine are better.'

'You need to practise more. Get Simone to help.'

'Oh, yeah, she'd really go for all that white flour, milk and jam.'

'Maybe you should add some chia seeds and flaxseed oil, or at the least some of that lavender or rosewater stuff. She's putting it in everything these days, have you noticed?'

Lily was proud of herself, and the way she talked jovially, normally about Simone with Jack, even though she recognised the flip-flops in her stomach in his presence as the kind generally reserved for Men She Quite Fancied. So what! Over the tour she had made a deal with herself that there was no harm in having an innocent, private crush on Jack. God, *everyone* did, from Mackenzie through to Sasha. Even Grimmo seemed especially fond of him. Nothing would come of it, no harm done, and it made work fun. Whatever.

Jack nodded slowly; his brow was creased, deep in thought.

'Jack?'

He bent down to switch on the oven, then stood up slowly turning back to look at Lily.

'You might have just given me an idea.' He started pulling things out of the small bar fridge bolted to the back wall: eggs, milk, butter.

'Flaxseed oil?' she asked, squinting up at him.

'Can you drive a manual?'

'Yeah . . .'

'Do you remember passing through that town about ten minutes back from here?'

'Yeah . . .'

'How would you feel about driving there in my ute, going to the deli across the road from the post office, and getting some rosewater? Love some apple cider vinegar too, if you can. I've run out.'

'Um, Jack, I can't drive that thing.'

'Course you can! I would do it but I need to start the mix' – he looked at his watch – 'to have the scones on the judges' table by three.'

'I could do that bit?' Lily offered vaguely.

He gave her an affectionate are-you-kidding look.

'It's near the van. It's a touchy clutch, go easy. And go slow on the dirt, it's a magnet for accidents.' He took a single black car key from his back pocket and handed it to her.

'Gee, sounds *fun*,' Lily said sarcastically. But he was back facing the bench, pulling still-drying mixing bowls off the drying rack – this was not a dishwasher zone – and yanking open drawers looking for the perfect scone-making utensils.

Lily didn't have a choice. She was going to have to drive that beast along a dodgy dirt road and get this fucking flower water. Great idea, dickhead, she chided herself. Key in her hand, she began walking in the direction of his ute, feigning confidence in the same way she might approach a large mare who could sense her fear.

Dale was packing the van when she reached it. He looked up at her. 'ETD is one p.m, correct?' Lily pulled her phone from her pocket and looked at the time: 12.17. Shit.

'Yep . . . Hey, Jack needs me to pick up something urgently from town. Mackenzie has done crowd-gifting, and the events team has pretty much cleaned the truck, which Jack actually now needs for a couple more hours. What do we think that might mean in terms of keeping Grimmo back to drive it home a bit later?'

Dale looked at her with the same blank face she assumed he was born with.

'He will want to leave at one.'

Lily hadn't considered that Jack might not have use of the truck for his scones. She called him, hoping he had his phone in his pocket and, more importantly, that it was at least on vibrate. TV types were forever forgetting to take their phones off silent.

'You haven't crashed her already, surely.'

'Thanks for the vote of confidence. No, I've some bad news. Crew, all of us are meant to be heading off in less than an hour. That means the truck. Your bakery.'

'I'll drive it back later on. Already cleared it with Grimmo.'

'Oh. Right. Okay then, I'll just get this poncy water for you, in that case.'

'Two bottles, just to be safe.'

'Yes, Nigella.'

She hung up the phone, impressed at his pre-emptive strike.

'Jack will drive it back; I assume Grimmo will be taking the ute. All sorted. If I'm not back by smack on one then *wait*.'

She was sad to not to be able to spend the afternoon watching Jack get competitive with seventy-year-old CWA dollies, but she had to head back to Sydney in the van, so there was no point even thinking about it.

Jack was generous in saying the clutch was 'tricky'. Lily muttered to herself as she bunny-hopped his big, shiny black ute off the 'good grass', trying her best not to knock over small children on her way out onto the dirt road that led back into town. Once she'd got more of a handle on it, she allowed herself to feel a tiny bit tough driving a car that made all the men double-take.

As she drove along the dusty trail in the perfect sunshine, she noted the car smelled like Jack, but squared. The leather, the faint trace of his aftershave; the mints he seemed to exist on for most of the day, lodged in the console between the two deep bucket seats. His iPod was connected to the stereo via the cigarette lighter and, when Lily turned on the ignition of the ridiculous V8, she was delighted to hear Paul Simon's voice filter through the speakers. How could a man who enjoyed a monstrous, petrol-guzzling chariot like this enjoy folk music, she wondered, secretly thrilled at the fact, and that she had also finally worked out the exact nanofoot-pressure to use on the clutch.

She realised suddenly and with shock that Jack saw her as a *runner*; she was doing errands for him. How did that happen, she wondered angrily; how did she fall into this role of reliable, asexual Producer Joe who'll do anything for him, just like everyone else in his life always had. She should've said no, she cursed at herself. Do you think Simone would've done this? Alice? No. No chance. Lily was a *fool*.

Lily returned with the loot at five past one, relieved she'd got the car back in one piece, but anxious about the fact her team were meant to be departing this second. She parked hastily on the forbidden grass, got out of the ute with the shopping bag and closed the door, clicking a button on the keys to lock it. A loud wail immediately emitted from the car, and the hazard lights began flashing. People looked over, shocked and horrified at this noise piercing their margarine-ad-perfect country fair.

'Fuck, *fuckfuckfuck*,' Lily swore as she clicked and double-clicked every button on the key. She opened the car door and closed it again, with no luck. The sound was horrific; it was cutting right through to her exhausted bones and infiltrating her poor skittish little cells.

One phone call and two horrible minutes of panic later, Jack was sprinting towards the car, smiling. Lily held the keys out to him, her face etched with humiliation and the unique brand of panic loud, shrill alarms cause.

He clicked something, and it all stopped. A few smartarses

nearby clapped. Fucking country folk, Lily thought, fuck off. Just because I'm not fluent in ute.

'Got her back in one piece! Well done!'

'A MASSIVE and unnecessary stress, that's what this whole thing has been. For fuck's sake . . . Anyway, here's your fancy water.' She thrust the bag at him, annoyed at his calm, joking manner when she had just been the villain of the fair, thanks to his stupid car. She made to walk off, but Jack ran to walk beside her.

'Hey, hey, Lil, I'm sorry. Happens all the time, the alarm is oversensitive. Thank you so much for doing this, I know the car is a bugger, and you probably have a hundred other things to do . . .'

She looked up at him with a half-smile, feeling a bit like a daughter getting a 'hey, you're a good kid' speech from her dad.

'Winners! Ay, you fuggin' idiot, whaddyoudoin'ere?'

Lily and Jack both turned to see who owned this twangy, aggressive voice. A short man in a shiny sports zip-up stood a few metres away. His balding was exacerbated by thin, shoulder-length hair and he was smoking a cigarette as though his life depended on it. He looked precisely like the kind of gent you did not want walking behind you at night.

'*Simmo*, how's it going!'

To Lily's shock, Jack went in for a tight hug with this louse, who patted his back in an equally friendly manner.

'Mate, so good to see you . . . You're living back here then?' Jack asked.

'Yeah, yeah, nah, it's good, ay. Got a small place out the back of Dad's I'm livin' in, he don't bother me, he's all right. Brooke's been living with me too, she's havin' a baby, ay, spin-out.'

'You're kidding! You got the girl and the baby. Living the dream.'

'Yeah, nah, it's all goin' good, you know, been stayin' out of trouble and all that, goin' to the meetings and stuff, yeah, it's all good.'

'Gleeson still running them?'

'Nah, he left, ay, went up north with his missus. You'd hate the new bird, ay, she's a real cold bitch, no offence.' He looked at Lily in apology.

'Oh, none taken,' she said, trying to figure what on earth the two men a) were talking about and b) possibly had in common. Gender aside.

'Jeez, you're doing all right, aren't ya! All a big telly star and in the papers and stuff. Brooke said you were here today so I thought I'd come have a sticky and see if I seen ya.'

'I'm glad you did, Simmo. And glad to know you're doing well. God, it's been, what, four years?'

'Yeah, easy. Anyway, youse look busy, I just wanted to say g'day, I'm on the Facebook and that now so if you're indathat send us a message or something. I dunno, I'm new to it, but Brooke made me do it. Be good when the baby comes, she reckons.'

'I'll do that. So good to see you, mate.'

Another affectionate hug, and Simmo turned and left. Jack watched him depart, then finally turned to Lily with a soft smile and a shake of the head.

'Your old hairdresser?'

He smiled.

'No . . . we used to go to the same group here but he, ah, moved away.'

'Drama group? Knitting club?'

'NA, actually,' he said, casually starting to walk again. Lily followed.

'NA?'

'Narcotics Anonymous.'

'You. *You* at NA.'

'Yep. Still go in Sydney. Just once a month.'

'What on earth for?'

'Because I had a drug addiction.'

'*You?*' Lily couldn't disguise her shock. That he knew and was friendly with Simmo was shock enough in itself.

'I was a drug addict. I had a bad car accident and became extremely fond of painkillers. Particularly Oxycontin, consumed with bourbon. It was ruining my life, so I got help. Well, my girl-friend at the time and sisters posed an intervention, to be honest.'

This was like hearing that the Pope dabbled in MMA.

Still walking, he pulled up his shirt to show an enormous snake of a scar across his left ribs.

'*Whoa.* Mr Clean-Cut Country Guy has a dark past . . . Jeez, it's all very Batman, isn't it?' Lily tried to process all of this as she shuffled along quickly beside Jack who was walking at Eliza-on-too-much-coffee speed.

'I wasn't clean-cut then; believe me. It took three rounds of rehab and two years of hard work training in Paris and London to get me focused again.'

'So this would be why you don't drink?'

'Correct.'

'Wow. You've obviously come a long way since then . . . Does Simone know?'

'I told her, yes. Thought it might help with her . . . similar tendencies. Doesn't seem to have had any influence, but you know how headstrong she is. I was exactly the same.'

'She's, yeah . . . Look, she's certainly not at NA level, but she could ease off.'

Lily at once felt guilty and relieved. She couldn't speak to anyone, *especially* Simone about her habits.

'Well, good luck for this afternoon,' Lily said sunnily as they reached the van, which was sitting obediently on the 'parking grass'.

'I won't be there to watch you win your Scone Queen sash and tiara but I wish you good luck and strong oven temps. God speed.'

'You're leaving?' Lily saw confusion in Jack's eyes.

'We have to get everything back to the events company and car rental by six or we pay for an extra day. Also, I just kind of need to sleep for about twenty-four hours.'

He put his hands on his hips. Looking at her, his eyes squinting in the sun, he said, 'You wouldn't want to stick around, would you? Help me win?'

There was no need or time for thinking music. She dialled Dale, who was back at the van.

'Dale? You guys go without me. I'm going to get a ride home with Jack.'

28

Jack was intensely nervous as he waited to hear how his scones scored, which Lily found hilarious. Two rotund women in dresses and cardigans, the kind that showed no evidence of natural fibres or trend awareness, and a short man wearing a bark-coloured suit were carefully judging and rating the twelve scone entries displayed on the long, gingham-covered table in front of a sixty-odd crowd. Each judge held a clipboard, which Jack informed Lily pertained to scoring the texture, appearance and taste of the scones, and there was a plastic plate and cutlery in front of each entry for them to use. Lily had to hold in her giggles when she saw a small dab of butter, cream and jam already splodged onto each plate, ready to condiment the hell out of those scones.

Jack was standing at the back of the marquee next to his amateur sous-chef, his right arm crossed over his body, his left arm bending at the elbow so that the thumb could rest gently on his lip and be nibbled at need. The judges gave nothing away when they tasted his rosewater scones, not even so much as a raised eyebrow. Lily took photos on her phone and with Jack's permission sent them to Siobhan for the *The Daily* social media, then texted it to Simone.

Did you know your boyfriend is actually a 74-year-old woman
named Shirl?

She received no response. Huh. Maybe she was still overseas.
Lily realised with some sadness that she hadn't seen or spoken to
her friend since the tour had started, just the occasional text. It
wasn't like Simone to be so off the grid. Lily quashed the bad feeling in her gut; Simone was *fine*, she was just busy.

On an adjacent long table covered in a cheap blue plastic table-
cloth were the vegetable competition entries: bulbous pumpkins,
gleaming squash, cartoon-perfect carrots . . . Some had blue rib-
bons, some gold, some white – none of it made any sense to Lily.
She had somehow found herself in a Christopher Guest film and,
in her sleep-deprived state, could not stop giggling.

'There she is,' Jack murmured, nodding his head in the direction of a woman in her sixties, wearing pale-yellow slacks, a white
T-shirt with a photograph of two dogs on it and the kind of stiff,
starched dark-denim jacket reserved for exactly this type of woman.
She'd entered the room with another woman of a similar age, the
two of them smiling and cackling congenially, linking arms as they
made their way towards the front of the crowd.

'Marg Milton, reigning champion.'

'Man. She looks like a *real* bitch,' Lily said, facetiously.

Jack shot Lily a Look. She laughed; he really was taking this all
far too seriously. He hadn't even been this worked up for his first
live TV segment.

'That's her partner, Beth. Been together forever. First married
gay couple in the district.'

'Good on them. Couldn't have been easy with all the country
boys hooning round in their utes, playing footy and sinking slabs
and picking up chicks at the pub.'

Jack laughed and turned his head to look directly at Lily. 'Is that who you think I am?'

'Ssh, they're about to make a decision.'

'Marg will win,' he whispered. 'Mum says she puts maple syrup in her recipe. Sure, I could copy and beat her convincingly, but Nan wouldn't want it that way.'

'And this is *all* for Nan, is it?'

Lily looked at Jack, her eyebrows raised. She was acutely aware of how physically close they were, of how his hand had occasionally brushed hers as they baked all afternoon. The fact they would be in the truck together, just the two of them, for five hours tonight. The fact that he wasn't just a wholesome rural bumpkin, but a reformed drug-addict bad boy, which, bizarrely, she found sexy.

'If you'd met Nan, you'd understand. She was incredible. Taught me to cook as a kid, inspired me to follow it through, and supported me even in my darkest days. She'd have loved you,' he said, smiling. 'You're a rascal, just like her.'

'When did sh—'

'If we could have your attention please,' Brown Suit's feeble monotone came over the microphone. He pushed his glasses back up his nose every ten seconds, a move Lily guessed he'd done since he was in school 500 years ago.

'We have selected the winner and runner-up. The winner will receive a plaque, which must be returned at next year's show, and a $100 cheque; the runner-up will receive a certificate and a $50 cheque. All contestants will receive a certificate of participation.'

'God, he's *all* razzle-dazzle, isn't he,' Lily murmured.

'Runner-up: contestant 27, Ms Marg Milton.'

A collective gasp went up, followed by slow, then robust clapping.

'Ohmygod, ohmygod, you've won, you have *so won*!' Lily said, clapping excitedly. Jack raised his brows and turned down the corner of his mouth.

Marg, laughing and gracious, walked up, a slight preference given to her left leg, Lily noticed, but otherwise beaming with youthfulness. She kissed Brown Suit and the other two women, both of whom seemed extremely apologetic, and then blew the crowd a kiss. Lily wished Marg was her grandma; she seemed like the fun type who would drink brandy and cheat at bridge.

'Winner,' Brown Suit said, raising his voice over a room full of people flying into gossip about Marg not winning, because Marg always wins, who could possibly have won if Marg didn't? Jack had both arms folded; Lily's hands were up over her mouth. She had not been this excited in – she couldn't remember how long.

'Contestant 22, Mr Jack Winters.'

'*AHHH!*' Lily squealed, jumping up and down on the spot, grinning at Jack. In an instant, he had his arms wrapped around her and was picking her up off the ground in glee. All too quickly their faces were suddenly level, their lips only centimetres away. Their eyes met, and Jack quickly blinked and placed Lily back on the ground. Lily was blushing, deeply, but Jack was already walking to the judges, and she was left alone to clear her throat, shake her head and try to calm herself. Don't overthink it; *under*think it, if anything, she warned herself. All friends hug like that in triumphant moments.

She clapped along with the rest of the crowd while Jack had his photo taken and accepted his plaque. Marg came out of the crowd to shake his hand and kiss his cheek.

When Jack finally returned to Lily, holding his small wall plaque, his face was set into a wide, genuine smile, and his eyes were filled with . . . *something*. Lily couldn't pick it.

He handed her a white envelope.

'What's this?' she said.

'Your prize money,' he said. 'Gerald said it was the delicate rose flavour that set my scones apart, and *that*, Woodward, was all your doing. I couldn't have, *wouldn't* have won without your help.'

She blushed, handing the envelope back. 'Not a chance. Here, let me get a photo for the show. And your mum.'

'Would you mind grabbing one on my phone too?' He pulled it out and handed it to Lily, who was beaming for him and his ridiculous new title. His wallpaper was a photo of his dogs. Of course.

As he sent the photo to his mum, Lily glowed in the knowledge she had helped Jack, a proper, professional chef, not only cook some lovely scones, ridiculous as that triumph was, but win a title that obviously, in its own silly way, meant a lot to him. *God*, she'd had a good day. *They'd* had a good day. Both of them. She didn't want it to ever end.

'I can burp on demand, you know,' Lily said, riding high on sugar and caffeine after the obligatory pit stop at McDonald's. Oh, good. She'd morphed into Alice.

'I don't doubt it, I saw how quickly you put away those nuggets.' Jack smiled, facing the long dark freeway ahead of them. The truck was rattling, and thanks to the rain, the wipers, fresh from 1976, screeched across the windscreen with the charm of a possum being strangled. Still, it was undeniably cosy.

'Just say the word.'

'Will do.'

'Was that the word?'

'No.'

'Okay, well, let me know.'

Lily felt incredibly playful. She knew it was probably the artificial colours and flavours and sugar spreading through her veins, compounded by the thrill of finally having finished the tour, but mostly she knew it was because she was on a road trip with Jack. In the truck. At night. In the rain. If they slid off the road in some horrible, unthinkable accident, she would die happy. She spied his iPod and headphones, which he'd grabbed from the ute before Grimmo had hooned off and, before realising the truck wasn't equipped with any speakers, had an idea.

'Let's play a game. I'm bored. How about I press shuffle on your iPod, and before I hit play, and I don't look, by the way, we both have to try and guess the song. No, the artist.' She popped one headphone in her left ear and switched the iPod on.

Jack laughed. 'You won't know who I have on there, that seems a bit unfair.'

Lily scrolled through the albums and artists quickly. A *lot* of rock, fair amount of moody folk, Bon Iver, Kings of Convenience, Grizzly Bear and The Shins, and more than enough soundtracks. *Millions* of soundtracks.

'Like soundtracks, huh?'

'That's how I find new music I like. *Natural Born Killers* is unbeatable. *Django Unchained* is pretty good too.'

'Hmm. It's going to make my game hard, but let's try anyway . . . Okay, shuffle, pause and . . . call it.'

'Um, Powderfinger.'

'I'll go with Destiny's Child.'

'I don't have any Destiny's Child on there,' he said, laughing.

'We'll see.' Lily looked down.

'Damn. Foo Fighters? Okay, go again.'

'*Okay*, Kanye.'

'Keeping in theme, I will go with Jay-Z . . . *damn*. Led Zeppelin.'

'I am starting to see flaws in your game. Also, I can't hear the song, so you could potentially cheat.'

Lily sighed. 'Give it a chance, the suspense will make the win even sweeter. Go.'

'Cold Chisel.'

'Ooh, *good* one. I will say . . . The Police.'

She looked down.

'OHMYGOD, OHMYGOD, *it's The Police*, I shit you not, I SHIT you not, look, look, no, no, definitely safer if you don't look, but here, if I press play, listen!' She popped one of the headphones into his left ear and the first strains of 'Roxanne' piped through. A smile spread over Jack's face. She gently removed the headphone, beaming at him.

'Very clever, you shonk.'

'I *promise* on Marg Milton's grave I did not rig that! That's why it is SO amazing, don't you see? Jesus . . . What are the *chances* . . .'

'*Right*, so you just made up this game and happened to nail a one-in-a-probably-ten-thousand song choice.'

'YES! And that's why I am flipping out! First the scones, now this. I gotta buy a scratchy when I get home . . .'

'You didn't cheat?'

'Eat a leek and chicken pie, cross my heart and hope to die.'

He said nothing, just kept a closed-mouth smile and watched the road.

'Unbelievable. Statistically unthinkable.'

Lily shook her head and stared at the iPod. A good luck omen? Who knew.

'Okay, well, when you're ready to marvel, let me know.'

'Are you always this chatty on car trips?' Jack asked, still smiling.

Lily most definitely was not. She had barely said a peep all week on the road, except to talk work, or chat *Homeland* plots with Mackenzie, who was equally obsessed. In fact, Lily usually put her headphones in and worked until the vague nausea of motion sickness kicked her in the stomach.

'I can shush now,' she said, trying to not sound defensive or wounded. Maybe she *was* being a bit hyper. She had a flashback to how she used to feel around Jack, back when he was mostly mute and rude.

'No, no, I like it. I've done this trip a thousand times, and it's usually so boring. It's nice having you with me.'

Lily went quiet. Wasn't that the kind of thing the guy said in the movie before some kind of 'I like you' confession fell from his mouth? Maybe this road trip was a bad thing. This whole day was a bad thing. She should've left with Dale and the crew.

'Hey, we should call Sim,' she said suddenly, guilt mingling with obligation in her head. 'It'll be fun. Tease her about all the cool baking contests she's missing out on.'

She pulled out her phone and called Simone's mobile. It rang out. She tried again. Same thing.

'Does she *ever* answer?' Lily muttered.

'Not for me either.'

'I haven't seen her for *ages*,' Lily said. 'Miss her.'

'Yeah, busy girl,' Jack said, his tone unreadable.

'Everything okay between you two cats?' Lily probed, telling herself she was not being disloyal to her friend, they were all friends and this was all fine.

He didn't say anything at first, and Lily figured he was also probably tossing up how loyal it was to Sim to discuss her with her friend. Guys who talked about their girlfriend to other girls were creeps.

'Never mind. Hey, so, I think I have some work news,' Lily said, knowing she had to drop a bomb to create a thorough and authentic conversational shift. The rain was coming down extremely hard now, and the truck had been expertly, carefully slowed to around 50 k's.

'You're quitting,' he said, face serious, the strength of the rain clearly unsettling him in an unfamiliar vehicle.

Lily reeled a little. How did he guess?

'Quitting sounds a bit harsh, I think of it more as *leaving*. And I haven't even decided for sure yet.'

'Is it because of Nikkii?'

'No,' she said, trying to sound believable.

'Do you have a new job lined up?'

'Well, no, not yet, but I kno—'

'Is it because you didn't get the promotion?'

'No!' Lily said defensively, giving herself away.

'Because of me?'

'Jack! Are you mental? No.' If only he knew that he was the one and only reason she was considering staying on.

'So you're quitting for no reason, then, is that it?'

Lily was silent. She frowned. When he put it like that, it did seem a little lame. God, he was such a bully. She regretted bringing it up.

'Look, I haven't made up my mind for sure yet. But to be honest, no, I don't want to work under Nikkii. I also don't love the new direction of the show, so there's that too. And Sasha and I had a good talk and she —'

'She thinks the world of you, you know.'

Lily let that sink in for a second, luxuriating in the words.

'I love Sasha too. She's the reason I wanted to work on *The Daily* in the first place; I wanted to learn from her. But then I got lumped with Eliza, who was sweet but grossly incompetent, and now *Nikkii*, I mean, I don't need to elaborate on that, surely. What could I possibly learn from her? I need to respect my series producer.'

'So you think you're above Nikkii?' Jack was just shy of yelling in order to be heard over the rain.

'Who are you? Dr Phil? What's with all the questions?' Lily started to get her back up. 'Jack, with all due respect, I've been here two years longer than you. It starts to wear you down.'

'I'm not saying it wouldn't. But I am interested to know the real reason you're leaving, because my concern is that it's not the right one.'

'Gee, Dad, okay, well, what *is* a good reason then?'

'The fact you're getting aggro means you're defensive about something. I'm just saying if you were completely at ease with your decision, you would have a clear conscience about it.'

Lily sighed.

'I liked this car ride better when I was eating fries and magically selecting Police songs,' she muttered.

'Look, obviously, *I* don't want you to leave. You're really talented, Lil. You've taught and helped me so much and, I mean, this whole food-truck idea, what a cracker. It'd be sad, disappointing even, for you to go just because you're annoyed at Nikkii.'

Lily was building up to such rage she forgot to properly hear all of the lovely things Jack was saying about her. Thankfully, the rain was starting to lessen, making the moment slightly less tense.

'Alice has been let go, did you know that? She was my saviour.'

'This is a *job*, Lil. Not school. You're here to do the best you can in your role, and I think you are doing that, will keep doing that, and will get even better, despite these changes. Survival of the fittest.'

Lily was suddenly feeling frustrated, claustrophobic and shitty. She didn't appreciate being lectured. What would he know, she thought bitterly.

'But where is there for me to go? I'm stuck in my role, nothing will change, there's no moving up now. Do you see that?'

'Do you even know what you want to do next? Have you got a clear idea?'

Lily felt embarrassment wash over her. She didn't. She just knew she wanted to be . . . higher up. With superiors she respected and some kind of goddamn professional challenge. Why was he being so *mean*?

'It's easy for you to say all this. You come in, do your bit, smile and cook, everyone loves you. You can't go any higher than —'

'You're kidding, right? You think morning TV is the pinnacle for me?' He laughed, but it wasn't unkind.

'See? That's what I'm talking about, wanting to reach higher! I want to do amazing things and test myself, but as long as I'm doing your segment, no offence, it's not going to happen.'

'I understand that part. I just want to make sure you've thought it through fully before I lose you.'

His words hung in the air. They were far too loaded and meaningful to simply fall to the ground with the corpses of all Lily's petulant but-but-buts.

He looked over at her briefly, an earnest expression on his face. She coiled up the headphones neatly, placed his iPod in the console and folded her arms.

'Mum's taking me to Greece for my thirtieth in a couple of weeks. I was going to use the holiday to think about what's next.'

'Is she! Oh man. You're gonna *love* it. What a great place to turn thirty.'

Lily much preferred excited-tour-guide Jack than stern-career-coach Jack.

'I *will* think it through. Promise. Even though I know deep down the reason you don't want me to leave is because I'm the only one who will deal with your burnt pans.'

Jack smiled. 'It's a bit more than that.'

Lily sat pondering his words, listening to the rain begin to pour down around them again. She loved the way he was quietly, protectively guiding the two of them home in the storm. It felt hyper real in that small, dingy cabin, just the two of them discussing her life and career. The reality of not seeing him every day suddenly struck her, hard. But feeling the way she was about him, particularly after the World's Best Day, and knowing how inappropriate and unfair to Simone that was, she realised with melancholy acceptance that it might just be for the best not to have him in her life any more.

29

'I can so get you a job here. This music festival is fucking mega. It's like Big Day Out and Future Music Festival and Lollapalooza all donated sperm and had a big, grotesque baby. Hang on.'

Lily could hear the phone being muffled.

'Is there a banana in here? DAMON. *No!* You *know* about the no-banana rule, why would you do that! Go outside. No, I'm not kidding. Do, yes, really, go, *go!*'

Alice was not overreacting. Lily had seen her vomit into a waste-paper basket once when Grimmo ate a banana on set.

'You'll have to let him go, obviously.' Lily cradled the phone between her neck and ear as she rearranged the small colourful bowls on Jack's cooking bench. It had only been two weeks since Alice had been retrenched and she had already snagged another job, as producer on a huge, touring summer music festival.

'I even made a sign with a banana and a big red cross over it. But do they care? Fucking creatures.'

'It took us a few months to get used to your anti-banana regime, they'll learn.'

'Damo's too cute and useful to release into the wild, sadly. You might even like him, he's got a bit of that layabout, vague muso vibe you love. Byron notwithstanding. Did you ever text him back by the way?'

'No . . . Got side-tracked with the tour. What a bitch I am. God.' Lily poured some milk into a small jug and water in another.

'What's happening with Jack? Did anything or anyone go down on your dump-truck voyage?'

Lily looked across the set, where Jack was chatting to Mel off to the side. The tour crew had all had Monday off to recover, but despite sleeping all day yesterday – in a blissfully empty house due to Simone being at work, presumably – Lily's fatigue had stuck with her into Tuesday. Jack was stirring the chilli oil he insisted on making fresh, even though the one Dale bought from the deli was totally fine. She lowered her voice and walked off set down past the edit room, hunching in the corner at the end of the hallway. Just to be sure.

'There were some . . . *moments*, but I'm reading far too much into it. And I've decided to stop all of it, out of respect to Simone. Can't be that girl. When he's not in my face every day, I won't be like this any more. He thinks I shouldn't leave, by the way. Says it's stupid.'

'Doesn't want his cute producer to leave. What a surprise.'

Lily sighed, still perplexed by the decision she had to make. 'I'm trying to be a good person here.'

'You have a friendship with him, and you respect each other. *That's* something. I think we just let what he has with Simone right now fade out; and it will, because that relationship has as much soul as a thumbtack, and then when all that's over, you can reassess.'

'Al, that's so *perfect*! Except for the bit where Simone has no reason to break up with him, and he's not into me like that; and even if they *do* split up, she hates me for being with her ex, whom she still cries for at night.'

'She can't quarantine him! Fuck that.'

Grimmo walked towards Lily and tapped impatiently at his watch. Lily gave the thumbs up and began walking back to set.

'Gotta go, can you email more about this festival thing?'

'Yes, but I need to know if you're in by tomorrow. And you *should* be in. It's good cash, and you get to work with your precious.'

'And I can start in a month, after Greece?'

'Yesyesyes.'

'Huh. Hey, how's Sven, by the way?'

'Had to let him go, he never showered. Never. Not after sex, not after work; I couldn't risk the diseases.'

'Cute. 'Kay bye now.' Lily hung up and got to work.

Lily picked at her cold noodles, wondering if she would miss having main meals for breakfast. She'd grown accustomed to eating fish, spices, lamb (always cold because they needed to take photos for the web rundown and recipe first) – before most people had even had their morning cuppa. She had to compile a report on the food-truck tour for Sasha, probably so she could justify the enormous cost of it – but most of it could be filed under the marketing budget, surely, Lily thought.

'There she is!'

Startled, Lily turned around in her chair to see Nikkii's face greet her. Lily had avoided her successfully since she had stolen her promotion, but the inevitable had arrived. Nikkii was wearing a patterned dress that flared out awkwardly at the waist, with cut-outs on the chest and shoulders, which was of course entirely appropriate for the workplace at 9.32 a.m. She seemed to have removed her hair extensions, Lily noted, which definitely looked better, but she still insisted on putting in those brittle, bridesmaidy curls.

In an act of next-level awkwardness, Nikkii seemed to be expecting a kiss or a hug, or something involving human contact, as she stood there for a few seconds, hands outstretched, black nail polish (so *edgy*) shining, luminous Hollywood teeth gleaming. Lily didn't stand or move, so Nikkii gave her a hug while she was still seated. Shocked, Lily seized up, making the hug even more wrong.

'Hey, an official congrats on the new role, Nikkii.' Lily regrouped. 'How's it all going?'

Missing the awkwardness with the same confidence that saw her ask Christina Aguilera in earnest how much happier she was when she was skinny, Nikkii put her hands on her hips and cocked her head to the side.

'You know what? I literally never thought I would be boss, like, I'm just not cut out for that stuff, but then I realised that the *more* you do, the more big-picture stuff you're involved in, the more creative control you have and now I have proof! It feels *amazing*, Lily. So compleeetely different. I am *so* looking forward to making some big changes, and really exploring some big things . . . it's just *so* exciting.'

Jesus, Lily thought. She'd already mastered the art of meaningless middle-management bullshit. And just how many changes could possibly occur when Never Say No to a Junket Nikkii was constantly off doing press trips or interviews?

'It sure is,' Lily said, with what she hoped was a convincing smile on her face.

'So, on to food stuff . . . Jack's bits are fantastic, obviously, and the truck thingy was amazing. We had *great* numbers, Sasha said, but I really do think there are some other cooler things we could do with him, don't you agree?'

She looked at Lily with a conspiratorial look, but Lily wasn't in on this, and Nikkii could tell she didn't want to be.

Nikkii switched the weight onto her other hip and ran her hand smoothly not through, but *over* her curls. It was her textbook I'm 'in front of the camera' move, designed to let you know she couldn't just mess her hair up, she was the *talent,* you know, she might be called to shoot something. On air. Where she often was. Being on TV.

'I was thinking we need more glitz, more *sex* appeal . . . What do you think about him having an assistant, like, oh, I don't know, some gorgeous young thing who helps him out and they chat and have fun and there's this kind of sexual chemistry going on, and you just have these two people having *fun*, which is SO what I'm all about right now. Just, like, real people *literally* having real fun.'

'Real people who happen to be extraordinarily good-looking and on TV.' Lily couldn't help herself. She'd started tapping her pen into the palm of her left hand, and the pace and ferocity was increasing with every frustrating thing Nikkii said. She never thought she'd admit it, but Lily in this moment missed Eliza.

'Ex*actly*' Nikkii said, missing the sarcasm. 'And also, we really need Jack to be more on social media. Can you try? He needs to be relatable, accessible, humanised. Literally even just Facebook would be amazing. Can you ask? You're his favourite, he'll totally listen to you.'

Lily savoured the idea of being his favourite for a moment before remembering it was *her* segment that was being massacred by the resident buzzword fountain.

'Can I think about all this? I'm not sure if that kind of assistant is that . . . appropriate. And Mel and Rob, they have a great rapport with Jack, and it keeps the flow of the show to have the hosts pop in to see what's cooking, it's always been that way . . .'

Nikkii looked at Lily very directly, a tiny, taut Botoxed frown forming on her forehead.

'Oh, you don't know? Rob and Mel are moving on.'

Shock, sadness and rage smacked Lily in one powerful hit. What was *happening* around here?

'*What?* Why, when?' Lily asked, gripping the pen tightly in her right hand, and gripping that hand with her left, mostly to stop herself from punching something. Maybe Nikkii.

'Oh, um, this week, I think?'

'Whose decision was it?' Lily asked, swishing her tail and baring her fangs.

'The powers that be. Siobhan is sending out the press release tomorrow.'

Perfect, thought Lily. The exact day I hand in *my* resignation.

'Yeah, we're actually moving to THREE hosts, two guys and a girl, all young and gorgeous. I don't want to say too much, because we're still waiting for the contracts to be signed, but you will literally DIE when you find out who we got.'

Lily had had enough of Nikkii's vacuous, hyperbolic waffling.

'Sorry, but I need to find Rob and Mel. I'll see you around.'

She stood up, threw Nikkii a tight, apologetic smile and pushed her chair in. She didn't give a fuck if Nikkii was her boss, she was 'literally' an unfeeling, insincere, superficial bag of shit and Lily wasn't going to sit there a second longer and pander to her tacky, fluoro-teethed vision of the future.

'I've sent you a meeting request for Monday morning to chat about Jack. So see you then.'

Nikkii's twinkly, confident tone indicated she knew she'd get that assistant. Lily could not STAND her. The new hosts, Lily guessed, would be about twelve, and about as engaging as the carpet she walked on. A perky young assistant for Jack? What was this, the '80s? Jack needed T&A on set now? No. No, no, no. Just everything, no. This was not an inspirational workplace, this was not the kind of show she wanted to work on, and that was not the kind of segment she'd be proud to produce.

Despite what Lily had felt after her talk in the car with Jack, that maybe it *was* childish of her to take her ball and go home because Nikkii was in charge and the show was changing tack, she now knew in her heart she had to go. Sorry, Jack.

Quitting tomorrow. I'm in. x

As she sent the text to Alice, she felt a surge of panic and adrenalin and excitement shoot through her. She would be freelance! *Freelance*. She'd never wanted to be freelance. Freelance to Lily seemed like the career version of a shitty relationship, minimal commitment, constant uncertainty and marginal satisfaction. *If you were lucky*. It didn't feel right, but neither did this Frankendaily that was evolving before her eyes.

Greece had better provide some answers, she thought, the familiar scent of anxiety wafting in. Soon she would be thirty, jobless, single, have her mum for a best friend and still be living in a sharehouse. This wasn't how it was supposed to be, she told herself miserably.

30

'Sim?' Lily yelled, opening the fridge to see what magical, delicious food might have appeared since this morning.

She spied some beetroot dip and pulled it out, grabbing some spelt crackers from the pantry and diving in straight from the box, to the dip, to her mouth, like the soon-to-be unemployed, loser slob she was. She honestly had no idea what she'd live on when she moved out – two-minute rice and sweet chilli sauce, probably.

'SCHIM?' Lily yelled louder, with her mouth full. She stopped crunching, cocking her ear for a response. There were candles burning; Simone *had* to be home. Taking a fully loaded cracker with her, Lily walked up the stairs towards Simone's room. The door was ajar and the lights were off, but when Lily got closer, she could hear quiet sniffing. Flicking the light on, she saw a track-suit-panted Simone curled up in the foetal position on the bed, clutching a bright-pink pillow, and crying. She flicked the light off again. Oh, Jesus.

Looking around quickly for somewhere to dump her snack, Lily put it on the hallway floorboards, next to the wall so she wouldn't forget about it and trample it as she left, and rushed back into the room, turning on the bedside lamp then plopping down next to her friend on the side of the bed, placing a hand lightly on her thigh.

'Sim, Sim, Sim, what's wrong? Are you okay? What happened?'

Lily tried to push back the thought that Sim was just coming down. She'd seen it before, and it was not dissimilar to what lay before her.

'I – I'm, I'm so glad you're home,' Simone managed to get out as she wiped her eyes and nose and made to surrender the pillow she was gripping onto as though it were a life jacket and she was at sea. Finally composing herself, she rolled onto her back and then sat up, her back against the bedhead, her knees pulled up to her chest protectively.

She looked through her messy blonde hair at Lily and then closed her eyes tightly as she cried a few more final tears. Lily hadn't even noticed how thin Simone had become; her chest and ribs were bony and her arms were rail-thin. Whatever Simone had been doing over the past two weeks, it hadn't included much eating.

'Sim, has something bad happened? What's going on?' Now genuinely anxious, Lily was starting to become angry at the idea that this might be caused by drugs, but at the same time she hoped it was, because then nothing *actually* terrible would have happened.

'No, it's just, I'm being, it's all, oh, God, Lil. I am such a FUCK-UP,' and the tears started all over again. She buried her face in her hands and sobbed, Lily sitting awkwardly on the bed, her hands clasped together in her lap, no idea what to do.

'I'm going to make you a tea. When I come back, we'll chat, 'kay?'

Simone nodded faintly and, pleased with her quick-thinking, nurturing solution, Lily took herself off the bed and into the hallway, quickly scooping up her cracker en route and jamming it into her mouth, and headed downstairs to make a pot of something herbal and soothing. There were so many boxes and jars of tea to choose from, Lily didn't know where to start. She picked one out called Divinity, which seemed to her a bit of an overstatement for tea leaves that smelled like wet dirt. She settled for one called Self-love instead, which had a nice pink box and a gentle font, and boiled the kettle. 'Add organic oat or almond milk to taste', read the packet. Give me a break, Lily thought.

Five minutes later, using a move she'd seen Simone do a million times, she presented to her flatmate a small bronze tray with a teapot and two small Moroccan tea glasses. Placing it gingerly on a dresser overflowing with jewellery, perfumes and make-up, she poured a cup for Simone. A rush of shame washed over her; Simone was *always* making tea for Lily, always offering her a wine, or a juice or some gorgeous, earnest, homemade dinner, and Lily *never* repaid the favour.

'Here you go. Hope I did it right.' Lily held the tiny blue and gold glass out to her shambolic friend and Simone, who had finally been granted dry eyes, took it carefully, a sad smile on her face.

'Thanks, babe.'

Taking her own cup, Lily sat back down on the side of the bed and waited for the Big Explanation.

'So, what's going on?'

Simone looked at Lily and tears immediately began welling again in her eyes.

'I did a bad thing. I'm a bad, bad, terrible person.'

'Unless you did a hit and run or something . . . oh God, you didn't, did you?' Lily's eyes were wide with fear.

'No, no, it's nothing like that . . . I, I don't even know how to say it and I know you'll be disgusted with me, and I am, I am SO angry with myself, and I, I —' The tears were back.

'Shh, just, relax. Take your time. I can come back in half an hour if you like? I might pop down to Nina's and get some Thai; would you be interested in anything, a soup maybe?'

Simone shook her head, eyes down, and then, in a flash, they were back up and on Lily.

'I slept with Michael.'

Lily's left hand flew up to her mouth in shock, and she inhaled sharply.

'Oh fuck, Sim. *Fuck*. Ohhh, that's no good. That's no good at all.'

Tears began rolling down Simone's face, and she had to relegate her tea to her bedside table to manage the salty streams. Lily noticed with disappointment that Valium, Xanax, Phenergan and some other unidentified foil packets were all fighting for space on the small surface area.

'I just, I don't even know how it happened. He was at Town having a few drinks with his mates last night and I was there having dinner, and we, we hadn't seen each other for ages, and I was in a really good mood cos I'd just got back from this awesome Hawaiian trip, and so we were chatting, you know, and we were both talking about our partners and just being normal exes. No funny business. And I don't know, maybe because he was being so normal, I, well, I started to feel familiar old feelings, and I SWORE to myself I wouldn't be with him again, Lil, not *ever* . . . So I wanted to go home, because if I'm being totally honest, I could sense something maybe happening, but I couldn't find Skye anywhere, and so he said he'd drop me home in a taxi, and I *shouldn't* have agreed, but then we . . . we went back to his place and I am so ANGRY at myself, Lil, I am such an *IDIOT*. Why do I always do this? Why can't I be strong for once in my fucking life? *Why?*'

She began sobbing uncontrollably, her whole body shaking; her head on her knees, hair covering her legs, her body looking roughly as small as she probably felt. Although Lily knew it was unkind to think so, Simone deserved to feel like shit. This was a girl who had been lucky enough to have all of the magical attributes to attract Jack Winters, and then she cheated on him. With Michael, the world's biggest nightmare. No, the hot steaming *shit* of the world's biggest nightmare.

Lily was furious with Simone, but she held it in. She also reminded herself she shouldn't be feeling more sorry for Jack than one of her best friends, even if all the evidence herewith suggested she was within her rights to.

'Oh, Sim . . . how could you let that dirty dog back into your pants . . .'

'Babe, trust me, if I could rewind the clock I'd take it back. I would give anything to!'

But Lily wasn't so sure. Simone had a history of this precise kind of fail, and she just didn't seem to learn the lesson. She seemed *predisposed* to messing things up just as they seemed to be going well, and life was normalising. She was a serial self-saboteur.

Lily took a deep breath and tried to calm down. After all, who was she to be judging? It wasn't like Lily was perfect. And yet all she wanted to do was scream at Simone, and say that maybe if you didn't drink so much and do so much coke, and take so many drugs, maybe you wouldn't make such shitty decisions. And *maybe*, maybe if you were more invested in your relationship with Jack, you wouldn't be out getting shitfaced every weekend; you'd make time to see him instead of stumbling out of clubs with your ex-boyfriend in tow. Jack was handed to you like a goddamn gift, *and you're chucking him away!*

'I feel for Jack. I know you don't want to hear that but I'm sorry, I do.'

'Babe, can you not? It wasn't like I wanted this to happen, fuck!'

'I know that, Sim. I do. But, well, you've got to take responsibility for this. You can't blame it on the alcohol, or drugs or whatever.

You know that. It's never an excuse.'

'I know, I know . . . I just, oh God, I can't believe I did it. And now I've probably ruined the one *really* good, normal relationship I've ever had.'

'So you'll tell him?' Lily asked, because it wasn't a given with Simone. Despite her waxing lyrical about being true to yourself and honesty setting you free and acai being the answer to everything, she took a slightly different tack when it came to her own life.

'Jack is such a good guy. This would kill him.'

That was a no, then.

Lily fought the temptation to yell that Jack deserved the truth, and furthermore, unlike Tom Cruise in *A Few Good Men*, he could handle it. She took a deep breath and said nothing.

'How are things with Jack anyway?' Lily asked, clearing her throat as she did. As far as she could ascertain, the shiny gleam of their relationship had become more matte of late. But for Simone to even be chatting to and hanging out with Michael, let alone sleeping with him, showed evidence of big cracks. Huge.

'Yeah, fine. I mean, obviously we've both been away lately, but we've texted heaps . . . He's just so . . . decent, babe. So good and nice and kind to me.'

'It kind of sounds like you're saying those like they're negatives,' Lily said, thinking back to her conversations about 'nice' Byron with Alice.

Simone looked at Lily, thinking. She roughly wiped her nose with the back of her wrist and thought some more.

'I don't think I'm used to it. The more perfect he is, the worse I feel about myself. Does that make sense? I'm not on his level, babe. I'm not who he needs. Maybe that's why I've been acting up lately; it's having this weird reverse effect on me, because I think deep down he knows he can do better, so why try to prove him wrong? Why should I change who I am when he won't stick around once he gets to know the real me anyway?'

Simone looked at Lily with her swollen, red eyes and Lily's heart broke. Here was a beautiful young woman, a genetically flawless, smart, spiritual, positive, kind, successful, generous, fun woman, who had no clue just how rare she was, and what a good person she was. Lily's eyes welled with sorrow for her friend, for the demons that continued to plague her.

'Sim, no more "I'm not good enough" talk. There is no one like you. No one. You have it all, anything you want to be, have or do; it's yours. You gotta start practising that self-help shit you spout. And as for Jack, or *any* man, of course you are good enough for him! He is lucky to have you. *So* lucky. He knows that. I know that. Do *you* know that? I fear you really don't, Sim.'

Sim sniffed and tucked some hair behind her ear, and seemed to process what her friend was saying. Lily knew Simone had tried to bluff her way into self-confidence a million times, but the truth was she would never feel good enough. Never feel as pretty as people said she was. Never be as successful or young or fit as the next girl. Never be the 'perfect girlfriend'. She had to work hard, harder than the others to stay afloat, and she always would. It was crushing, this pressure, and it was what propelled her need to escape so often.

'I have to go back on my antidepressants, I think. Can't sleep or relax without a few barbs and I can't feel good without something helping me up.'

Lily was quiet. Simone hadn't been on antidepressants for years.

'Have you, would you talk to Jack about this stuff?' Lily thought Jack would be the perfect ear for this, Michael stuff notwithstanding. He'd been down his own path of addiction after all.

Simone laughed. It was a bitter, unhappy, sarcastic laugh.

'Oh yeah, cos confiding in boyfriends worked a treat with Michael!'

'Oh, come *on*. They're incomparable, gender aside. What about that therapist you had? Mrs Whatsername, with the big nose?'

'Do you know Michael hasn't even called or texted since last night?'

It was becoming obvious that while Simone was upset, she wasn't exactly remorseful. She seemed to view the whole episode as inevitable. And it pissed Lily off. She wasn't going to enable this any more. She stood up and walked around to the other side of the bed. She snatched the foil packets from the beside table, and then, yanking open the drawer underneath, found a few more telltale white pharmacy boxes and packets, and small plastic bottles, and snatched them up, too.

'What are you *doing*!' Simone shrieked, a mother having her baby stripped from her.

'Don't take those! I need them to sleep – they're nothing, those ones, people use them all the time, on planes and whatever, babe, what are you *doing*!'

Lily cradled the packets in close to her chest, lest Simone lunge at her.

'I can't change the way you think about yourself, Sim, but I can tell you that I no longer support this. It's dangerous. I won't stand by and watch it any more. I support you, I love you, but you need to sort your shit out.'

With one last look at Simone – a small, shell of herself, outrage and disbelief flashing in her puffy eyes – Lily sighed and walked out of the room, closing the door behind her.

31

Lily stood in the shower, slowly massaging the shampoo through her hair. Her day loomed ominously in front of her. She planned to tell Sasha she was leaving today, and on top of that she would be forced to work with poor Jack, whose girlfriend she knew had cheated on him.

She hadn't heard or seen from Sim since last night; her bedroom door remained closed, but the sound of thumping to the bathroom and back earlier this morning reassured Lily that her housemate wasn't in the wrong/tragic/eternal kind of slumber. Lily was pissed off that she had to think like that at *all*, before remembering she needed to be there for her friend, not judge and admonish her. She'd said her piece last night; Simone knew where she stood.

On set an hour later, Jack was making pork belly, and for some reason, even though it was a meal Lily loved, and one often used in her and Alice's game of Death Row Meal, today it was making her nauseous. The syrupy caramel scent of the sauce was burning her nostrils, and the look of the uncooked pig was turning her stomach. The segment was sliced in half for an ad break, and Mel and Rob started chatting to Jack as he prepared the cabbage and chilli side dish. They were in remarkably good spirits despite being 'let go', but rumour was it they were being paid out handsomely for the remainder of their contract. Mel winked at Lily playfully as she was wont to do, and Lily realised just how much she'd miss them. She'd miss all of them. Especially Jack.

At that very moment Jack looked up at her, and they locked eyes. The knowledge of Simone's misdemeanour felt like an enormous clown nose on Lily's face, and she immediately looked away. She was being a shitty producer this morning, absent and distracted, but she couldn't seem to normalise. There was far – *truckloads* – too much going on in her head to hang around the kitchen bench and chinwag with the talent today. They'd all understand once the news got out.

'Lily?'

Lily spun around to see Sasha, a picture of layered, ruffled perfection with emerald-green earrings and vibrant red-orange lipstick.

'I got your email, what's up?'

'Oh, um, I just, I needed to speak with you about something.'

'Can we speak now?' Lily couldn't tell if Sasha knew what was going on and was being deliberately nonchalant, or if she genuinely thought Lily wanted to discuss something insignificant, such as Jack's need for more fancy Le Creuset casserole dishes, which the budget, like everything fancy he asked for, wouldn't permit.

Lily flashed a look at the set, which was due to light up with live, porky magic in sixty seconds. Sasha knew better than to interrupt mid-segment. She clearly hadn't put two and two together yet.

'Um, is it okay if I come and see you after the show?'

'I'm around til eleven. Come by my office.' She nodded towards the set. 'And if there's any of that pork belly left, do bring it with you.'

Lily smiled. 'Of course.' She would miss Sasha, she realised with regret and a stab of fear about making the wrong decision. She'd wanted so desperately to impress her and advance and advance and advance, and she'd failed. She'd come to *The Daily* full of hubris and entitlement, expecting a promotion in six months, and to be on her track to EP within two years, and she hadn't even been able to beat a twit to series producer.

Lily tried to smile, focus and enjoy the remainder of the segment, but all she saw was a blazing red FAIL sign. At least she had Greece. Greece would be exciting, inspiring, sunny, invigorating. Maybe she would even have a summer fling . . . Mimi was always banging on about how gorgeous the Greek boys were. The less blonde-haired and blue-eyed the better, frankly. She checked her phone for the time; Mimi would already be at the airport, soaking up the cheese and champagne in the business-class lounge, all decked out in her finest travel cashmere tracksuit. Good for her. She knew how to live.

A text buzzed in her hand as she was replacing her phone.

Hun, I'm so sorry about last night. And everything ☹ I know
I have work to do. xoxo

She was still alive, Lily thought, releasing a breath she didn't even realise she'd been holding. Thank fuck for that.

She wondered when Sim and Jack would speak, and whether Simone would tell him what she'd done. She figured she might feel compelled to since Lily knew, and might just pull the moral-crusader, I'll-tell-him-if-you-don't card.

I love you, Sim city. Always here for you. Xx

Lily walked back down the hallway, past the kitchen, to check her emails before meeting with Sasha, pork in hand, and taking a guillotine to her job.

'Woodward!'

Jack's voice rang out from the kitchen. Shit. She really didn't want to face him right now. *Fuck fuck fuck.*

He was casually sipping on a coffee from the gleaming new coffee machine Nikkii had insisted on, and looked exactly like the kind of guy you wanted to take you to a movie and then snuggle on a lounge with. Especially on this kind of disgusting day.

'Hey,' she said, popping her head back into the kitchen and smiling in what she hoped was a convincing manner.

'Everything okay? You seemed a bit . . . distracted this morning?'

'Oh, yeah, totally, no, everything is fine, totally.' She stayed outside the kitchen to signal she wasn't up for a chat. No light chats with Jack today. No, thank you.

He frowned slightly.

'You're quitting, aren't you? I saw you chatting to Sasha.'

Why today, why *everything* today! Lily exploded internally. And how could he tell from that tiny moment she and Sasha shared this morning. It was nothing! Pork belly chat! Lily's unnaturally fake chirpy demeanour buckled, and her chest slumped. She looked down. He was disappointed in her and it felt horrible.

'I wanted to tell you, but I, well, I needed to tell Sasha first, which I'm about to do now. And *then* I was going to tell you. I've thought about it a lot, Jack, and it's the right thing for me to do at this time. I know you don't agree with it bu—'

He smiled and chuckled, his eyes softening.

'What I think doesn't matter. What you're doing is brave in its own way.'

'Well, *you've* changed your bloody tune.' She exhaled in surprise and relief, but couldn't help feeling a little bit disappointed he no longer felt compelled to fight for her to stay.

'I'm starting to understand your reasoning, I guess you could say.'

Aha! Perhaps he was starting to feel the squeeze of Nikkii's vulgar tentacles. Maybe *he* would even leave too . . . Lily couldn't decide if that was a good or bad thing; at least if he was here she could still stalk him easily. She looked down, suddenly remembering what awaited this poor guy when he next caught up with his girlfriend. As if reading her mind, Jack spoke up.

'I know you need to go, but just quickly, is Simone okay? She's sent some very . . . odd texts over the past couple of days, but then her phone rings out. I was thinking of going over to yours tonight – if she's home, that is?'

A tiny gulp involuntarily slid down Lily's neck. She might have to hijack whatever Alice was doing tonight, freezer yoga or erotic book club or whatever it might be.

'Yes, I think she'll be there. Um, maybe give her some notice though.'

Jack's eyes searched Lily's for what that might mean, but she wasn't giving away a thing.

' 'Kay, well, see you Monday, I guess . . . Wish me luck,' Lily said, and ducked off to her desk. She had to get her game face on. And she *definitely* had to stop her mind from skating over to the fact that Jack might well be single again soon. It was irrelevant. No-go zone. *Enough.*

32

Sasha was openly appalled by Lily's decision. She'd immediately questioned whether it was a reaction to being passed over for the promotion, which Lily had adamantly denied, but Sasha seemed to have made up her mind. Given Lily's lack of immediate prospects, Sasha felt she was being a quitter, and in Sasha's eyes, there was nothing worse, except perhaps nude lips.

Reluctantly holding Lily's exit-interview form, Sasha looked at Lily, not saying anything for a few seconds.

'Lily, I'd like for you to stay.'

Lily wasn't quite sure she was hearing correctly.

'I'm not going to piss in anyone's pocket, but you are by far our top segment producer. Lord knows what I'm going to do with your shadow of a co-worker. And as for Jack, he clearly adores working with you. The food segment is a genuine *Daily* highlight. Lily, what I'm saying is the show needs you. Now, I know you'd still like to work in TV, and I'm not saying I have something specific in mind to offer just now, but don't think you'll be stuck producing gnocchi and chitchat in a fake kitchen forever if you stick around.'

Lily, unused to hearing praise from Sasha, flushed with awkwardness. Did this mean Sasha was *finally* going to promote her? Or was she just saying that to keep her on? Lily knew better than to fall for gilded boss talk, the type that promised whatever it took when faced with an unsavoury turn of events. Even Sasha wasn't immune to this, she realised, slightly dismayed.

Her brain started hurling glorious possibilities at her before a) remembering who the new sheriff in town was, and b) becoming angry that it took Lily's resigning before Sasha told her she was an asset.

'I'm sorry, Sasha, and thank you, that's very kind of you to say. I just, I really do need a fresh start right now.'

Sasha nodded, disheartened. Oh well, thought Lily, annoyed. Too little, too late. Lily wasn't just some puppet Sasha could manipulate as she pleased. As she watched Sasha sign the form, Lily felt something rise within her. Pride? Self-assurance? Sure, she was now jobless and had refused a fictional but potentially better position from the woman she admired most in her industry, but it was on her terms, and somewhere deep in that part of the soul or gut or symbolic golden butterfly chamber that existed in self-help books, it felt *right*.

Sasha took off her glasses and handed the form back to Lily, peering at her in a puzzled fashion.

'Are you sure this is the right thing to do, Lily?'

'Yes,' Lily said softly, hoping to Heston Blumenthal she was right.

'Very well. I assume there will be formal goodbyes soon, so we won't entertain that portion of this particular ritual just now.'

A small smile, and the glasses were back on, her sleek computer screen again her focus.

Lily nodded and smiled, feeling like a slave who'd upset her master. A common feeling when it came to Sasha. No! Actually, suck it, Sasha, she thought defiantly. I tried my best and you never noticed until now. Next time maybe value your staff more, Lily thought as she walked out of Sasha's office and back to her desk.

Running her eyes over her leaving papers, Lily discovered that contractually she was only required to give one week's notice. Which she had just given. That left her a full week at home to organise her hairy, pale body, and buy a decent bikini before she flew out to Greece in a fortnight. Perfect. At a slight loss as to what to do next, Lily sat in her chair and started compiling a handover document for whoever would be taking her role. She stuck her head up over the partition and looked at Dale, who was busy picking something out of his teeth with one of the laminated fire-safety cards that were stuck onto everyone's desk.

It seemed highly unlikely he would be the next in line, even if technically he was the most knowledgeable and competent. Jack seemed to like him well enough, but Jack was now so confident in his role, he barely required anything more than his brief and some help making space in the set fridge.

A text from Alice interrupted Lily's thoughts.

Yes!! Would love to see your head tonight. Going with Carlos to see a band at the Nash, see you out back at 7 for a schnitz first x

Lily smiled with relief. She was *so* glad Alice was free tonight, and that there would be ample alcohol available for consumption. She missed Alice so much; her energy was such a positive, playful force in the office. She couldn't wait to work with her again and be in a judgement-free environment of daily M&Ms and Fanta once more. She had no idea who Carlos was – he could be a trapeze artist Alice had met on set that week, or he could be her new fiancé, it was hard to say.

> Just quit . . . Sasha was not happy. But I AM! And we are going
> to celebrate tonight Xx

Lily realised she should text Sim so she knew she had the house to herself. And text in a way that didn't imply Lily knew Jack would be going over.

> I'm going to The National tonight seeing one of Alice's ridiculous
> bands, you are so welcome to join Xx

Pleased with her gentle deception and knowing full well Simone would *never* come to the inner west, Lily stood up and went to tell Dale her news.

'They are gonna be the new big thing, for *real*,' cried Alice, whose hair was now peroxide-blonde, evolving roots notwithstanding, and cut into a wispy, elfin bob that seemed to make her eyes bigger and her cheekbones even more extraordinary. With her red mini tunic dress and knee-high flat boots she looked like she should be on stage, possibly sometime during the Beatles' reign, but she was a sight to behold on the filthy beer-slippery dance floor nonetheless. Men brave enough to dance tried to sidle up next to her, and others content with nursing their lagers by the wall watched her dance joyously to the music; this strange, beautiful nutbag who didn't seem to quite fit the 'from Earth' brief.

Carlos turned out to be a nuclear dud: a classic suit hunting for a manic pixie dream girl to transport him from the banality of his dreary, stressful existence to a movie montage of wild sex and happy-go-lucky living. He was on his phone constantly during dinner, and then excused himself to go outside for a call for so long that Alice and Lily bought a bottle of wine and set off to the dance floor without him. It was packed, he would never find them, and that was completely fine. Why he'd come at all – he was *clearly* more of a scotch on the rocks/cocaine/oysters guy than a pub live-music guy – was a mystery, but such was the Alice effect.

'The drummer is a good sort. A VERY good sort,' Lily yelled to Alice over the noise, waiting until Alice spun one of her ears in her general direction. She swayed and danced to the music, drunk enough to forget her high heels were killing her, and gazed upon the lovely dark-haired drummer, who remarkably, seemed to be looking back at her, and smiling, too. She looked behind her, but Alice had made sure they were at the very front of the dance floor, and there were only drunk, glazed-eyed guys behind her. It was definitely Lily he was smiling at.

She looked back at him and he smiled again. Now, suddenly self-conscious despite at least five glasses of white wine, Lily reigned in her dancing and tucked her hair behind her ears. It was touching her collarbones again, she really should get it cut, she thought. Or should she? She was a wild and carefree freelancer now, who *knew* what might evolve, appearance-wise! Maybe she would buy a bike and start wearing wide-rimmed black spectacles and collared shirts with men's loafers and backpacks. Anything was possible.

The singer, a Johnny Depp doppelganger who seemed happiest when his hair was completely covering his face, announced the set was over and Lily burst into rapturous applause and whistling. Alice joined in as much she could while holding a wine glass.

'Drink, drink, drink, need a drink,' Alice said, eyes wild, skin damp with sweat and joy.

'Yes, yes, let's go, the wolves are circling.'

'Good! One day they won't, and then we'll wish they were.' Alice winked at a cute boy in a beanie behind Lily and then started walking off to the bar, yanking Lily's hand as she went.

'How about that *singer*? I would do him in the fucking fire stairs this *second* if he asked. He's got that mystical rock-star vibe, hasn't he? Wouldn't look twice at him on the street, but up there . . . he's like a musical Jesus.'

The two girls reached the bar and gently pushed their way into a front-row-ish position. Alice whisked a wine list out from underneath a guy's almost empty beer glass without it so much as tipping the glass and he turned to stare at her, slack-jawed. She grinned at him and started reading the list.

'I like the drummer, actually,' said Lily. 'He smiled at me, I think. Or maybe his girlfriend was behind me or something, but I —'

Alice stopped reading the wine list and turned to face her friend.

'He smiled at *you*! Where is your self-confidence, Woo? You spend all your time pining over a guy who's banging your flatmate: WHAT CAN POSSIBLY COME OF THAT? What's gonna change? You're cock-blocking your*self*, for fuck's sake.'

Alice was looking at Lily as though it personally insulted her that Lily had a thing for Jack.

'Well, no, hang on a seco—'

'Don't you want more? More men, more from Jack, just more *something*?'

Alice's words rang loud and true, even over the terrible house music. Lily had no defence. Alice was right. She did want more. *Why was she wasting her time on Jack?* He was off limits. Always had been. He was never going to go for her. And whether he was with Simone or not, Lily couldn't go there. Lily suddenly became furious with herself for allowing this charade to have run this long. What was she hoping would happen? Jack would one day mysteriously fall out of love with his blonde goddess and go for his ratbag producer? Yes, because *that* happened all the time.

Even if Simone had irrevocably ruined things by sleeping with Michael, Lily couldn't very well collect her heartbroken leftovers and think it would go karmically unnoticed. Lily was shocked at just how pointless her feelings for Jack were. *It would never amount to anything.* And there was no better time to get over him than right this second.

'You're right. No, you really are, *don' look at me like that*, I mean it! I've thought aboudit, and I'm *done*. No more. Egh, it's such – a – fucking – waste – of *time*.'

'I will hold you to this, Woodfart. Now you can start letting men fall in love with you, instead of the other way round. Deal? *Hi!* Yes, two double-vodka pineapples, please.'

Lily had forgotten Alice's love for doubles. Saved you going back to the bar, she maintained, forgetting the way Lily's body liked to handle spirits, which was with extreme resistance and, quite often, rapid and violent expulsion. Alice pulled a glittery purple wallet out of her tiny black messenger bag and dumped it on the bar, before suddenly squinting at something over Lily's left shoulder.

'Okay. So. The drummer's over there by the back bar, some bald guy too . . . he's with some busty wench, forget him. *OOH*, Musical Jesus is there. How wonderful. They're drinking beers . . . mingling . . . The drummer keeps looking over here. A LOT. Lucky him; he's about to meet his dreamweaver. Why did you put your hair back? No, no, no, out, out, give me that.'

'Cos I was hot, from danci—'

Alice leaned over and yanked the elastic from Lily's hair.

'Ow! *FUCK!* Why'd'you have to be sucha goddamn maniac all your life?'

'Shh . . . Okay, here's your drink, yum-yum, have a *big* sip, now we're going over there and you're going to flirt with Drums like you're a professional lap dancer.'

Yes, she was, Lily confirmed to herself. It would act as the perfect full stop to the Jack business, and if all went well, and Drums didn't have an adoring wife or girlfriend back in bloody Nimbin or wherever he was from, Lily might even be able to clean the slate thoroughly tonight.

She took a swig from her tall glass of potent, sugary juice and nodded affirmatively.

'Rock'n'roll.'

33

Lily opened one eye and tried to locate her bearings. Even *one* bearing would suffice at this stage. She was in a nondescript room, and she was in a bed, and there was a guy's naked torso, untanned and slightly freckled, next to hers, and he was facing the other side of the bed and snoring lightly, and every pore of his body reeked of alcohol.

Or maybe it was hers.

Lily noted with an unwarranted amount of self-pride that she was still wearing her bra and knickers, but the memory of removing those items in a drunken, wild session with the gent laying next to her came back like a swift punch. Fucking Alice and her double vodkas, Lily thought as she wiped her eyes with both hands in an effort to see and think and do the kind of normal activity non-hungover people took for granted every day.

Before she beat herself up like she usually did after letting her hair down, she permitted herself a smile. She remembered the fun of the night, hanging with the band like a couple of misfit groupies, drinking and dancing, then kissing the amorous drummer (whose name Lily thought *might* be Kai but she couldn't be sure), then the ugly lights coming on, and the whole group, all of the band and some of the crew, Alice and Lily and a handful of twenty-year-old model types who'd laid claim to the band well before Alice and Lily strutted in, moved back to this weird, sterile serviced apartment the band were staying in and did shots of rum and smoked joints and danced.

It was a very, *very* fun night, Lily had to concede, despite the fact her body was seconds away from shrivelling up in dehydration. As she carefully unwrapped herself from the sheets and tiptoed around the room looking for her jeans, top, bag, *anything*, she wondered if Alice was still here. If she *was*, she would be ensconced in the arms of her latest soulmate. She and the singer had kissed within around three minutes of being introduced, which would have been Alice's instigation. Most girls would be labelled unstable if they told a guy they'd just met they were about to kiss them, but when Alice did it, it seemed somehow normal in its abnormality. Like she was just playing her role in a quirky rom-com, and he was just playing his, and everything was perfectly as it should be.

Dressed and thankfully in possession of her bag, shoes and phone, Lily carefully opened the door and crept into the living room, home to three million empty beer bottles and as many overflowing ashtrays, and more shoes than Lily remembered there being people with feet to own them. One of the young girls, Jessica, or *Mess*ica, as the drummer referred to her while watching her make out with two separate roadies, then dance/cry/vomit at various stages of the night, was sleeping daintily in a foetal position on the enormous lounge, and the band manager, a huge, bald, burly guy in a Lakers shirt, was squished into a small armchair, snoring with the power and roar of an industrial generator.

No Alice. And all the other bedroom doors were closed. Lily feared what she might find should she open any of them, and with her phone out of battery she couldn't text, so she made an executive decision to leave the apartment and hope that Alice was still sound asleep in the arms of her Musical Jesus. Thankfully, it was early enough that Lily could get away with only the very earliest of dog walkers' judgy eyes on her atrocious appearance and humiliating taxi hunt.

Once home, Lily removed her heels and placed them by the door, snuck inside, and crept upstairs to her bedroom. She plugged in her phone and left it to charge as she showered, letting the hot water wash over her body. She scrubbed her skin and washed her hair and found herself having flashbacks of her early-morning session with Kai. It had been a *long* time between drinks, she conceded, but that didn't take anything away from his impressive skills. She'd never really enjoyed men going down 'there', but he seemed to have read a secret manual no other guy she'd been with had. She smiled, her face flushing at the memories popping up without warning or invitation.

She was grateful Alice had bullied her into getting her rascal on. She never needed to see or speak to Kai again, she confirmed, feeling strangely empowered in her decision to have a one-nighter and not feel emotionally bereft in her sleep-deprived, hungover fog, which was how it usually panned out. No, in fact she felt GOOD! Her mojo seemed to have finally returned; all that was missing now was an upbeat disco track and a buoyant street strut.

For the first time in a long time, life felt exciting, and fun, and full of potential. Like she had been neglecting her carefree, spontaneous side for far, far too long, stuck in a day-to-day existence of work/home and secretly pining for a man who was never going to pine for her. She had, as Alice brutally but correctly pointed out, lost the plot. And it only took three litres of booze and a frisky young drummer to find it again.

Towelling off her wet hair, which, despite two rounds of shampoo, still reeked of cigarette smoke, Lily checked her phone. A text had come through, sent at 4.25 a.m.

Took Jesus back to mine for a holy rogering ... Think ur busy
doing same with Drums, AS IT SHOULD BE xxx

Lily quickly tapped out a reply.

You guessed right. Just got home now. Your bad influence rubbed
off finally, well done! Your trophy's in the mail xx

Smiling, Lily chucked the phone back on the bed and rustled through her drawers for a T-shirt and tracksuit pants to cocoon herself in and sleep this atrocious, thirsty, blissful body back to health. But first, something sugary and watery to coat her mouth and poor, suffering liver.

A thought popped up: Jack wouldn't be here, would he? Would he have stayed last night? Maybe, if Simone hadn't told him the truth. Or maybe he left in a daze after being told his girlfriend had cheated on him. Or maybe he'd never come over and nothing had happened either way. Lily considered putting a bra on in case he galloped down the stairs on his way out, as he had done a couple of times in the past, but then, remembering she no longer cared about him Like That, kept on walking downstairs. What happened between those two was of no consequence to her. Concern because they were both friends, but not consequence.

Reaching the fridge, a wave of nausea rose in Lily's stomach, and she realised she needed something in that poor, acidic, gurgling pit or things might get *really* unsavoury. Dear God, let there be some normal toast in this freezer, she thought, as she waded through frozen berries and pre-cooked soups from Baroness von Healthypants. There were brown rice and spelt gypsy wraps; that would have to do. She could slather them in peanut butter and honey.

'You're home,' she heard Simone say on her way down the stairs. Lily looked up to see her flatmate, all three kilos of her, in gym leggings and crop top, barely covered by a small purple Victoria's Secret hoodie. Lily looked at the oven for the time; it was not even seven yet.

'Just. Well, in body anyway. It was,' she exhaled through dry lips, 'a big one. Too big. Alice led me astray.'

Simone smiled faintly; her eyes were sad and devoid of their usual spark. She wasn't sporting her usual year-round fake tan, and her hair was greasy. This wasn't the Simone Lily knew. She was clearly still in a bad place. A stab of guilt pierced Lily, was she a witch for going out last night? Should she have been home here with her friend in need? But Jack had mentioned he was coming over . . .

Simone walked down the stairs, sitting on the second-last step to put her shoes and socks on.

'Good. It's been too long since you've had some fun, babe.' Her voice was weak and full of false energy.

'Off to the gym then?' Lily asked, wondering how to get past platitudes to ask how her friend was doing. *Really* doing.

'Mmm, doing TRX then pilates. Double hit. Got a shoot Monday, need to firm up.'

'Are you kidding me? Sim, you probably weigh less than that sneaker right now.' The words were out before she realised how inflammatory they might be.

A cloud fell across Simone's face.

'It's not *deliberate*.' Her voice trembled and she lowered her head so that she was facing the floor as she yanked her shoes on roughly.

'I'm sorry. I didn't, my brain, I just . . . I'm sorry.' Lily walked over to Simone and stood awkwardly by the bottom of the banister, wondering where to from here.

'Are you – how are you feeling today, about you know, just, everything . . .?'

Simone, still with her head down, wiped a tear from her face.

'Jack broke up with me last night. No surprises there, I guess.'

'Oh, Sim . . . oh shit. I'm so sorry . . .' She sat down next to her friend and placed her right arm around her tiny frame. Simone nuzzled her head into Lily's armpit and cried. Lily, operating at about fifteen watts, sunk to around three, her eyes filling with tears in sympathy for her friend. Her heart broke for Simone, for a thousand reasons. Her friend was blessed and cursed in such equal measure.

After a few minutes, Simone, sniffing and wiping her nose and eyes, lifted her head. She shook her head.

'I deserved it. It was always going to happen. The Michael shit was just the nail in the coffin, babe.'

'Do you really believe that?'

'I do. He liked me because I was friendly and he was new to the city and I was a bit of an accelerator, to be honest. You know what I'm like . . . And me, I thought I wanted a guy who was settled and stable and . . . *normal*, but we're just such different people, you know? He's so set in his life. Like, we have fun, and he's gorge, and he treats me well, but I just, I'm more about living in the present, and having fun, and with work being so full on and all the travel and —'

'Sim, you don't need to apologise for your life. It's an amazing life; people would kill for it. Plus, you're only twenty-six. This is exactly the time for you to be partying hard and livi—'

'Do you think I party too much?' She sounded wounded.

'Are we being honest or polite?'

Simone sighed. 'Honest, I suppose.'

'It's not even really the partying. It's the constant self-medicating. Uppers, downers, sleepers, wide-awakers ... You take something to clean the house, for God's sake. I find it confusing, I guess, since you're so pure and holy about everything else you put into your body.'

'Jeez, you make me sound like Anna Nicole Smith.' She laughed hollowly.

Lily could only look at her friend. Simone's smile faded and her eyes registered what Lily was saying.

'What have you taken today, as an example? From last night to right now.'

'Oh, come *on*. Find me someone who doesn't take a few Benzos after a break-up.'

'Anything else?'

'And then I couldn't sleep so at about two I had some ... I think it was Ambien. Yeah. That's all though.'

'I honestly don't even know how you're up and functioning. Did you have anything this morning?'

'The contraceptive pill; is that allowed, Sergeant?'

Suddenly, Simone shot up and started walking to the door, grabbing her keys from the bowl on the way.

She whirled around as she opened the front door.

'You know what, babe? I don't need this. Not today. I really thought you might be a bit more supportive, to be honest.' Tears made it a struggle for her to talk, but before she could clear her throat, she was gone, the door closing loudly behind her.

Lily sat on the stairs and slumped her head onto her arms. What a big fucking mess she'd made of that.

34

Lily repositioned her phone, smiling like she was having the best time in the world and wasn't aware there was a camera being held by her very own hand capturing this moment, and clicked again. She checked the photo. So . . . *smug*. And too close! Her nose looked enormous. How come when Simone and Nikkii and all those girls did it they looked perfect? Probably because they did a hundred takes and employed strenuous filtering and editing, things Lily had no clue how to do.

Lily tried again. Just as she was about to take the photo, a couple of old men chatting loudly walked past Lily and down the steep cobblestone path, one leading a donkey with a vibrant rug and several crates of bright fruit and vegetables on its back. She quickly snapped the scene, marvelling at how everything on Santorini looked like it had been sent in by a TV props team.

She looked back to the view she was trying to nonchalantly capture in her selfie and took it in for the eightieth time that day. Her T-shirt flapped gently in the sea breeze, her arms were warm from the sun and her smile was full of pure joy.

Even after several days here, she found the view before her

absolutely breathtaking. Enormous terracotta cliffs played host to higgledy-piggledy rows of restaurants, crisp white and azure-blue villas, and postcard-perfect spherical chapels, all facing the most spectacular, vast sea Lily had ever seen. It defied imagination, especially the enormous cruise ships that zoomed in and out of the vista all day, unloading wealthy Texans for lunch on the caldera before whisking them off again in the late afternoon. On the day Lily had arrived, she and Mimi had enjoyed some seafood and a couple of bottles of local white wine at a rooftop restaurant and soaked up the world-famous Santorini sunset. The sun shimmered on the horizon like a magnificent burning red orb, sending the clouds into a spin of pinks and oranges and red, each of them outlined with iridescent gold and bronze. Mimi had failed to tell a very jet-lagged and confused Lily that sunset was not until after nine p.m., despite the fact they began drinking at six p.m. What eventuated was a completely disoriented, giggly Lily, who, as Mimi had planned, slept soundly until seven a.m., therefore 'kicking jet lag's arse'.

Lily had been here only a few glorious days, but instantly understood what Mimi had been on about all these years. The Greek islands were *special*. The people were warm and genuine, the sea and the sun and the sky played in a breathtaking visual symphony, and the food was outstanding. It was the perfect place to turn thirty and become a Proper Woman, Lily conceded. Which, just this morning – on Australian time anyway – she had. Annoyingly, because she was a clueless novice traveller, she hadn't set up her phone for international roaming before she left, so there were to be no birthday texts or calls, but she had put an autoreply on her work email sending people to her Gmail account before leaving *The Daily*, and hoped that when she checked it on Mimi's iPad later there would be at least one well-wisher.

This morning Mimi had requested two hours to 'set something

up', and Lily was banned from their small B&B until then. It was a peculiar little place, more like a cliff-side cave than functioning accommodation, but their caldera-side balcony came with a breath-taking view of the sea, and it made the sparse, dark interior worth it. Plus, the husband and wife who owned it, Paros and Eleni, were wonderful, generous, kind hosts, and the yoghurt with honey and quince they served for breakfast was unlike anything Lily had ever had before. She'd taken to having two bowls, with extra honey, and a sweet frappe each morning. It was possibly her favourite part of the day. The Greeks seemed to really understand sugar. She appreciated that.

It was finally time to head back. As Lily walked back along the top of the caldera, past the chintzy jewellery shops and overpriced dining options catering to the many cruise ship tourists who poured off the enormous boats anchored in the vast sea below, her mind snuck over to Jack. Their last week together at work had been a strange one. It was furiously busy, which was a relief, and not a word was uttered about his breaking up with Simone. Lily had to hand it to him, even if it did secretly annoy her; he was excellent at keeping his personal stuff personal.

'Won't be the same without you,' he'd said at her lame, in-office leaving drinks, which was nice, professional enough. But when he'd followed it with 'we're a good team, you and I', all the old feelings Lily had been stuffing down began to bubble back up. She told herself it was simply a throwaway line pertaining to the daring and inventive recipes and food-truck tours they could've masterminded. But there was something about the way he'd said it . . . Lily stored it away quietly for later analysis – to pull out slowly, like a precious photo – when she allowed herself a small, occasional moment to think about him.

'Lilia!' Eleni came out from the small front room of the hotel and greeted Lily with wide-open arms.

'Happy birthday to you! We will miss you!' And she hugged a surprised Lily, her short arms barely meeting around Lily's waist.

'Thank you, Eleni . . . Uh, why, where are you going?' A frown settled on Lily's face.

Eleni laughed. 'It is you who is going.'

Lily scrunched up her face. That was weird. They weren't due to check out for another four days.

Eleni smiled and winked. 'It is surprise. Panos will be here in a moment to take you.'

'Oh, okay. Do you know where Mimi is?'

'Here is Panos now.'

Lily turned to see a tiny three-wheeled Mr Bean-style vehicle approaching down the narrow alleyway, a gruff-faced but kind-hearted Panos at the wheel. It sounded like a motorbike but looked like a shrunken truck, complete with a small tray on the back.

Panos stopped the 'car' suddenly and got out, tipping his straw hat theatrically to Lily.

'Yasou, yasou. Come, we must go.'

What the hell was Mimi up to? Lily wondered, a bemused smile on her face.

'Jump in, jump in, is safe, go on.'

Lily surveyed the ridiculous truck cabin before her. Panos was not a large man, but he'd eaten his fair share of feta and could barely fit in himself, let alone with room to spare for a (just) thirty-year-old woman.

'You will be safe, sit in the front there. Sit, sit!' Eleni took Lily's hands and walked her, bewildered and confused, to the toy car.

Lily realised she was genuinely not ready to leave this funny little cliff cave and her substitute grandparents yet. The whole island was just starting to feel real; it wasn't time to move on yet.

'Okay, oh God, thank you, thank you for everything, I *really* loved my time here. You're wonderful hosts, the view is incredible, we'll write great things about you on TripAdvisor!'

'Mention the new mattresses!' Eleni yelled over the sputtering vehicle, which was ready to reverse – there was no space to turn – back up to the main path.

Laughing, Lily gingerly opened the side door and perched on the edge of the seat before closing it again. Seconds later, Panos was inside, his legs crouched up under him like a clown in a box, and the two of them masterfully zoomed up the narrow alley in reverse. He shot out onto the street with a few beeps of warning and then put the truck into gear and tore forward, people scattering around him as he went, horn tooting wildly at each new turn and alleyway. Lily could not wipe the smile off her face. If someone had asked her whether, on her birthday she'd be in a truck-bike-car with an old man, hooning through the streets of Santorini, she would've guffawed. Yet here she was.

Twenty-five minutes later, having driven over hills and past small homes and rocky paddocks, the shops and hotels were getting more condensed, and she realised they were in Oia, at the far tip of the island.

'We are here!' Panos reported suddenly, and yanked the brakes on. Lily put her hands out instinctively to stop herself from flailing seatbeltlessly through the window, but Panos only laughed.

Lily got out, stretching her legs urgently, as a handsome young man dressed all in white arrived at the bottom of some winding white steps.

'Welcome, Miss Woodward,' he said, smiling at her with perfect, gleaming teeth set against a perfectly even, genuine tan.

'Hi,' she said, smiling shyly.

Panos and the young guy exchanged some rapid Greek, then

Panos came around and shook Lily's hand, looking her in the eyes, 'Yasou, Lily, na'sai kala,' before tearing off in a sea of dust.

Lily raised her eyebrows, smiling, and looked at her host.

'Please,' he said gently, motioning for her to begin her ascent up the winding steps before her.

'With pleasure,' she said, meaning it with every cell in her body. He was rather lovely-looking, she noted. Greek men *were* a handsome bunch, she had to concede. Eleni had told her they made good lovers but terrible husbands, and Lily was forbidden to marry one.

Arriving at the top of the stairs, Lily was greeted by a chic, white open marble lobby offering a view of not only the most glorious, uninterrupted expanse of sun and sky she'd ever seen, but just in front of it, the kind of infinity pool high-fashion magazines plopped gleaming swimsuit models in.

Everything about the scene before Lily screamed luxury. Or honeymoon. One of the two. Lily saw a green and gold sparkly-kaftanned Mimi chatting to the receptionist, who immediately turned her head to Lily's direction.

'Happy birthday, my darling girl!' Mimi cried, racing over and grabbing her daughter and pulling her against her glittery muumuu.

'Welcome to your new home.'

'*Mimi*,' hissed Lily quietly so as not to ruin the moment. 'You SO can't afford this, what are you doing? Have you gone mad?'

Mimi pulled back to look at her daughter, her face glowing with happiness and calm.

'I *didn't* do it,' she said, smugly.

'What do you mean?' said Lily, confused.

'*Simone*. Darling Simone did it all. She contacted me last week and told me her plan, that she wanted to treat you for your thirtieth since she couldn't be here with you, and I told her we'd be in Santorini, and so she went and booked this place for us off the internet. Isn't it incredible? *This* is how you do the Greek islands, Bean. I mean, would you look at that *view* . . .'

Before Lily could answer, a small voice interrupted from behind.

'Would you like a fresh mint cocktail?' A petite, pretty waitress advanced gingerly, her eyebrows raised, her smile wide.

'That would be lovely, thank you,' Mimi said on their behalves, taking the two drinks from her and passing one on to Lily. Lily was still trying to get her head around Simone doing all of this. Especially since they had not parted on the best of terms. Simone had spent the week after her break-up coming home extremely late and leaving well before Lily woke. Then a hair commercial in Singapore took her away for the week Lily had off before she went to Greece, so they didn't even get to say goodbye in person. Lily could feel tears well in her eyes. She had been such a wretched friend to Simone. She'd lusted after her boyfriend, and she'd allowed her to spiral back into her old ways, and then, as the finale, had lectured her and made her feel like a piece of shit. And how had Simone responded? With this.

'I know, Beany, I cried too. What a *beautiful* thing to do. She's a keeper, that one.'

Lily wiped away the rogue tear that had slipped down onto her cheek and sniffed. If only Mimi knew what a friend Lily had been back. 'I should call her,' Lily said with urgency. 'Do they have wi-fi? I can Skype her – *we* can Skype her.'

Mimi laughed. 'It's the middle of the night there, darling. How about for now we send her a photo of us with our drinks? She'd like that.'

Lily shook her head in disbelief. This was paradise; absolute paradise. And all thanks to Sim.

'Perhaps you would like to drink this by the pool, and then we can show you to your room?' Lily nodded, as did Mimi and, linking arms, mother and daughter walked through the atrium and out to the pool and the heavenly blue vista. Lily had thought the view exceptional back in Fira, but this, *this* was the premium version, uninterrupted, untainted by competing villas jutting out either side, just cliff and cruise ships crisscrossing the sea below.

'I quite like being thirty,' Lily turned to Mimi, a smile spreading across her face.

Mimi giggled then reached up and kissed her daughter on the forehead.

'Life begins at thirty, my girl. It really does. And there could not be a better starting line than this. Aren't we *blessed*.'

They clinked their glasses, sipped their drinks, and Lily said a silent thank you to Simone. She was a lucky, lucky girl. And surveying where she was, both geographically and in life, she felt very strongly that everything was just as it should be. That everything was going to work out for the best.

'Do you feel it, Bean?' Mimi asked.

'What?' Lily said slightly too fast, wondering if Mimi was reading her mind.

'There's a . . . *vibe* I always get on these islands. A feeling of beauty and calm, but also of freshness, of invigoration. A lot of people say it's because this is a volcanic island. Women in particular seem to sense it.'

'S'funny, I *was* just reflecting that I'm about to start an unknown new chapter but it's not scary . . . It just feels right, you know?'

Mimi looked at her and smiled softly.

'That's exactly what I'm talking about.' She reached her arm around Lily and the two of them looked out at the sea, smiling.

35

'I'm just going to do some emails. When are we going to lunch in town? One, did you say?'

'If that suits you,' Niko said, smiling at Lily.

'*Per*fect. Mimi, you need sunscreen, your back is burning.'

'I think I know someone who might be able to help with that,' Mimi said, salaciously winking at Niko, who moved his eyebrows up and down several times in a sleazy Pepé Le Pew manner.

'*Gross,*' Lily said, and walked away from the table, leaving the lovebirds to it. She secretly couldn't be happier, though. Since the two women had met Niko in Dubrovnik two days ago - a last min-ute decision that Lily hadn't minded one bit - Mimi had been like a sugared-up foal, buzzing with delight in his company, laughing and joking with him constantly and being far more tactile than Lily thought appropriate in front of her daughter. Niko was equally smitten, and fluent in several languages including witty bon mot, romantically suggestive and adoring flattery. Lily approved. A lot. If this was New Dad, then one who was utterly enchanted with her mother, cooked like a demon, and could pull off boat shoes and pastels on holiday was fine by her.

Lily schlepped back to the hotel room, which was more like a small house, with two levels, three bedrooms and two bathrooms and a wonderful view over the striking blue-green Adriatic Sea. Niko had booked it, wanting to impress the girls, which he had.

Lily found her mother's iPad and, settling into the couch, opened up Gmail. She needed to check Alice knew she was starting work next Monday, and to make sure Alice hadn't chucked in work altogether to go on the road with her Musical Jesus, whom she had fallen deeply and predictably in 'love' with after their night of passion a few weeks ago. Lily doubted the longevity of the fling for several reasons, like the fact Alice wasn't familiar with the word longevity.

There were a bunch of emails, she noticed briefly, before seeing that the first one was from Sasha. Which was *very* odd. Maybe that breadboard she'd nicked from the set was coming back to haunt her. She opened it right away.

To: Lily Woodward
From: Kirk, Sasha
Subject: Question

Lily,

I trust you've been enjoying your time in Europe.

Wanted to gauge your interest on something. *Iron Chef* starts filming here in a couple of months, and they're looking for a senior producer. Thought it might be something you'd be keen on. I think you'd do a great job. Be a big role, baptism of fire, etc., but sometimes that's the best way.

Let me know your thoughts. I know the EP very well, he is a

dear friend, and my recommendation will be taken seriously, just as I hope you know I expect you would take the role seriously.

S

Lily read the email three times, trying to make sense of the electronic gift from above.

Iron Chef.

Senior producer.

HER.

Did she want this job . . .? It would be very full on. Terrifying, quite possibly well above her skill set but still food-based. She realised there was no choice to be made when compared with a temp job producing a music festival. *Of course she wanted this fucking job!* She immediately replied to Sasha, so excited her fingers kept tapping the wrong letters. Alice would understand. Thank GOD she hadn't emailed her first.

To: Kirk, Sasha
From: Lily Woodward
Subject: Re: Question

Hi Sasha,

Currently in Dubrovnik, home of the clearest and most clean water you've ever seen. And no stingers or biteys at all! A huge treat for a girl from Oz. Thank you for your email. What an exciting prospect! I am so grateful you thought to ask me about this, and want you to know I am definitely keen.

Do you have any idea when it might start? I had some freelance work about to commence and just wanted to check.

Thank you again for thinking of me, I am so flattered.

Lily

High on adrenalin and excitement, and unable to believe her good fortune, Lily shook her head, smiling. Man. Sometimes it just does all work out, she thought, thinking fondly of Simone's prophecy. Maybe she wasn't *meant* to get the job at *The Daily* for this exact reason. If she had, she'd be stuck there for at least another year. Who even knew if the show would be something she liked by then? But now she had a chance to be a senior producer on an internationally known reality show, which could lead to multiple seasons or even just awesome new contacts or skills, or just, God, ANYTHING. Her heart was racing. This was her dream outcome. She felt a powerful and immediate urge to tell Jack, to prove that she *had* made the right call to quit. (And to impress him.)

She went back to her inbox and looked at the other emails. She'd been waiting on one from Simone, who had, over a mutually teary Skype a few days ago, revealed she was looking at a rehab place in Arizona. A model friend had been to it with great results, and Simone was waiting to hear back from them. Lily was so relieved. Simone finally seemed to be doing something about her problem.

'Hey-hoo, are you decent?' she heard Mimi holler as she opened the front door.

'Where's Niko?' Lily asked.

'He ducked to the spa to book us a massage for this afternoon.'

'Get you two . . .'

'I know! And yet, for some reason I thought it might be odd, being away with Niko like this. An overseas trip after only a few months is . . . quite *accelerated,* after all.'

Mimi walked over to the table, sunlight streaming in from the huge sliding doors facing out to the balcony, and took off her wide-brimmed straw hat, gently tousling her hair as she did.

'Pah, life's too short, especially for geriatrics like you two. I'm *kidding*, don't give me that face. Just enjoy it. He'll be gone soon and you'll be Nigel No Mates eating fettuccine in Rome and missing him like mad.'

A grin crossed Mimi's face.

'That's true, I suppose.'

'So. I have news. Sasha, my old boss, emailed me about a job. They're doing an Aussie *Iron Chef* series! And she thinks I could be a senior producer!'

'Oh, how wonderful! What's *Iron Chef*?'

Lily laughed. 'It's a stadium type cook-off, where top chefs battle a new chef each week. It's *awesome*.'

'Right up your rue. When do you start?'

'No, no, she's just recommending me to the EP. Hopefully I can meet up with him next week. Production starts soon, so I think they'll need to get moving . . .'

'I'm SO happy to hear this, Bean. Didn't much like the idea of you all jobless and broke.' Mimi walked to the kitchen and poured them both a glass of water.

Lily clapped her hands and did a little jump, her face beaming with glee.

'I've bloody well got my mojo back, Mimi!'

Lily thought her jet lag when she *arrived* in Greece was bad, but that was only the baby sister of the jet lag she'd been feeling since she'd arrived home three days ago. She was trapped at the intersection of fatigue and confused, and couldn't seem to shake it. Waking at four a.m., gasping for naps at four p.m., showering three times a day in order to 'reset', Lily was not quite the jetsetter she'd like to think she was.

And now, as she sat in the reception of the production studio she might soon be working for, her eyes lined and wearing a simple navy dress she'd picked up at Zara for this very appointment, she began to feel the demons of fatigue start clawing at her.

'Excuse me,' she said to the receptionist, a woman in her late forties with immaculate, shiny pink nails and an airline-hostess-worthy chignon.

'I'm a little early; I'm wondering if there's somewhere I could grab a coffee nearby?'

'There's a coffee cart down by the foyer, it should still be open,' she said kindly.

'Thanks, I'll be right back.' Lily stood up and walked to the lift, pressing the button with urgency. The reception phone rang.

'Yes, Mr Riley. She is. One moment.' The receptionist hung up.

'Miss Woodward? Mr Riley is available to see you now.'

Fuck, thought Lily, shaking her head slightly in a dismal attempt to clear the cobwebs. Ever since she'd replied to Sasha's email, this process had been set to warp speed. The interview had been immediately set for Tuesday, the highly confidential show outline had been emailed through for Lily to familiarise herself with, and straight-off-the-plane impressive haircuts had been urgently booked.

Lily, wanting to be straight up, had emailed Alice about what was happening. Alice had been half excited for Lily, half sad they might not be working together again, but mostly concerned with dribbling and gushing about Musical Jesus and his extraordinary penis.

'Wonderful!' Lily said to the receptionist, painting a smile on her face and spinning on her heels. She'd noticed when she'd put them on they were still a bit trashed from her big night out with the band a month back, but hopefully Evan Riley wouldn't notice that.

Within seconds of being in his office, Lily realised he was precisely the kind of person who'd notice that. Apparently the male version of Sasha, Evan wore thick-rimmed, round glasses, had a shiny bald head, and sported a light-grey suit with a lilac shirt and mint tie. He looked impeccable.

'Lily, hi, thanks for meeting me so quickly. Sash told me you were in Greece, and I know how hard it is to drag yourself away from those boys, let me tell you,' he said, followed by the kind of bawdy, staccato laugh that flirted between hysterical and highly irritating.

'Oh, gosh, my pleasure. I am so excited to even be meeting with you.'

'Well, you have some good experience. I mean, you probably don't quite have the *skill* level I need, and you will need to get it *tout de suite*, because you'll have a team looking up to you, but I believe good people can learn anything technical – it's finding the right personality that's hard, and *eesh*, if I could teach personality, let me tell you, I'd create a full-time college.'

Lily's tiredness only compounded Evan's manic conversational speed and delivery. She started to feel a bit like she did when she took too many cold and flu tablets.

'Ha,' she offered, smiling as he looked at her from his chair, across a lovely wooden desk featuring several small rubber rabbit toys. He caught Lily looking at them, and picked one up.

'Kidrobot; amazing store in New York. My partner Matt buys me one every time he goes, which is far too often, as you can see from my zoo here. Anyway, so you like food, you're into food, you worked with that *gorgeous* human being Jack Winters on *The Daily* . . . Tell me, which team does he bat for? It's yours, isn't it?'

Lily was taken aback before realising he meant men or women, not Lily *specifically*.

'Oh, yes, he does, I'm afraid. Had a girlfriend for some time.' She was careful not to mention that she knew her, or that they'd broken up, aiming to appear distant and professional.

'Figured as much. Terrific talent though, hard to believe he's fresh off the farm. So, you want to stay in food? It's easy to find a good producer, but when they're passionate about the content, it flows better, you know? And I think it shows, personally. Dreadfully obvious when you're lacklustre.'

'I do, yes. I produced cooking at *The Daily* for just over two years, and before that I did it for six months on *The Barbara Bates Show*, filling in for Naomi Giles, who was on maternity.'

'Och, Babs, what a dame. True star, she was. Such a pity they took her off. Never mind, that's how the margarita shakes, and she *was* nearing 200, I'm told. So, look, Lily, you know all about the show, you told me on email you're a fan of the format, I think you're pretty fab, Sasha gives you her golden thumbs up, which let me tell you, she does *nay* hand out to everyone, so you should feel very lucky. If you're available to start next week, then I would love to see you back in here Monday morning.'

Lily looked at her new boss, wide slightly agape, her eyes wide.

'Really? Ohmygod, thank you, that's incredible. Thank you, Evan. Thank you so much, this is all, it's just amazing timing, for one —'

'Sasha's loss is my gain.'

'Thank you, Evan, I won't let you down.'

'No, you won't. Now, before you go: Jack Winters. Do you think he will – and this is terribly out of school, and obviously not for Sasha's eagle ears – but do you think he's happy over there? Wouldn't consider a station jump like you, would he? I don't imagine it will come off, but *oh*, the idea of him as a host, it's too much.'

Lily gulped, her heart racing as she immediately fast-forwarded to working with Jack again.

'Oh, I have no idea; I'm sorry, Evan. You might need to talk to his management?'

'Yes, of course, just being a weasel. Never mind.' He stood up, puffing out his chest ever so slightly, which, with his paunch, was mildly reminiscent of the fat controller from *Thomas the Tank Engine*. Walking around to open his office door, which featured a print of an old bar sign saying 'Beware of Pickpockets and Loose Women', he smiled at his newest staff member.

Lily stood up and took the hand he held out to her, shaking it with an enormous smile on her face, in utter disbelief at what had transpired for her professionally in the last week.

'Stephanie will email you all the details, pay, contract, blah blah blah. You know we shoot out at the old Wonderland, yes? I recommend spending the weekend making a couple of new playlists for the drive.'

Lily laughed and bid Evan farewell, jubilant about her new job, but also thrilled that she now had such an effervescent, theatrical boss. Sasha was great, but she was so . . . *understated*. One thing Evan certainly was not.

36

With a half-eaten cheeseburger on her passenger seat and a caramel thickshake wedged between her thighs, Lily drove home, excited because Simone should be back by now.

The rehab place had no spots for now, apparently, so Simone had been staying at her mum's for the past week, to stay out of temptation's way, and be nurtured following the break-up and generally pretty shitty time. She'd come back this evening for an early-morning job tomorrow. Lily couldn't wait to see her, and had bought her a beautiful silver bracelet in Greece she wanted to give her.

Simone's mum was the original Earth Mother: she owned a small co-op and health food shop in Yamba, on the north coast. She chose to be called 'Luna' over her actual name, Debbie, and signed off all correspondence with 'Blessings to you', or 'Love and light', a practice Simone had dabbled in, but wasn't able to commit to. It was the right place for Simone to be.

Spying Simone's BMW coupé in the driveway as Lily pulled up across the street, she realised that the feeling in her stomach had morphed from excitement to anxiety. She and Simone had not once discussed Jack since the split, but it was bound to come up tonight. They might have even got back together, Lily thought with a sharp intake of air. After all, Jack would no doubt be impressed with Simone's action to remedy things in her life, and maybe he was the forgiving type . . .

Opening the front door, Lily hollered a big 'Yoohoo!' and heard a delighted scream from upstairs, followed by rapid footsteps.

In moments, Simone, in leggings and a tight white hoodie, was on the stairs and racing down to greet her friend in the lounge room.

'OMG, she's *home!*' she yelled before grabbing Lily, still clutching her shake and handbag, for a big hug.

'How ARE you?' Simone asked emphatically, squeezing Lily tight.

'I am so good, Sim. You won't believe what's just happened. I am so, so good.'

Simone pulled back, her hands still grabbing each of Lily's arms. 'What?' she asked, smiling widely, eyes huge and pupils enormous. Lily quashed the thought that Simone had probably taken something for mood bounce. She wouldn't be so stupid – not now, not after she was trying so hard to stop all that.

'I got a new job! Senior producer on *Iron Chef*!'

Simone squealed and clapped her hands.

'Ohmygod, LIL! That is AMAZING! You were out of work for what, one week? Way to manifest, hun; you created that, you know. Oh! I'm so happy for you. We should celebrate!'

This was the part where Simone usually skipped to the fridge and grabbed some champagne, but obviously now she wouldn't. Only, right before Lily's eyes, she did, and it wasn't until she was reaching for the champagne flutes that Lily spoke up.

'Um, Sim, I don't mean to play warden, but are you, should you be drinking right now?'

'It's a *special occasion*,' she said with emphasis. 'I think it's allowed this once.'

Lily bit her lip, watching her flatmate rip the foil from the top of the bottle, not sure where to go from here. Was she a bad friend to allow this? Or was she a bad friend to stop it?

'Actually, maybe I shouldn't. I just had a thickshake and it will mix and I'll feel spewy,' Lily said, marvelling at her genius and subterfuge.

'*Um*, I've seen you pour Red Bull INTO a thickshake before, I don't think you' – the cork was popped – 'care about mixing dairy and fizz. Plus, babes, I never got to toast you for turning dirty thirty, and I damn well am now.'

Simone poured two glasses, replacing the bottle in the fridge and kicking it closed with a playful little tap of her foot. Lily knew she wasn't going to win here. She dumped her bag on the dining room table and sighed quietly.

Simone walked over to her and handed her a glass.

'To your new job, and your flirty thirties. You're tanned and you're hot and you're smashing it. Love ya!'

They clinked glasses and Lily sipped the champagne, feeling sick to her stomach about letting someone trying to go clean have a glass of champagne on her watch.

'*Oh*, I have *missed* you,' Simone cooed to the glass, savouring the taste in her mouth before placing the glass on the table. 'Both of you.'

'Okay, I have to ask or I will never forgive myself; are you meant to be drinking?' Lily blurted, acutely aware she was potentially igniting the wick of some powerful Simone dynamite.

Simone looked straight at Lily. 'No. I'm not.' And she took her glass and poured the remainder of it into Lily's.

'But I wanted the ritual and the fun, just for a second.' She smiled sadly. 'I know what I'm doing, babe.'

'*Jesus!* I thought I'd let you relapse or whatever it's called. So, how's it all going, Sim . . . how are you?' While Simone pulled out a chair to sit, Lily took a quick sip, not wanting to be the girl eating chocolate cake in front of the dieter, but now enjoying the champagne too much to stop. She sat down on the chair opposite and looked at her friend; still very skinny, she noticed, but slightly less . . . gaunt.

'Yeah, better. I know I deserve a better existence and true joy, and pure self-love, and I'm dedicated to that . . . I was trying to replace real things, genuine things that were missing with partying and drugs, and I kind of always have.'

Lily nodded.

'I found this great guy near Mum's, Dashi, and he's inCREdible, Lil. Like, he's this amazing yogi who studied in India, and he taught me that transcendental meditation I'd been wanting to do for ages, and I've been doing healing and yoga with him almost every day, and I truly believe I was meant to find him, you know?'

'A spiritual saviour.'

'Uh-huh. I wrote a huge post on him yesterday, you should read it. He's amaze, Lil.'

'So will you drive up and see him still?'

Simone looked at her friend in a way Lily recognised from when she was confessing to having slept with men she shouldn't have.

'Well, I'm kind of moving up there. To live with Mum for a while. The agency is willing to give me six months off, but I don't think I'll need it. I feel so much better already.'

'You just opened a bottle of champagne so you could have a sip,' Lily said.

Simone nodded solemnly, her eyes big, her bottom lip pressing up over her top lip in a way that had been driving men wild since she was about thirteen.

'And that's why I need to remove myself from ALL temptation. All of it. All my friends, work, men, clubs, booze, this city, the
whole lot.'

'Speaking of men, have you heard from Jack?' Lily said, as nonchalant as possible.

'Mmm. So I didn't tell you this, but I had a bit of . . . an episode
just after you left for Greece.'

'Episode? Like back-to-the-hospital episode?'

'Not quite. I mixed too many things, basically, then went hard
on the rosé, fucking idiot. *You* were away and the girls weren't
answering, and so he was my SOS call, and he was amazing, Lil, he
came straight over and was just the *best*. You know he's had his own
drug battle, don't you? Hard to believe . . .'

Something began to twist and turn into the sides of Lily's stomach. A javelin, apparently.

'He's a good man,' Lily said in earnest.

'Yes, he is, isn't he, Lil?'

Simone was looking at her strangely, her head tilted on an angle,
and a tiny smile was playing on her tightly pursed lips.

'What? What is that look?'

Simone smiled in full and placed her chin between her hands,
elbows on the table.

'We talked about you a lot that night, actually. Or the following
morning, really, once I had stopped all the vomming and was able to
converse like a human being. And, well, if I didn't know any better,
I'd say he had a little thing for you, hun . . .' Simone said, playfully.

'What? Don't be stupid, Sim. What are you on about?' Lily's
breath quickened immediately, she hoped not visibly.

'Oo-oooh, bit defensive, babe!' Simone raised one of her perfectly thick, full eyebrows.

Lily crossed her arms and shook her head irritably.

'You don't know what you're on about.'

Sitting up straight in her chair, Simone crossed one leg over the other.

'I think you'd actually be a really cute couple; is that weird?'

Lily shook her head erratically and sipped deeply from her glass.

'It's funny . . . I went out with Jack because I thought he would be my knight in shining, normal armour, and he kind of was in the end, like, literally a lifesaver.' She laughed. 'But I was never present with Jack. I tried to go for Michael's opposite, then basically treated him how Michael treated me.'

'Speaking of the devil . . .?'

Simone swallowed before she spoke.

'I still have some . . . stuff I need to work on there. We're talking again, and, look, he has been making a *real* effort, Lil.'

So much for no men, Lily thought to herself.

'He's helping me get better. He drove up to see me on the weekend, and met with Dashi, and, I don't know, if *he* can heal and *I* can heal, and we're in it together, I feel like, maybe this was all for a reason, in a fucked-up way, you know?'

'So you could get back with Tony Soprano.'

Simone sighed.

'I know it doesn't make sense. But I have to work it out for myself. All part of the process. And I trust the process. Whether he's in my life or not, I need to get this closure.'

'I thought you were moving there to get away from men?'

Simone sighed, this time with frustration.

'Where's that strong, powerful, earth-sister girl?' asked Lily. 'The one who blogs about always moving forward and making sure you're happy and that you love *yourself* before you attempt to love others and don't forget to eat wheatgrass, and teach people how they treat you and why not knit some socks for the homeless and the —'

'I get it, I get it, stop!' Simone laughed.

'I want you to get better, Sim. He's not right for you just now.'

'There is *one* other thing, actually,' Simone said, suddenly very interested in chipping some candle wax off the table runner.

'Go on,' Lily took a sip of her champagne.

'I'm going to rent this place out. After Mum's, I'm thinking of relocating to LA for a while. Remember my friend Kitty? She's got this huge house there, and she's said she can get me some meetings, and I've always wanted to try it, you know?'

'We're not going to be living here any more . . .' The truth and sadness of this realisation hit Lily hard. Ups and down, ups and bloody downs; it was like this day had been on some of Simone's pharmacueticals.

'Are you mad at me? Please don't be, and it's only for now, you never know what will happen down the track, babe. I'll miss you too much!'

Lily looked up quickly to stop the wetness pooling in her eyes. 'No! No, it's all good.' And it was, Lily realised. She was thirty now; she *should* be living alone, like a grown-up. No more bumming off Simone any more.

She cleared her throat, hoping the large lump would go with it.

'When would you need me out then?' Lily prayed the answer was one that would make her life easier right now, not harder.

'Um, well, I *am* actually showing two families through tomorrow morning . . .'

It was not.

'Are you kidding? Am I going to be homeless by the weekend? Some five-year-old in my room when I get home from work on Monday?'

Simone laughed weakly. 'Is two weeks okay?'

Well, it would bloody have to be, thought Lily, wondering if she had accidentally 'manifested' her way into this by dreaming of living alone a few months ago. Fucking wishful thinking, she thought. Just be less alarming for once.

'Totally fine,' she said, because deep down she knew it would be. She felt confident that this was all part of the Bigger Picture; new home, new job, new attitude, new Lily.

37

'She ditched me, she ditched me, I can't believe she ditched me, she chose them calves' testicles, over music festivals —'

Alice was rapping disapproval at Lily's career move, even though it had been almost a month since Lily had been at *Iron Chef,* and Alice seemed to care about her music festival about as much as cats cared about swimming.

'That's one tight jam, Jay-Z.' Lily was busy trying to find some scissors in the third drawer of the kitchen bench, which, like so much of her new home, was an illogical mess of rushed unpacking and this-seems-like-the-right-spot-for-this-for-now.

Alice had been reading magazines on the floor as Lily pottered for the past hour but now came to life. 'What is *this*?' she said, holding up by her thumb and index finger a wet pair of undies that she'd found in the kitchen sink.

'Relax, they're clean. I needed a plug and I couldn't find one.'

'So you used undies.'

Lily turned to look at Alice, whose dark roots were angrily molesting her peroxide blonde. She seemed to prefer it that way.

'Well, aren't *you* just a tall glass of judgy water? I am pretty sure you'd do the exact same thing if it was the first item you could find, which it was, cos my washing was on the sofa, which if you squint, you can just see in my living room all the way over there.'

Alice laughed, the joke being that the lounge backed onto the bench in the kitchen, which acted as a partition between the two 'rooms'.

'This really is the smallest apartment in the world, Woodfart.'

'The real estate agent called it a view with a room. At least he was honest.'

'View is good. View is worth it.' Alice walked over to the huge windows facing out to the sea and raised the blinds fully. She whistled in appreciation. It was a wet, wild, miserable day, but the angry dark waves with an ominous grey lid of sky were impressive.

Lily gave up on the scissors and attacked the stems of the flowers with a steak knife. Alice had brought them as her housewarming gift, along with a bottle of tequila and a multicoloured salad bowl. Satisfied, she jammed them into a jar that had been the home of some ready-made spaghetti sauce up until very recently and plumped them out. She really was so shit at this domestic stuff, she noted. Simone had been the perfect friend-mother for the past three years, and now Lily was being forced to know things about cleaning and cooking stuff. It was horrible.

'So how's the line-up for the festival?'

'Oh, who gives a shit,' Alice said and flopped down onto the sofa, which although Lily had spent $900 on it was far too stiff and small. She'd wanted one she could sleep on as she watched movies, or make out with boys on, but *that* required a three-seater, and her new home simply wouldn't allow such indulgent use of space.

'I'm thinking of going on tour with Jesus. Not in a groupie capacity, although *Almost Famous is* my all-time favourite movie and I would be an *incredible* fucking groupie, but as assistant stage manager. Can't tell if it's a great idea or a really shitty one. He's pushing me to do it, which is cute, I s'pose. Did I tell you they're playing Splendour in the Grass? Do you wanna come? We won't even have to sleep in a tent this time, because the band has apartments . . . come on. You *know* Kai will make it worth your while.'

Lily shook her head.

'I won't be able to get time off. And I hated it last time. It rained, and Pete took mushrooms and went AWOL for two days. What a dick.'

'Fine, don't come. But do you plan on having sex ever again? Can you at least come to a gig with me once in a while?'

'One day. Hey, do you want popcorn? I feel like popcorn.' Lily set about putting a bag of microwave popcorn in the microwave and rinsing out Alice's salad bowl to serve it in.

'Kilos of butter, please,' Alice said. A pause and then: 'He's still on your mind, isn't he.'

Lily didn't answer straight away.

'I just need to get over him, and I am subconsciously trying to do that.'

'But you said the other week that Simone basically said you should be together! Blessing! Open gates!'

Lily took the still-popping bag out of the microwave and shook it around a bit before pouring it into the bowl.

'I think we are both conveniently forgetting that Jack hasn't exactly been banging my door down.'

Lily was getting frustrated at Alice's ineptitude to see the electric fence around the Jack situation. She came around and placed the popcorn on the small glass coffee table Mimi had said Lily could use until she found one she liked.

'He hasn't emailed? Called? Nothing, nada?'

'Nope.'

'Then email *him*, FFS!' Alice said, as she jammed two fistfuls of popcorn in her mouth and wiped her hands onto her black high-waisted jeans.

'I'm not from your school of Stalk Men Til They Fall in Love With You.'

'One email,' Alice said with a mouthful. 'Ask him out for a mocha frappuccino.'

'NO. If anything *ever* happens between us, and it really, really won't, *he* will need to start things so I don't forever live in guilt.'

'And *this* is why you are eternally single.' Alice checked her phone for the time and sat up, tucking some of her wispy hair behind one ear with nails that about two weeks ago had sported a fresh coat of blue nail polish.

'My overpriced beach parking is up. I gotta go.'

She stood up and put her green Paddington coat on, buttoning it up slowly, like she'd just learned how to do it.

'Stop being such a loser. Just email him and say hi. That's not creepy, that's normal and friendly.' Alice slung her bag over her shoulder and took two handfuls of popcorn for the road.

'Yeah, yeah,' Lily said, popping a few more pieces of popcorn into her mouth as she confirmed to herself she would do no such thing.

38

Lily took a deep breath and tried not to let panic tumble in. Sophie, one of her assistant producers, had failed to advise Takeo, Melbourne's three-hat Japanese superstar and star of the show, that he would have to use the knives provided by the show's sponsor, and would not be able to use his own, and now he was threatening to pull out. Lily understood that Japanese chefs, in fact all chefs, were incredibly particular about their knives, but she also knew Takeo was sponsored by a rival knife brand, and this was far more likely the reason.

And they started shooting next week. And they needed him. *Bad*.

'I'm just asking you to help me understand, Sophie. This was one of the key points all the chefs needed to be told. How is it that he didn't know until now?'

Sophie, reminiscent of a gleaming panther with her long black straight hair, heavy black eyeliner and black leather motorbike jacket, looked at Lily as though she had just asked her if she was a boy or girl. Discussions with her were always arduous, but when she was indignant they quickly escalated to infuriating. Sophie refused to take any responsibility for anything, ever. Lily had even heard her tell one of the other producers the cyclist she'd knocked over in her car recently ran into *her*.

'I mean, he *has* all the notes, I definitely emailed them to his assistant, and it says it on them,' she said, the incredulity ringing in her words.

'That's fine, Sophie, everyone got the notes, I know that. The fact is that each participating chef needed to be told very clearly about our sponsors for this very reason, and Takeo, who is one of *your* chefs, was not. And hence, I draw a conclusion that perhaps you failed to tell him.'

'But he *knew*! I swear to God, if he and his manager read that document properly, he had to know about the knives.' Sophie spoke to Lily as though she were a small, naughty child who could not understand why she wasn't allowed cookies right before dinner. Lily tried not to put it down to her being twenty-two and grossly over-entitled, because Mackenzie was the same age and had been a dream. Also, now that Lily had reached a position of management, she needed to learn how to *manage* people, not just be pissed off with them and walk away calling them fuckstick under her breath.

'Okay. What's done is done. Now we need to fix it. Fast. Call his people, and very delicately apologise for not making this clear, and ask if there's any way we can make it work.'

'His assistant already said he can't do it now.'

'Yes, but the amazing thing about being a producer, Sophie, even an assistant one, is that we never take no for an answer, and we always find a way. That's our job. That's what Evan needs, that's what the show needs, that's what the network needs: for us to make sure, no matter what, we get the talent and the content required.'

Sophie crossed her arms and looked to the right, her foot tapping almost imperceptibly on the ground in either fury or outrage or even inrage; who knew, she seemed to have a whole archive of rages ready to fire.

'Fine, but I don't like our chances. I don't even know why we are bothering with Takeo; he is like, the most precious person I have ever dealt with in my *life.*' And she clip-clopped off to her desk, swishing her mane as she went, a million reasons as to why she was better than this undoubtedly swirling through her mind.

Lily shook her head. She wondered if she had ever been like that. She had certainly *felt* like that back when Eliza was casually claiming credit for all of her ideas. Suddenly Lily wondered if she was at risk of being an Eliza, and that was why Sophie was being such a pain in the arse. She thought about how she spoke to her, and tried to help her, and assured herself that she wasn't a terrible senior producer. But still, it was worth keeping an eye on.

Back at her desk, which was tucked away in the corner of an open-plan office that buzzed and hummed with people, laughter and far too many YouTube clips, Lily sighed and opened up her shiny new Apple laptop. She'd had to run off and buy one after work on her first day after discovering they weren't provided – you were assumed and expected to have your own. No clunky, chunky desktop dinosaurs on Evan's watch. *Everyone* had Macs, so she'd copied, pretending she'd always intended to pick up her new one that evening as her old one had exploded over the weekend.

As always, when she left her desk for more than half an hour, a stream of bold names had snuck into her inbox, most of them Evan's. He was incredibly hands-on but thankfully in a funny exciting genius way, not an overbearing, interruptive way. She saw his most recent email – the copy in the subject line as was often his stream-of-conscious thinking – asking them to all work Saturday. Amazingly, Lily didn't mind one bit. She felt so much more invested in this show, so much more passionate than she had been at *The Daily*.

Double-clicking her way through the emails at lightning pace,

Lily suddenly saw the name Jack Winters pop up. Everything went completely still for a moment. All noise faded away.

To: Lily
From: Jack Winters
Subject: Hey stranger

How are you? How's the new job going? Long time no speak. That's my fault for being rude. I finished up at *The Daily* last week (long story) but Siobhan filled me in on your new gig before I left. Bet you're enjoying working with all those *real* chefs instead of a guy who can't caramelise sugar without burning the pan.

Hey, love to pick your brain on something... wondering if you're around the next few days if you have time to grab a coffee?

Jack

Both unsure of and unwilling to heed the protocol regarding aloofness when it came to response times and general keenness, Lily hit reply and started thumping out a response as fast as she could. Oh, she'd *missed* him! She'd missed him so much. And the joy she felt seeing his name in her inbox again and reading what he'd written was stark and irrefutable proof of just how much. She missed him as a workmate and she missed him as a friend, but she also missed him as the guy who made her take in a sharp little hit of air every time he entered the room.

To: Jack Winters
From: Lily Woodward
Subject: Re: Hey stranger

You LEFT! Let me guess, Nikkii asked you to do the segment topless and it was the final straw? Can't wait to hear all the juicy details.

New job is amazing. Challenging too, which I'm loving. Not *quite* the slap-dash affair *The Daily* was, put it that way. There are all these international-format rules in place, most of which drive me mental, but it's a good learning curve.

Funny you should mention our chefs, as the EP actually threw your name up in the early days. (I told him to contact your management. And also that you were always burning pans.)

I could catch up Friday afternoon for a coffee? At about three? Tell me where and I'm there.

Lily

Before she could analyse her tone and exact word choice to the point of crippling indecision, she hit send. She was a friend, she was just being a friend, and a friend wouldn't overthink it, she told herself as she calmly checked that it had been sent, so that he wouldn't not get her response and think she was rude, and also, so she wouldn't miss out on this magical coffee date come Friday.

She propped her elbows on the desk and leaned her chin into the palms of her hand for a moment, smiling widely, her pulse still racing. He'd emailed and he wanted to see her. Even if it was just nothingy work chat, she was going to see him, and that was all that counted, really.

Friday morning presented Lily with a spectacular vacuum of sartorial choices. She had bought a few new clothes for the job, but it was a workplace that approved of flats – practically demanded them – so she was back into her habit of ballet flats and jeans. She'd kept the blazers though, and under the tutelage of one of the other senior producers, Katie, who was fast becoming a good friend, she was now experimenting a little more with necklaces and bright little jumpers with collared shirts underneath. Casual but polished, and most crucially, comfortable for the long hours. It wasn't *sexy*, though, not that she wanted to look 'sexy' per se for Jack, but she wanted to look a bit cuter than he was used to.

She settled on a little cherry-red sweater that always earned her compliments with a white shirt underneath, and black jeans that stopped just above the ankle. Her hair was growing so quickly, it was down to her collarbones, but it softened the look a bit, she decided. A bit of eye make-up, some tinted lip balm and she was good to go. Remember, Lily, she warned herself. This is not a date. This is just a catch up with a friend.

Her phone buzzed with a text. It was Simone. Lily blinked with the coincidence and creepiness of the timing. Was it a sign that she was doing the wrong thing? *Was* she doing the wrong thing catching up with Jack? No, surely not . . .

Hi babe! Just a lil hi and I miss you xx I will send a full email soon but Mum has banned me from the web for a while, prob a good thing!! I hope job is great and can't wait to see your apartment soon as I'm back down xoxo

Lily could only shake her head in amazement. Crazy timing. Too much. Too, too much. She punched out a reply quickly.

Miss you too. How are you?? You'll be shocked to know I haven't eaten a single leaf of kale since you left. New job is so amazing, apartment is cute, roughly the size of our old bathroom. I'll buzz you over weekend for a catch-up. xx

Lily wondered if it was deceptive to not tell her she was catching up with Jack, but then pushed the thought out of her mind *because they were just friends.*

A response buzzed quickly.

☺ I feel great, totally clean 4 weeks now. Started teaching the local mums yoga, which is hilar . . . LA is a no-go. I might be moving back to Syd soon . . . Most likely with Michael. He's been living up here with us. He's changed so much. NEW man. New me. New everything, babes! Life is good. xoxo

Lily sighed. Michael. God knew how *that* would turn out. Perhaps they had some kind of 'past life' connection, which was generally what Simone put anything inexplicable down to.

Later that day, Lily was checking Google maps to make sure she had the right address. She was where Jack had told her to meet, but all she could see was a florist, a gift shop, a Japanese restaurant and a place being renovated that was boarded up with building signs. Surely that couldn't be it?

She went back into her emails to check the address once more, before hearing a familiar voice call from her left.

'Woodward! Over here!' She looked up and there stood Jack. He was wearing a dark-blue hoodie with a zip, black jeans, Converse and an enormous grin.

Smiling like a doofus, Lily walked towards where he was standing, next to what appeared to be pretty much a construction site. She stood awkwardly in front of him, clutching her phone with a steel grip of nerves. They were not kiss-hello types, she'd already told herself, just be cool.

'This is the cafe? Jesus, they've really taken the deconstructed trend a bit too far, haven't they?'

Jack laughed, throwing his head back, the spicy, smoky scent of his cologne hitting Lily; something she'd completely taken for granted when they had worked together, but now she drank it in as if she were an airport sniffer dog looking for gear.

'Come in, I'll explain.' And he beckoned her to walk into the work zone, his hand gently resting on her elbow as he guided her. She ignored the sensation of her arm tingling at his touch.

'You should wear red more often, Woodward, it really suits you.' Lily blushed furiously, which thankfully he couldn't see.

The first thing she saw was a small courtyard at the back, which was separated from inside with huge warehouse-style steel-beam windows. Two men were outside working away on the pavers.

'Wow, *cool* spot,' Lily said, taking it in. They stood on wide, dark, imperfect floorboards, and the walls were covered in beautiful dark green and blue ceramic tiles. A black bar stretched the entire left wall, with an old, rusty mirror as its backdrop, making the relatively small place look twice as big.

'It's getting there,' he said, walking past the lone table and chairs to the back end of the bar.

'What kind of coffee would you like? We just have a little Nespresso thing at the moment. The real one is being shipped over from Milan. It was meant to be here last week.'

'How *fancy*. Anything with milk is great, thanks.' Lily was taking it all in, the dark bronze pressed-metal ceiling, the vertical gardens in the courtyard . . . everything was so cool, and so well done. What *was* this place? And why did Jack say 'we'?

'So, what is this place?'

'Do you like it?'

'I do, it's very . . . dark and hipstery.'

'It will actually be pretty bright once we take off the boarding at the front. We're north-facing, which is good.' He talked loudly over the noise of the coffee machine.

'We?' Lily yelled just as it stopped, sounding stupid.

Saying nothing, Jack carried the coffees over to the table and beckoned for Lily to sit down. Lily couldn't stop her body from tensing in his presence. She was giddy being near him again, and realised with certainty it would take weeks to get back to Not Thinking About Jack again after this. Oh, fuck it, it was worth it, she thought as she followed him over.

He placed the coffees down and took a seat.

'This is actually my restaurant, Lil. It all happened pretty quick. The week you left *The Daily* I walked past this place and saw it was for lease. I'd heard this is a growth area, all these great restaurants and cafes are opening up around here, so I thought I'd give it a shot. Also, and this was a bit of a clincher, my mate Billy had just moved back up here from Melbourne. He's a total gun, and he wanted in, so we're doing it together.'

'*Jack!* This is amazing! Your very own Sydney cafe! It's going to be so so good . . . Can you imagine how many of your groupies will come here once word is out that it's TV Jack? Awesome for business . . .'

He smiled. 'Hope so. We'll, uh, need to do pretty well to break even. But even if it all fails, we want to give it a go.'

'So is it dinner and lunch? Fancy stuff?' Lily looked at him, eyes wide with excitement, and not just because she now had a brand-new local. On the other side of the city.

'Just breakfast and lunch to start. Licensing is a bit of a bugger, so we'll hold off on dinner for a bit. But that suits me . . . Never liked working dinner. Screws up your life too much. And also, we opened it up because no one is doing a *really* good brunch around here. We want to be *that* place.'

'The place no one can get into on weekends cos you're too full?'

'Exactly.'

Lily smiled at Jack. So this was why he hadn't been in touch – he'd been flat out building his new cafe. A sense of relief washed over her.

'So, will your ricotta, peach and plum hotcakes be on the menu?'

'Absolutely. Billy's famous French toast will be there too. You'll love it: bacon, almonds, mascarpone.'

'Just a couple of tough guys, aren't you.'

He grinned, his eyes resting on Lily just a second longer than they needed to.

'Hey, wait here for a sec? I want to show you the menu.' He stood up and walked through the small door at the back, returning a moment later, laptop cradled on his arm, his eyes on the screen as he tapped away.

'While I find this, tell me about your new job.'

Lily crossed one leg over the other. 'Well, it's pretty nuts. I got out this afternoon because we're shooting all weekend, but I honestly don't mind. Such a fun team. I hope people watch the show, I really do.'

'You kidding? I love *Iron Chef*. Everyone does. *Allez, cuisine!*'

Lily laughed.

'Okay,' he said, placing the laptop down onto the small wooden table. 'See if you can see anything you recognise.'

Lily scanned a PDF of the cafe menu. It was very, very good, despite being a tight edit. She would have real trouble ordering here, which was always a good sign. Corn and bacon fritters with avocado and feta mash, Spanish baked eggs with haloumi and red capsicum salsa on rye, polenta with honey, almonds and warm milk . . .

'Shit, Jack. This is phenomenal. I would eat here every day.'

'Go to the bottom,' he said, looking at her strangely, taking his seat again, this time right next to her, at the end of the table. He sat forward and folded his arms loosely while she read. She tried not to notice his body being so close to hers. She failed.

Lily scanned on past the pain au chocolat, the buttery croissant with gruyere and ham, and saw what he was referring to: 'The Lily' – *award-winning rosewater scones with homemade three-berry jam and vanilla bean whipped cream.*

Lily cocked her head to one side, a quizzical look on her face. 'You have a dish called The Lily?'

He smiled widely, his eyes soft. 'After you, of course! You created that scone, you deserve the credit.'

Lily blushed, which seemed ridiculous, considering they were discussing baked goods.

'Wow. I've never had anything named after me . . .'

'Billy thinks scones are uncool, but I insisted.'

'How dare he,' Lily said playfully.

'Truth is,' Jack said, and then stopped. He ran his hands down over his thighs towards his knees uneasily. 'I've missed you, Woodward.'

Lily's hands found each other in her lap, and she began fiddling with her fingers wildly in anxiety. *He missed her.* Could he have missed her in the same way she missed him?

'It was – we had a good time at *The Daily*, it was fun,' Lily said nervously, then cursed her stupidity. Just let *him* talk, she scolded herself.

'I'm guessing you know what happened between me and Simone a while back.'

'Mm-hmm,' Lily said, looking at him, wondering what might fall from his mouth next.

'It was a bit of a funny one from the start, that one. I was lonely and looking for some company in a new city, and I guess I was excited by the attention of, well, you know, a —'

'Stunning bikini model?'

'Anyway. We gave it a nudge, but we never really . . . I don't know, *connected*. We lead very different lives, we're different people, even blind Freddie could see that. And then, well, you know what happened.' He cleared his throat.

'Yeah . . .' Lily said, nodding slightly.

'If I'm being brutal, it kind of provided a clean exit from the relationship,' he said quietly.

Lily nodded and said nothing. She didn't want to ruin his flow, but she also knew she had nothing to say here that wouldn't completely give her feelings away.

'I feel for Simone, you know? I know what she's going through; I've been there. I was a mess. After her incident a few weeks back I tried to get her to join NA but she wouldn't hear of it. Not her style. Far too prescriptive.'

'That doesn't surprise me,' Lily said.

'But above and beyond all that, I realised that we didn't really have any *fun*.' He paused, looking at the ground for a second to gather his thoughts. Lily was about to combust with impatience: *where was this heading?*

'I have fun with *you*, Lily. And I think that only really hit home once you weren't stealing my leftovers and rousing on me for requesting expensive French cookware all the time.' His dark-blue eyes were locked on her now. His eyebrows were raised slightly and Lily took small delight in noticing he actually seemed a bit nervous. *She* was making Jack nervous! Things might never be better than this moment, she told herself. *Relish it.*

'I —' Lily's voice snagged and she cleared her throat. 'I have fun with you too, Jack. And I've missed you being around. No one even makes me peanut-butter cookies at the new job. But, you know, with the whole Simone thing I just, well, you know . . .'

He nodded. 'I know, I know. I really do know, trust me. There's a good reason I've kept my distance. Even if I didn't want to.'

Lily's pulse was now at Formula One speed. All the things she'd dreamed of him saying, all of them, falling from his mouth, all at once.

'So . . . what if we just caught up again in the next month or so? Just, you know, took it slow. Very slow, whatever you're comfortable with . . .'

Lily suddenly felt compelled to blurt out that Simone was back with Michael but didn't. When the time came, *if* the time came, she would have a long, gentle, honest and awkward discussion with Simone about Jack. But for now, it wasn't required.

'If it's to another building site, count me in,' Lily said, smiling, trying to act nonchalant even though her whole body wanted to leap off the ground at what Jack had just said. *He wanted to see her more. Whatever she was comfortable with.*

He laughed. 'I might even take you to an *operating* cafe, if you're lucky,' he said.

'I'd love that, Jack,' Lily said in earnest, looking into his eyes before getting nervous and looking away quickly. Maybe in time she could even get used to looking at him directly, she thought, the idea leaping around in her brain with confetti and glitter.

'So are there any hotshot chefs at your new job stealing your kettle?'

'No.' Lily laughed. 'You know, I thought you were SUCH a pig when I first met you. Couldn't tell enough people how much of a pig you were.'

He shook his head. 'Lily, Lily, Lily.'

'What? You were. Stole my car spot, my kettle, you were nice to everyone but me, told me I had stuff on my shoe at the provedore, you were —'

'I was shy, Lily. Just trying to keep it together at my new job. You think having a cute, bossy producer makes it any easier?'

'You thought I was cute?' Lily beamed, and she didn't even care if he noticed.

'Angry, but cute. Like a little Tassie devil.'

'Not *that* cute, if you went for Simone.'

'You don't ask your workmates out, Lily. And especially not your producers. Plus I figured you weren't the least bit keen on me anyway. I seemed to be mostly a nuisance to you. Except when I made desserts.'

'Huh,' Lily said, thinking about what he'd said. He was probably right.

'But all was forgiven when I helped you win the bake-off, right?' Lily asked cheekily.

'Or when I caught a glimpse of you dancing in your knickers that night,' he said, looking at her wickedly, playfully.

Sexual innuendo? From *Jack*! Lily didn't say anything. She couldn't. She became acutely aware of their knees touching under the table, and how close they were. *Was he going to kiss her?* she wondered, thrilled and anxious and feeling sick in the gut.

'So,' he said, voice soft and low, 'would you say tomorrow is too soon for our next catch-up?'

ACKNOWLEDGEMENTS

First of all, I must thank my dear friends Jamie Oliver and Curtis Stone, who spent hours, many hours, with me detailing how exactly chefs operate on a day-to-day basis, as well as the inner workings of live TV production. Second, I must retract those thanks, because I've never met either of those men. But I think they'd both definitely be very lovely and helpful.

With regards to people I *have* actually met and who were genuinely helpful in the creation of this book, I must mention my editor and publisher Kirsten Abbott, who encouraged me to perform some exquisite surgery on my story and make it into the tight, fun package you just read; my ever-reassuring agent, Tara Wynne; and Chantelle Sturt, the best publicist and cutest strudel to ever roam the earth. Finally, and most importantly, I want to thank my beautiful husband for his unwavering, 1000-watt support, his brilliant ideas, his joyful, pure enthusiasm for my work, and, perhaps most crucially, the peanut butter sprinkles cupcakes he presented me with when I finally typed 'The End'.

Air Kisses

If the devil wears Prada, then God wears La Mer.

'Everyone knows that a beauty editor's headshot has to be
a masterpiece of shiny, bouncy hair, lacquered lips, twinkling eyes,
and well-blended eye shadow so that the readers believe that the
woman instructing them on bronzer application actually knows how
to apply bronzer. I looked at my headshot again. Gross. In a way,
it was symbolic: I was always going to be the girl with unblended
foundation and a wobbly trail of liquid eyeliner. In fact, the more
I thought about it, it was an absolute farce that I was advising women
on how to look perfect. But somehow, somehow, I had managed
to hoodwink everyone into thinking I had a clue about this beauty
thing. Until now, anyway.'

'*Air Kisses has launched Zoë Foster as a stylish, witty author
of chick-lit.*' SYDNEY MORNING HERALD

'*Air Kisses is written in such a sexy way that it's difficult to put
down . . . Clever and cheeky.*' SUN-HERALD

'*Its wit-strewn pages will give you a smile from ear to ear.*'
SUNDAY AGE

Playing the FIELD

In the glossy world of footballers' wives, love is the toughest game of all.

'I turned from the bar and prepared to navigate my way through the mass of heaving, loud, beautiful people to our seats in the courtyard. I was doing a brilliant job, nursing the drinks to my chest and caving my shoulders to protect them, until I was knocked from behind. Half of each drink went flying onto the back of the guy unlucky enough to be standing in front of me. He turned slowly around. With my hands full and covered in vodka, I was unable to do anything but offer what I hoped was a sincere apology via my eyes. His mouth was open and his fingers were pulling his shirt out from his substantially wet back. And somewhere high above, God was high-fiving someone on his incredible handiwork.'

'Zoë Foster tells an engaging and fun contemporary tale with her fabulously wry wit.' **NEW IDEA**

'This glam and "fictional" exposé of the lives of WAGS is a rollicking read.' **NW**

THE
Younger
MAN

He was only supposed to be a bit of fun . . .

When Abby enjoys a memorable night with a delicious 22-year-old,
she easily waves him out of her life the next morning. She doesn't
have time for these sorts of distractions. And he's only 22, after all!
A child. But the charming young Marcus isn't going to let her get
away that easily. He knows what he wants and takes it upon himself
to prove that age is irrelevant where the heart is concerned. Abby,
though, isn't convinced. She feels certain she should be with someone
her own age, someone more impressive, someone more . . . settled.
Surely nothing can ever come of this relationship?

Textbook
Romance

Wouldn't it be great if there was a textbook with clear
lessons on clever dating and how to build that Perfect
Relationship? One that tells it straight but lets you laugh
at yourself too? One that leaves you with your dignity
and your personality intact? There is!

Zoë Foster Blake, relationships guru, provides whip-smart
step-by-step lessons in successful romancing, with male
commentary from self-confessed male, Hamish Blake.

From 'Never Drink and Text' to the secrets of avoiding the
'Thai and Tracksuit Pants Curse' and the meaning of 'Engaging
the Apricot', *Textbook Romance* is essential reading for
every girl looking for love that lasts.

*'Serious moments provide dating gems but along the
way there are loads of giggles.'* SUN-HERALD

Amazinger Face

Fully revised and updated! Over 60 new pages! New longer title!

Sometimes a lady just needs to know the most flattering lipstick for her skin tone, or how to correctly use sunscreen, or a very quick hairstyle to conceal her unwashed hair. And there's no reason she shouldn't know which foundation or mascara is best for her, either.

All the answers are here, in this top-to-toe beauty extravaganza. Former *Cosmopolitan* and *Harper's BAZAAR* beauty director, and the founder of Go-To skin care, Zoë Foster Blake suggests makeup colours and brands for every occasion; useful, practical skincare routines and products for every age; and step-by-step instructions for winged eyeliner, arresting red lips, foolproof tanning, simple updos, sexy-second-day hair, and much, much more . . .

> *'A beautifully written book with thoughtful explanations, helpful step-by-step instructions and even a healthy dose of humor.'*
> **FASHION JOURNAL**